Charlotte Mary Yonge

The Release

Caroline's French kindred

Charlotte Mary Yonge

The Release
Caroline's French kindred

ISBN/EAN: 9783337313180

Printed in Europe, USA, Canada, Australia, Japan

Cover: Foto ©Andreas Hilbeck / pixelio.de

More available books at **www.hansebooks.com**

CAROLINE'S FRENCH KINDRED

BY

CHARLOTTE M. YONGE

AUTHOR OF "THE HEIR OF REDCLYFFE," "DAISY CHAIN,"
"THE LONG VACATION," ETC., ETC.

New York

MACMILLAN AND CO.

LONDON: MACMILLAN & CO., LTD.

1896

All rights reserved

Norwood Press
J. S. Cushing & Co. — Berwick & Smith
Norwood Mass. U.S.A.

PREFACE

It may be objected that the two parts of this volume only adhere through the individuality of Caroline; but having provided her with French kindred, it was tempting to make her the connecting link, especially as those who care to do so may trace her pedigree in the *Chaplet of Pearls* and *Stray Pearls*.

Both sets of adventures have a foundation. The defiance of the French fleet actually took place, and the head-dress, so proudly worn, is minutely described in the memoirs of the court of Louis XVI., and may be found in Lady Jackson's history; but I fear it was a wife and not a maiden who thus audaciously manifested her patriotism.

The second story is not in print, but it was told to me by Monsieur Guizot five and twenty years ago, — of the reluctant nun appealing to the Pope and obtaining her release. I have since had permission to use the circumstance for a plot, only withholding the names.

C. M. YONGE.

November, 1895.

CONTENTS

PART I

CAROLINE'S DEFIANCE

PART II

THE RELEASE

CHAPTER I

CHAPTER XX

CHAPTER XXI

CHAPTER XXII

CHAPTER XXIII

Part I

CAROLINE'S DEFIANCE

CHAPTER I

"WHAT shall we do with her?" sighed Mrs. Darpent, a lady with a large muslin cap over her as yet unpowdered hair, and a loose grey wrapper over her quilted tiffany petticoat, long-waisted stays, and well-stuffed, embroidered pockets. She was a fair, handsome, comfortable-looking dame, though somewhat tending to portliness, and the cheeks which once had been apple-blossom asserting their hue of the ripened fruit. She sat in an upright chair, without touching the back, in a room with a little carpet in a space of polished oak, wainscot panels on the walls, and a shining table on which stood her work-basket full of household linen.

Her sigh was scarcely breathed, before there entered, riding-whip in hand, with boots and spurs, a trim, neat-looking gentleman in a black coat and long waistcoat, with marked features, black eyebrows, and dark eyes under them, his powdered hair tied in a queue, and his three-cornered hat just removed as he entered, and catching her words, asked —

"What has she been doing now? — since I conclude that you mean my unlucky niece. What has she been

3

doing?"—and there was a twinkle in his eyes that showed an expectation of amusement.

"Doing? Did you not see a disreputable rag over the pediment? She has been climbing out on the leads of the north garret to hang up what she calls the Union Jack, and taking poor little Clem with her. What do you think of that, Mr. Darpent?"

"I think that Nature made a mistake when she was born a girl."

"To my mind the mistake was your poor brother's, in taking her to sea with him."

"He could not bear to part with her."

"And so he unfitted her for decorous life at home! Ah, you never can bear to hear a word censuring him. No, not if she had broken your son's neck."

"I conclude that his bones are still entire. What have you done to the children?"

"Whipped them both soundly and sent Caroline to bed. But if no worse comes of it, you may make up your mind that Clement will never be satisfied without becoming a sailor."

"There are worse professions."

"Mr. Darpent, you do not mean to say that you would wish to see your eldest son and heir wrecked, and shot down, and thrown into a French prison, and eaten by the sharks."

"They do not haunt French prisons, my dearest life."

"Now, Mr. Darpent, you are in your teasing mood——"

"Hark! there's the postman's horn." Wherewith Mr. Darpent darted out, "like quicksilver," as his lady was wont to say. "But there, what could be expected of a man with French blood in his veins?"

For Squire Clement Darpent was the grandson of a
French lawyer, who had given umbrage to the Court
during the Fronde, and coming to England had married into a family likewise of French extraction settled
there in the days of the Reformation. Though the
family had thoroughly embraced English life, he bore
the ineradicable impress of his Gallic blood in his
features and his vivacity, though his mother and wife
were absolutely English. His brother Eustace had
been in the navy, and in the course of the various
encounters in the West Indies had captured a vessel
from Guadaloupe containing as passengers the young
Chevalier de Bellaise and his bride, together with her
sister Marguerite de Mericourt. Of course the captain behaved to them with all chivalry, and won their
hearts by showing himself so nearly a Frenchman;
nor were they slow to discover the old connection
between the families. He was young, handsome,
and distinguished. Marguerite was portionless, and
was to be taken home to a convent, and before the
Spider had reached a harbour, the web was woven
round them; they discovered that they could not be
parted; and while Monsieur and Madame de Bellaise
were sent ashore near St. Domingo, Captain Darpent
and Marguerite de Mericourt were married by a chaplain at Jamaica.

This was before the presence of officers' wives was
forbidden on their husbands' voyages, and for several
years Marguerite Darpent sailed with her husband,
till she was cut off by fever, leaving him one little
girl of five years old. Her foster-sister, a Guadaloupe negress, had never left her, and continued in
charge of the child, with whom her father, now an
Admiral, would not hear of parting till, when she was

about eleven years old, as he was reluctantly bringing her home, allowing that the time when she must be educated had really come, he fell ill, and died just as his ship doubled the Cape of Good Hope.

Little Caroline was fetched to Walwyn, with her nurse Zélie, by her uncle, taking leave in floods of tears of the *Corcyr*, which had been her home for four years past, and where indeed she had reigned like a little princess over the crew. Her aunt at Walwyn had expected a little savage. This she was not, for the Admiral had, with old-fashioned punctilio, been very careful of her manners, and his flag-captain's wife had taken up her education in feminine arts. She could sew and do some reading and writing, and she could talk French much better than her cousins, though theirs was fairly good, for it had never been allowed to die out of the family. She had pretty manners on occasion, but she had been the pet of the whole crew, and her chief companions and friends had been the young lieutenant, son to the motherly Mrs. Aylmer, her playfellow Harry Norton, a midshipman of her own age, and also the old boatswain! It must be owned that she had not learned much positive harm by her strange associations. Every one had respected their little lady, the Admiral's daughter, and her father and Mrs. Aylmer had been very careful of her in essentials; but her daring, her dancing, her climbing, and her sea-phrases were a terrible trial to Madam Darpent, whose view was that girls should be bred up in the prim decorum of the eighteenth century.

The girl had been at Walwyn about three months. At first she was depressed and shy, missing her father's tenderness, and perhaps missing still more the free life which she had led at sea; but as her spirits revived, she began to teach her cousins all she had learnt on board, and as they were all boys, this was the more congenial. To tie sailors' knots might be useful and convenient, but what were the feelings of Mrs. Darpent when Caroline was discovered whistling a horn-pipe and teaching little Eustace to dance one, on the hall table, with personal illustrations, her skirts held up high so as to show her steps. Or when she was found trying to rig up the old boat for a voyage on the pond, and was found on the top of half the trees, and of all the walls in the Dutch garden, with Clement, Philip, and Eustace following in her wake.

One wet day a tremendous noise in the attic story led to the discovery of Neptune and Amphitrite cross-ing the line in a superannuated arm-chair, Neptune holding aloft his three-pronged fork, and his father's cocked hat put on wrong side foremost, and an ancient blue cloak enwrapping him, while Amphitrite wore a bunch of red and green parrot's feathers and an Indian mantle, and carried a sceptre of swordfish's spike! Waves were furnished by mats and carpets, in which the gardener's children and the dogs wallowed and kicked up their heels, and Caroline, in a sailor's coat, was engaged before the throne in shaving Clement with a big old wooden sword over a washing tub of water, into which the startling surprise caused him to plump at once!

It was a time when to climb three steps of a ladder was not thought decorous in a young lady; and to have the heads of her four boys filled with sea-stories was beyond the bearing of poor Madam Darpent, more especially as her husband was much more disposed to laugh at than to punish the enormities of the children.

So he hurried out, at the excuse of the postman's

horn, into the large paved court with handsome gates,
which formed the entrance to Walwyn Court. The
servants had been before him, and were refreshing
the postman with a horn of ale, which he was drain-
ing before proceeding to look out his budget for the
Squire. Meantime, Mr. Darpent, while waiting,
looked up at the great carved pediment which finished the front of the house, with the Walwyn and
Ribaumont arms quartered together, and above them
hung, or rather drooped, a not very artistic flag of
England. The passage to it, from the adjacent window, looked so perilous that, whatever he had said to
his wife, he could not help shuddering and turning
away his eyes when he thought of his son and niece
encountering it.

The postman claimed his fee, no less than a crown
piece, for the letter, which had an enormous black
seal with a coroneted coat-of-arms, was from France.
Mr. Darpent knew it well, for connection with the
French cousins had never been entirely dropped, and
family events were always communicated. He had
written to inform Madame de Bellaise of the death
of his brother, and had no doubt that this was the
response.

He had spoken French easily when a child, for his
grandfather had made a point of keeping up his parents' native tongue; but for want of use, he was not
so ready therewith as his niece, and the tall, slender,
pointed, and flourished handwriting of the Bellaise
de Nidemerle family cost him always an effort to
read. Besides, he supposed it would be only condo-
lence for a loss that could hardly be very present or
afflicting to the sister-in-law. So he put it aside till
he had opened his newspaper, where he was anxiously

watching for news from America, dreading a revolt of
the colonies, though supposing that it would be easily
put down.

It was not till he had settled himself in his arm-
chair in the study — a room with more books than
were usual for a country gentleman, but with a considerable proportion of guns and pistols — that he
applied himself to deciphering the tall, pointed,
flourishing hand in which the lady, who signed herself his cousin, Mericourt de Nidemerle, expressed
her condolences for the death of *ce bon et honnête
amiral*, whose *courtoisie* and *bienveillance* she should
never forget. After a good deal more of this kind,
she proceeded to relate that two years ago her brother-
in-law, the Marquis de Nidemerle, had died, so that
her husband, who had been known as the Chevalier
de Bellaise, had succeeded to his title and become
head of the family. Then she went on to propose
that she might be permitted to adopt the daughter
of her beloved sister, who would find loving friends
in her own daughters, and to whom she would be a
mother, no doubt finding an excellent marriage for
her, since a *dot* should be provided for her; and there
was at present such an Anglo-mania, and such talk of
liberty and philosophy, that her descent from an exile
of the Fronde would be rather an advantage to her
than otherwise. If Monsieur her cousin would bring
her over, he would see for himself how welcome she
should be — all the more if she brought with her the
dear old Zélie who had nursed both the sisters.

Mr. Darpent gave a long whistle. "My little Caroline! Poor Eustace's little Carry — to turn her over
to foreign parts! It is not what I meant — or he
meant! Papists, too! It is against my conscience."

Here he was interrupted by the entrance of his wife, now in full splendour, in case of afternoon visitors, in a full brocade dress, with hair powdered and rolled over a cushion, short sleeves, and long mittens.

"So, Mr. Darpent, there you sit at your ease, not caring while your niece is disturbing the house with her pranks, and ruining your sons."

"What now? I thought you had whipped her and sent her to bed?"

"So I had; but what does the brazen hussy do, but twist up the sheets like a heathen Indian woman — more shame for her! — and call the boys to make a feast, or some nonsense, on the nursery floor, — make-believe dishes, of course; but there they sat, all cross-legged, with her prating away, and ordering about, in French, that horrid Zélie, who always gives me the creeps. When Betty called me, and I came in on them, what do you think she had the impudence to say to me? — 'Oh, Aunt Darpent, I thought, when I had been flogged and mast-headed, that I need not be under arrest any longer!'"

"What have you done now?"

"I could not whip her again, but I sent her to bed again, and ordered off the boys to learn their lessons; but I expect to find her in some mischief, in spite of me. I protest she must go to school. She is past me. Only, where are we to find means to send her up to Queen's Square? And even Miss More, at Bristol, has her prices."

"What say you to this, madam?"

"You have one of your French letters? It is time, indeed, they took notice of their own sister's child."

"Listen, then." And he proceeded to translate,

for madam had forgotten the little French she had ever known.

"Ah," she cried, "it is perfectly providential! They will provide for her. Oh yes, let her go by all means! They ought to do it."

"The sister ought to take some interest in her, certainly; but I do not like sending my poor brother's child among the Papists."

"Why, the child is a Papist already — or half a one! She has got a crucifix and a string of beads in her room."

"Her mother's, of course."

"Yes, of course, so I did not take them away."

"But she goes to church; and did not I hear her saying the Catechism to you with the boys?"

"Oh yes! Her father had taught her the Catechism, and she has read the Bible with him every day, she says; but she stood and gaped when I asked her what she was; and if she has ever been to church before, it was with the black woman, or maybe her mother, in some Popish place. She will not see the difference."

"I do not know that I can answer it to myself, when I remember what my father fled from."

"I thought you always told me they were political exiles?"

"The Ribaumonts ——"

"Oh, never mind all that! You can have her back again when she has been educated, and do what you please with her. But I should like to know how you propose to bring her up as a young lady here, among all these boys, when she is ready to be the veriest tom-boy of them all."

"You spoke of school."

"Ay, and it would cost as much to send her to any good ladies' seminary as it would to educate one of your own boys; and you know yourself that it will go hard with the estate to educate five sons — and your first duty is to your own, Mr. Darpent."

"Poor Eustace! He is my own, and so is his child."

"What can you do better for her than this? We cannot give her female companions, which is what she wants to soften and tame her. Any school we could send her to would be far inferior to such an education as she would get in France; and, as to her staying here, it is bad for herself as for the boys."

Poor Mr. Darpent! He saw fate before him, and contested no farther, for the time, though he was not without hopes in the great force of delay and non-contradiction. But, without knowing it, Caroline sealed her own destiny, or Clement did so.

The boys gravitated towards her, for she was by far the most amusing person in the house; and no sooner was their mother safe in the study, than they crept back to her again. She was a fair child, with grey eyes and flaxen hair, which was cut short and tucked away under a little unfrilled nightcap, but peeped out in tight little curly waves, as she sat up in her narrow wooden crib, with a broom in one hand and a poker in the other, swaying herself backwards and forwards with the motions of rowing, and crooning out a sea-song.

"That's right!" she cried, as Clement peeped in. "I knew you would not forsake a comrade."

"Papa and mamma are shut up in the study, consulting," said the boy. "I wonder what it can be? Sending you to school, I expect."

" If they do, I'll run away, and go to sea."

" You, Carry ! "

" Why not? I know all the ropes."

" But you're a girl ! "

" Well, what of that? I could borrow your clothes and get to Weymouth, then I'd ship me on board a coaster going to Plymouth, if I could find nothing better — and there I should meet some of my papa's old friends."

" I wish you would take me with you."

" So I would. It would be much better sport than going alone. Then we would walk — not meddle with a lubber of a coaster, but take a boat from one port to another. Oh, what fun it would be ! "

The two children romanced together, without any real idea of putting their scheme into practice. But Mrs. Darpent was not a woman of imagination, and, catching a few words of the eager picture, was horrified as she stood at the door. She ordered Clement out of the room, and not to go near his cousin again, locked the door upon her victim, and betook herself to her husband with her story, and from that time she gave him no peace till his preparations for getting rid of this dangerous inmate were put in hand.

CHAPTER II

It was late in the afternoon of a November day that Mr. Darpent and his little niece rattled through the streets of Paris, in the calèche de poste which they had taken at Calais, drawn by two big, heavy, dappled-grey Norman horses, and ridden by a wonderful-looking postilion in enormous boots and wild hair.

On the whole, both had rather enjoyed the journey. Caroline had shed a few tears, and Clement many, at their parting, but the hope of her return was not taken from her, and the girl was so much used to change of place, that she was impatient of Walwyn, and glad, whatever might be coming, to move on. The crossing was absolute joy to her; she only wished it could have been infinitely prolonged. The smell of the sea and the motion of the vessel were felicity to her; and the strange voices, and Calais, looking as we may see it in Hogarth's print, was a new experience, much more amusing than Walwyn, even with the company of Clement and Eustace; and she had no trouble with the language, nor indeed had her uncle, so that the journey was an amusement, in which he enjoyed making acquaintance with the land of his forefathers.

They drove under the porte cochère into the great paved courtyard, with the house opposite to them.

14

A crowd of lackeys, in brilliant livery, stood about the steps to receive them, and ushered them up a broad stair, where, on the first landing, stood M. le Marquis, a handsome spectacle in his laced coat and long waistcoat. He bowed low to Monsieur son cousin, and then, with "Permit me, mademoiselle ma nièce," kissed Caroline's little gloved hand, hot and dusty as it was, and holding it, led her up another flight, to a lofty salon door, where stood a tall, majestic-looking lady, in a great hoop, and with her powdered hair in little curls.

"Ah! ma chère nièce. Sweet reminder of my beloved Marguerite," she cried; and in a moment Caroline was in her arms, pressed to her bosom, and her cheeks watered by a shower of tears. There was something in the tone and the embraces which brought back to the child the remembrance of the mother she had yearned for, and never found again; and with a low cry of "Maman, Maman!" she clung to the lady, who sobbed over her, not, however, without whisking a curl out of her way, but so deftly that it was no shock to the child.

She was treated to a little glass of *eau sucrée* and a biscuit, and then conducted to her chamber through that of Madame de Nidemerle. She looked for her cousins, but she was told that they were in their convent, where she would find them in a few days' time.

The idea was not so alarming to Caroline as might have been expected. Twice she had spent a few weeks with her mother in a nunnery, where she had been petted by the Sisters, and she had a delightful remembrance of kisses, oranges, sugar-canes, and all that was delicious. It was so far connected with her old life that it seemed congenial, and if she could not

be at sea, the alternative seemed preferable to hemming and sewing under Aunt Darpent, and being
whipped and sent to bed whenever she got a little
enjoyment with the boys.

As to her uncle, it is a curious fact that the mutual
antipathy between Roman Catholics and Protestants
was a good deal in abeyance in the latter years of
the eighteenth century. It seems to have died down
in the general indifference. Roman Catholic priests,
educated at foreign universities, were cultivated gentlemen, friends of the more educated gentry. Dr. Milner
and Dr. Lingard are examples. Hannah More was the
intimate friend of Mrs. Garrick, and Mrs. Jean Moore,
the sister of the hero of Corunna, was educated in
a French convent before the Revolution. Besides,
Mr. Darpent was uncertain what his brother would
have wished, or what he might have arranged with
his wife; and he made no objection to the scheme.

Zélie was delighted to have met Coralie and Cesar,
the old black comrades of her youth, from whom
she had parted to follow her mistress. She brought
Coralie to see "la petite mamselle," and there was
immense jubilation over her in queer negro French,
only marred by the fact that the two black nurses
had to remain at the Hôtel de Nidemerle, instead of
being with the young ladies at the convent.

They were in full chatter when Madame de Nidemerle, full dressed in primrose brocade laced with blue,
and with her hair raised to a preposterous height and
width, came to conduct her niece down to supper.

Young ladies were not expected to be thus richly
arrayed, so that Caroline's simple mourning, long-
waisted dress, with elbow-long sleeves and long, drooping crape cuffs, and her hair drawn up by Coralie in

the newest fashion of youth, was held as suitable to
her age, and really affected one or two of the emotional
ladies to tears; while she was studying their head-
dresses with amazement, perfect castles and gardens
as some of them were, — and even one lady wore
Mount Parnassus, with little waxen figures of all the
nine muses, and Apollo playing on the lyre with
Pegasus by his side.

The lady who wore this wonderful arrangement was
something of a student, and was talking eagerly of the
system of Rousseau.   Indeed, the name Emile sounded
so often that Caroline began to listen to discover whose
child he was.   However, the lady turned round to her
with "Ah! mademoiselle, you have had experiences!
You have seen the lovely countries of the tropics and
lived a sweet natural life."

"I have lived chiefly in a ship, madame," said
Caroline, in careful French.

"Ah! you belong to *ces braves Anglais.*"

For at this brief interval, the English were greatly
the fashion in France.   Their institutions were immensely admired, as one form of liberty, and their
horses, their carriages, and the simplicity of their
country life came in for the enthusiasm.

Caroline was surrounded by a whole party of ladies,
questioning her eagerly upon her life on board ship,
and receiving every bit of information with little cries
and exclamations, very different from Aunt Darpent,
who had always treated these doings as something to
be hushed up and to be ashamed of.   "Ah! she has
seen those noble islanders!   She has eaten cocoa-nuts!
She has watched the flying fish!   Do you hear, *mon
ange?* mademoiselle says the sea is full of coral."

Probably her auditors thought it was red coral,

c

ready to become necklaces on the spot! If she could only have seen the diaries in which some of them recorded the revelations of *la petite Anglaise, vrai enfant de la Nature*, who was supposed to have grown up in a perfect Eden of simplicity, and witnessed the dances of a tropical Arcadia if not joined in them.

That one evening was a perfect success, and the child was like a new toy among the ladies.

However, Madame de Nidemerle considered such successes as prejudicial to the young lady's disposition and prospects, or perhaps she thought what once in a way had been an attraction to her salon would not bear repetition.

A cup of milk and a little roll were brought by Zélie to the little cabinet where Caroline slept within her aunt's room, in early morning, while she was still asleep, after her journey and evening's dissipation. She had begun to dress herself, when Madame de Nidemerle looked in.

"Ah! that is well, my child. You will be ready by the time I return from Mass. Thou hast slept well, my angel? Ah, thou art as fresh as a rose."

Caroline had no time to answer, only to exchange an embrace with the lady, who wore a large blue calèche or hood over a mob cap, which entirely concealed her hair, and a loose sacque, her morning undress, in which to attend Mass at the nearest church. Indeed, bells were ringing in different directions all over Paris, and wafted a sweet, mingled music to Caroline's ears, as she leant on the window-seat and looked out. Here she could see nothing but high roofs and chimneys, with the swallows flying about and perching on them, but when she peeped into her aunt's room there was no lack of entertainment. It was a splendid place. The bed was in an alcove, railed in, and shut off by curtains of the most beautiful brocade, representing sheep, shepherds, and shepherdesses on an azure ground, and the toilette-table opposite was a perfect museum of wonders. There was the great mirror, with the gilded and ebony frame, a marquis's coronet on the top, and the arms of the family enamelled on the elaborately adorned sides, and all around were beautiful chased gold and silver or ivory and enamelled caskets and trays, with china or glass bottles and jars for scents or cosmetics; fans, too, of beauteous device; and on one side a cage with a green parrot, on the other a little marmoset. To Caroline this last was like an old acquaintance, and she was talking to it and playing with it, when Cesar entered with a tray of chocolate cups, followed by another lackey bearing a tablecloth and other appliances for the more solid déjeuner that was to be served on the return of Madame la Marquise; and a little silky white dog followed them, so that she hardly knew on which playmate to bestow her attention.

"Ah! fi donc, he bites, *mon ange*," was the first thing she heard as her aunt entered, while she was scratching the little monkey's frilled head.

"Ma tante, no; I know how to manage them. I had one from Cayenne, and it loved me, and slept in my berth, and I was desolate when it died. The carpenter made it a little coffin of sandal-wood, and the boatswain (oh! how do you call a boatswain?) made a little Union Jack to wrap it in."

"What is that? Un Jaques d'Union? Ah! my friend, they will tell you in the convent that it is not polite to laugh at a mistake."

"I beg your pardon, aunt. The Union Jack is our flag, the flag of Britain — the crosses of St. George, St. Andrew, and St. Patrick united. It is our pride. All sailors are buried with it; I mean, it is over their coffins when they are sunk in the sea. Ah! I should not" — and there was a gush of tears, while her aunt, surprised, asked, with kisses, what grieved her.

"Ah! it came back," she sobbed. "It was used when — when — my dear father was — committed to the deep — out in the Atlantic."

Madame de Nidemerle drew the child into her arms and caressed her fondly, bathing her handkerchief with scent; and in the meantime the breakfast continued to be brought in, and Caroline fled back into her room to compose herself, and her aunt made a little coquettish arrangement of her undress garments, Mr. Darpent was ushered into the room together with M. le Marquis, and the various dainty dishes prepared for the first meal of the day. The lady told them that she wished to receive them here for the breakfast "en famille," because she wished to talk about *la petite*, whom she found charming, and *si sensible*, by which Mr. Darpent had to recollect that she meant something very unlike what his wife understood by sensible; and only when Caroline returned with the red mark not entirely effaced from her cheekbones, did he quite understand madame wished to take her to the convent that very day. It would suit with her own engagements, and on the next, there would be a review at Versailles, which Mr. Darpent would certainly wish to see. And in truth the child was too charming to be continually in the salon (whereat the Marquis laughed with a little *malice*), and ought to go to complete her education.

To which the good Squire assented, not indeed
thinking the salon the most wholesome place in the
world, nor one which he would like to have seen fre-
quented by a daughter of his own.   He left the question of religion — not without a qualm, but he was not
at all sure whether her parents, at least her mother,
had not meant her to be a Roman Catholic ; and if she
was to be bred up and married in France, she had
better conform to the faith of the country.   He did
not much like the notion of being conducted to the
convent, but he felt it due to his brother to see what
sort of place it might be.   Zélie was to remain with
her compatriots in the great establishment of Nidemerle.   She cried bitterly as she packed Caroline's
small properties, though her young mistress largely
promised that when her education was finished they
would go out to some West Indian island and live
there under the palms.

"But it shall be an English isle, Zélie ; I will never
live under any flag save the English."

Zélie's chief consolation was the present one of
being with Coralie and Cesar — with whom she was,
of course, far happier than in the English household,
where the servants had called her " Blackamoor " and
Blackie, and had avoided her, while the French, even
the white ones, were always civil to her.

So when Madame de Nidemerle had completed her
toilette, and appeared with a turned-up hat and
feathers on the top of her powdered hair, she, with
Caroline and Mr. Darpent, entered the gaudily
blazoned carriage.   It was a very lofty one, but
madame's head-gear made it needful for her to sit
on a cushion in the bottom of it, instead of on the
seat.   Thus, with four horses, two postilions, a

coachman, and four lackeys hanging on behind, in
gorgeous liveries, progress was slow through the very
narrow streets, where projecting upper stories almost
met overhead, and linen hung out to dry from them.
Sometimes there was a space of wall, with trees looking over it, belonging to some great lordly house, but
even here the vantage ground was occupied by booths
or stalls of vendors of all manner of goods, which they
proclaimed at the top of their voices. Every cabaret
or café had tables in front, where people sat eating
and drinking; at the corners were charcoal stoves,
with old women roasting and selling chestnuts, and
how the horses steered their way through the crowded
thoroughfare of strange figures was a continual wonder
alike to Caroline and her uncle.

CHAPTER III

THE convent of Ste. Lucie stood outside the walls, higher up the Seine, which flowed at the bottom of the gardens, but with a wall between, less high than the other bounding walls, but quite high enough to shut out the inmates from the view of fishermen or boat-passengers.

Very tall and very grim looked those same walls to Caroline, not to say to Mr. Darpent, and they squeezed each other's hands, almost as if he expected to be shut up, while Madame de Nidemerle rattled on about the dear nuns and how happy she had been there. She nodded to the lay sister who came to the entrance of the outer court and peeped out at a little window in a huge nailed door under a ponderous arch.

"Good day, Sister Anne, I have brought you a new pensionnaire. Run and tell the ladies; only first you may let us in — you know me well."

"Ah, madame, indeed, I fly."

She first, however, unlocked the gate, and the carriage rolled in at the great paved courtyard, and up to another door, where a nun in black hood, white veil, and scapulary and dress of dark blue, was listening to her, and a young girl, with hair tied with blue,

23

was peeping behind her. The girl was promptly sent off running on a message, while the portress greeted Madame de Nidemerle, and the doors of the house and of the carriage were opened.

Madame embraced the portress, and all were admitted into the parlour, where there was not much furniture on the parquet floor, only a table with a paper-case and inkstand, and a cross on the mantel-shelf, while prints, chiefly of martyrdoms, hung round the wainscoted walls. One side had a panel fitted with wide-open bars, the *grille*, at which the English Squire looked with some awe.

Presently, however, from another door two girls, one a little older, the other a little younger than Caroline, in dark, stuff dresses and black aprons, one trimmed with red, the other with white, like the ribbons in their hair, came forward.

"Maman, Maman," they cried, while she embraced them fondly. "Mélanie, my dear; Cécile, my sweet. Welcome Monsieur votre oncle and your new companion, your cousin."

Each made a graceful curtsey to Mr. Darpent, and then proceeded to embrace Caroline, who was rather taken by surprise, and stood, shy and awkward, while they declared themselves transported with joy to receive their cousin.

Then, on the other side of the grating, the Mother Superior appeared, not at all the dignified and stately dame for whom Mr. Darpent was prepared, but a little, bright, black-eyed, eager-faced creature, evidently a capital woman of business, with whom there was a most affectionate greeting as of old intimates.

Caroline was introduced and was welcomed as a dear daughter, and the two cousins were sent to in-

troduce her to her companions, and to fetch their
work to exhibit to their mother. Then there was a
refection, *goûter*, or luncheon, served up, of the most
dainty and delicate description, though Mr. Darpent's
English appetite, after his *déjeuner* on small *cotelettes*
and salads, could not help longing for something solid
that he could understand; nor, indeed, could he follow
or fully comprehend the rapid French of the two
ladies, though he knew enough to be aware that the
gossip exchanged was fully equal in quantity to and
was far more in rapidity than that which his own
good woman exchanged with her neighbours over a
"dish of tea."

He did not go away quite happy, nor quite convinced that he had done the best for his brother's
child; but, poor man, what could he do in the face
of his wife? He had given her away, and all he could
do was to forget all about her as soon as he could.

Convents had, a few generations ago, in the days
of Madame de Chantal and Madame de Maintenon,
been made in many instances admirable places of
education. Madame de Maintenon's system for St.
Cyr is worthy of study for all concerned with girls,
and her plans had been adopted in many nunneries.
But machinery slackens without living and enthu-
siastic agency, and the more considerate ladies of the
early times of Louis XVI. were beginning to question
whether the best training for their daughters could
be obtained from women who in general had not the
slightest experience of family life, not even of their
own childhood, but had been pensionnaires from in-
fancy, and nuns because they could not be conven-
iently disposed of otherwise, taking the care of the
young girls in rotation, without any special fitness.

Thoughtful mothers and readers of Rousseau had begun to keep their daughters at home, though this involved the sacrifice of society, or else introduced the child to the world much too early, since there was no idea of a maiden being left to herself for a moment. The convents, however, remained the favourite boarding-schools for all the daughters who were to be kept off their parents' hands till their marriage, and as this comprehended most of the fashionable society of Paris, they continued to be full.

So Caroline found herself introduced to a lively band of some three and twenty girls, superintended by a good-natured old lady, who, if the truth must be told, let her pensionnaires do pretty much as they pleased, provided they comported themselves like well-bred ladies at table, at church, and in public generally.

They were divided into three classes, and all dressed alike, except that the little ones wore white trimmings, the middle ones red, the elders, *les grandes*, blue. Each class had a superintendent, who watched over the lessons, reading the simplest books — compiled and weeded for them a hundred years before — and learning a few other easy studies, among them, and of great importance, *le blason*, or heraldry, which really was not useless in after-life, since it enabled them to recognise any sedan-chair, carriage, or livery of the *grand monde*. Their breviaries and the Lives of the Saints were their religious books, but not much handled. There was a library, and the convent had once been inclined to Jansenism, and the bishop on his last visitation had sealed up all the translations of the works of St. Augustine, and decidedly discouraged study of any kind, except the Lives of the

Saints and *L'Histoire Sainte*, as prepared for the conventual reading of the pensionnaires.   Nobody did
read, in fact, but Sister de St. Jean Baptiste, an old
nun, who loved *L'Imitation* and other books in the
library, and Sister de St. Hilaire, a much younger
nun, who somehow had books smuggled in from outside.

Caroline's English Bible and Prayer-book disappeared with her ordinary wardrobe, when she was
put into the uniform of the second class, and, in fact,
she did not trouble herself much about the loss; it
was recently too much connected with Aunt Darpent,
and her father's big books were safe at Walwyn.
Controversy had not dawned on her mind, and when
she was walked into chapel, the services and surroundings recalled her mother and Zélie.

Music and dancing lessons were given from without,
and "les grandes" took it in turns, a pair at a time,
to assist the Sister Sacristan in the care of the ornaments of the chapel, the Sœur Lingère in the superin-
tendence of the linen of the establishment, the Ména-
gère in kitchen and confectionery work, the portresses
in taking messages — the occupation most esteemed
of all.   Needlework and embroidery were also well
taught, and the girls were generally turned out excellent and accomplished housewives, whatever else
they were taught or not taught.

Indeed, on the whole the influence was good, al-
though some of the management was very peculiar.

On going into the refectory with her cousins, Caroline was amazed to see a little one of the white
division set apart with an enormous pair of ears, cut
out in grey paper, erected on either side of her head,
and Mélanie whispered —

" Poor little thing, *elle a menti*."

Then Cécile added, " Darpent, my dear —— "

" Darpent! — why do you call me so?" exclaimed
Caroline. " It is like the men on board ship."

" No one uses the baptismal name," replied Mélanie.

" Yes, one does," added her sister, "but she is
Polish, with a name all *zy*'s and *sh*'s, which no one
can pronounce, so she is Mademoiselle Ludmille."

" True; but thou, my cousin, must be Darpent.
I am Nidemerle — Merle, if thou wilt, among ourselves — and my sister is Bellaise."

" Mademoiselle is too long to utter each time," said
Cécile de Bellaise; "and I know we shall be true
friends.   Is it not so, my sweet Darpent?"

So Caroline was kindly welcomed, and she did not
meet with less courtesy from the other girls, especially from " les rouges," with whom she was placed,
and to whom Cécile belonged.

They were merry, joyous girls, under very slight
control, as long as they behaved well when in sight,
and to Caroline, who had been used to nothing but
the society of boys and men, the free intercourse with
creatures of her own kind was at first almost intoxi-
cating.   The girls were good listeners, and her stories
of her own adventures, and the yarns she had picked
up, were perfect fairy tales to them, and they would
hang round her in the garden, or cluster about her in
the long evenings in rapt attention, though sometimes
there would be a little quarrel when she exalted the
English flag.

" Ah, if a French ship had been there!"

" The fleur-de-lys would soon have been lowered!"

" No, no; Frenchmen never surrender!"

"Do not they? How about La Hogue, and Ushant, and Quiberon Bay, and —— "

"Ah! deafen me not with your names. It is very impolite. I know the French flag never gives way."

"And I know that we can make it always strike. My father was in the fight off Cape François, where seven French ships were beaten by three English. What do you say to that, mademoiselle?"

"I say that you are a vilaine, naughty English-woman, whom nothing will convince."

This was in such a scream as to bring ma Sœur St. Martin on the scene, demanding what was the matter, and just in time, for the young ladies were on the point of tearing each other's hair.

Each shrieked out at the top of their voices, and so did all the rest of "les rouges," but by and by, through the babel, it was known that Mademoiselle Darpent had been so arrogant as to maintain that the French flag always was lowered before the English, which was preposterous, and Mademoiselle de Solivet had only maintained the honour of the nation.

"And falsely," broke out Caroline.

Whereupon Sœur St. Martin became extremely shocked.

"It is impoliteness — brutal impoliteness," she said. "Mademoiselle Darpent must apologise."

"Apologise! Never, when the British navy is insulted!" cried Caroline, stamping her foot. "They ought to apologise to me."

"Mademoiselle, this is out of all rules. I must send you to penitence in your cell, and make you fast on bread and water, unless you will beg the other demoiselles' pardon."

"Never! It would be lowering the flag."

So Caroline walked off, holding her head very high, to her tiny compartment, where she sat brooding on the possibility of sending a letter to her uncle, to tell him that the English were insulted in her person; but she had absolutely nothing to write with, unless — but that was only in case of extremity — her own blood. But even with that resource, she had no paper, and no means of sending the letter. Then she thought of escape, and struggled with the window, which was apparently never opened; and when at last she was able to crane out her head, she did indeed see cornice and spout enough for her sailor-foot to use in the descent, but it would have been only into the convent garden, and though she might there, by the help of the trees, have climbed to the top of the wall, what could she then do? If she reached her aunt's house, it would only be to be sent ignominiously back to the convent, and without money even her ardour could not reach England alone.

A lay sister opened the door to bring her refection of bread and water, and to ask whether she would apologise and submit; but the honour of the British flag and of her own father were at stake, and she shook her head.

When she had eaten her scanty meal, she amused herself with making a plan of the battle off Cape François with the very scanty appliances at her disposal — such as her brush and combs, a piece of soap, very small and scented, her shoes and — when driven hard to make out ten ships — her garters and stockings rolled up; and these contrivances, and the various manœuvres she made them execute, occupied her so well that she had hardly taken the last French ship before the door was opened, and Sister St. Hilaire came in with —

"Well, my child, I trust you are in a better frame. But " — in amaze — " what is this *déménagement* ?"

"I will show you, Sister. See here. This soap-dish is my father's ship the *Vanquisher;* this slipper is the *Bienvenue.* This is the harbour."

"Peace, peace with all this folly, child!" exclaimed the nun, kicking the *Vanquisher* out of the way with her foot. "Put your room in order, and make your *amende,* and the Mother will forgive you, as a penance."

"Never," cried Caroline, with clasped, not to say clenched, hands. "Nothing will ever make me say what is not true, or that England and my father, the Admiral, have ever been beaten by you French."

Sœur St. Hilaire really believed that the French were invincible, and she had not the wit to see that the national question had better be set aside, and the refractory pupil simply attacked on the score of impoliteness; so, after more wrangling, she retired, shutting her up for the night as hopelessly headstrong. And it was the same the next morning. Caroline was absolutely resolved that no word should concede that English ships had been beaten, and, in fact, she expected to tire out the nuns and gain the victory; so, with morning energy, she shut her lips obstinately against Sœur St. Hilaire, who came to see what could be done by persuasion and coaxing, but, as to the matter of fact, was quite as firm in her belief of her countrymen's victory as the little Englishwoman could be.

However, at about noonday, when very weary of her imprisonment, Caroline was summoned to see Monsieur l'Abbé de Pont de Loire, the spiritual, and often the temporal, adviser of the convent. He was a

good man, but a man of the world, and knew a good
deal better than the excellent ladies how affairs had
really gone at sea, and his *mais elle a raison* had
shocked them dreadfully, less for their own injustice,
or for the national glory, than because the naughty
girl would be maintained in her arrogance and con-
tempt of authority. He had undertaken to arrange
this for them, and when Caroline came down and
made a curtsey, with an odd, half-sullen, half-resolute
face, she was quite startled by being accosted with —

"Here is my daughter who stands up for her father
and her nation."

She felt as if the wall she was going to batter had
suddenly fallen down before her.

"Ah! Monsieur l'Abbé, you know better; you would
not have me deny the truth, and the honour of my
father and his flag, to please these senseless women."

"Hush, my child. It is only in nature and in true
nobility that each should defend his own country, but
it need not be done with bitterness and violence."

"They would not believe me. They made me
angry."

Nevertheless the Abbé succeeded in getting from
her an avowal that she had been uncivil and violent.
She was really tired out with the vehemence of her
resistance, and with her long fast and imprisonment,
and not sorry to be able to give way, provided she
had not to compromise the honour of the British
flag, nor to confess that her father and his *Vanquisher* had ever been defeated. So she agreed to
apologise for having spoken rudely and contradicted
flatly, and the good-natured nuns, who did not quite
know how to act in case of persistent rebellion,
were willing to accept her submission graciously.

CHAPTER IV

YEARS had gone on, and Caroline Darpent was among the "blue" section of the pensionnaires, and so much habituated to the companionship and discipline of the convent, that the time when she had sailed with her father, or when she had romped with her cousins at Walwyn and spoken English seemed like a dream, or, indeed, recurred as a dream, when the wind was high, and she fancied it whistling in the shrouds, and woke to realise slowly that she was in the partitioned dormitory. Sometimes, too, would come a deadly weariness of the monotonous sound, and of female society, and a longing to "break her mind," as it were, against something harder, rougher, and in fact masculine — something not so petty as all the interests and avocations around seemed to her; and even for a few moments a kind of frenzy against restraint within walls, and a longing for the open sea and sky would seize her. In this mood she contrived to climb a tall lime-tree in the garden, and get a view of the river and the country beyond; but this was discovered, and she was punished for "making a scandal."

There were merry times when the married pupils were invited to dances, and came, mostly joyous

young girls delighting in their emancipation, though
still under the rule of their "belles-mères," and petting
and even patronising their old mistresses, the nuns,
as well as their younger sisters and comrades, whom
they dazzled with accounts of the balls and soirées.
Once it was so delightful that the girls could not part
at night, and three of *les mariées* remained, hidden in
the dormitory, where they talked and were made much
of half the night, exultant in their naughtiness.   But
that was not by any means the frame of mind of the
Abbess when they were discovered in the morning.
She sent a note to each of the three mothers-in-law,
who arrived in full state, and carried off the three
culprits in a very limp and dejected condition.

Belles-mères were more the subject of speculation
to the young pensionnaires than the future husbands.
These three visitors had told such different stories.

One had a dear, good-natured mother-in-law, who
would let her do anything she chose, and attended
to her very little, being in fact quite taken up with
the philosophers and the politics of the encyclopedists
and the Academy.

Another had a belle-mère, belle, indeed, who had not
done being a youthful beauty herself, and was fright-
fully jealous of her son's wife, trying to keep her out
of sight, and to make her dress unbecomingly, and
scolding her whenever any one talked to her.

The third, who had been dragged into the frolic
without understanding what was going on, and was
the only one who showed any sorrow, had a really
kind and conscientious mother-in-law, and was very
happy.   Her young husband was *en garnison*, and she
had hardly seen him since the first few days; but his
mother had treated her as her own daughter, taught

her kindly household ways, introduced her to society
with tender, sympathetic care and protection, and
made her house a thoroughly happy home to her.

"All turns on the belle-mère," was well known to
the girls, and when it came to the turn of Mélanie de
Nidemerle, and she was told that the next day she
would have to come down to the parlour to see her
mother and Madame la Comtesse de Limours, great
was the excitement. Her parents had long ago arrived
before Mélanie was dressed, very passively, in the
white dress and blue ribbons that she wore at festi-
vals, and instructed how to comport herself. She listened in a dazed, dreamy sort of way, not half so eager
as the population around, who were wild with curiosity. There was one window that looked out on the
court, and here every available pane was filled with
young heads in tiers one above the other — kneeling
on the sill, standing looking over the heads of the
first, and the last now doing their best to peep over,
mounted upon chairs!

"Hark! is that the carriage?"

"No, that is only a cart."

"There's a trampling."

"Depend on it that is only a regiment of cavalry."

Cavalry could be seen through a scratched corner of
a fan-light, which was ordinarily in great request, but
now was left to such of "les petites" as chose to spy
through it, and one of whom called out, "It's outriders; it is a coach and six."

Politeness — yes, true politeness allowed the little
ones such a first view as they could get through their
small post of observation, and, indeed, the coach and
six, outriders and all, soon clattered into the outer
court, and the coach itself came forward into the

inner court when the prime moment of observation came.

"That is he! Oh! his perruque!"

"No; it must be his father!"

"See, he is handing her out."

"Oh! the belle-mère! Her toupée is *à la nymphe*."

"And what a brocade! How it glistens!"

"See! Ah! that must be her son — *le futur*. White satin — ah, that is appropriate! But, but — oh horror! he has no powder!"

"C'est à l'Anglais, the fashion!"

"But to come wooing without powder! 'Tis disgraceful."

"How could his mother allow it?"

"You are so old-fashioned, ma mie. This is the newest mode."

"Ah! ah! men will come next to woo without shoes."

"Ah! they are gone while you were quarrelling. Now I saw him bow to the mother portress, *à ravir!*"

There was no more to be seen except the servants and outriders, enjoying their *pourboire* in the courtyard; and their liveries and the coats-of-arms on the doors of the carriages were splendid to behold, to eyes accustomed to the monastic blacks, greys, and blues.

By and by Mélanie and Cécile returned, but Mélanie only came to reclaim her own possessions, and to take leave of her companions. She was to be taken to Paris at once to be fitted with her *trousseau*, and to sign the marriage contract. She was in high spirits. Madame de Limours was evidently very amiable, the old gentleman already called her "*Ma fille;*" and as to *le futur*, she demurely professed to have barely seen him, but no doubt he was "*très aimable*" too!

Then came an eager description of the intended
dresses, and how Mademoiselle Bertin was coming
to measure her that very evening. But messages
hastening her movements were followed by floods of
tears at the separation from her sister and her companions. Mélanie cried in the embrace of each, and
of all the nuns in turn, and they wept and wailed in
response, till·finally their sobs were suppressed in a
general rush to the window, to see the departure in
Madame de Nidemerle's carriage.

They had a fête on the wedding-day, and once
Mélanie came to see them, and dilated on all the
gaieties to which she was introduced, and the witty
conversations she heard. This small peep into the
great world filled Caroline with a vague longing.
She was seventeen now, one of the eldest of the
pensionnaires. She had been two or three times
through all the various practical lessons required of
them, and they had become routine, her first friends
had been married off, and she was becoming extremely
weary of her monotonous life, and thought with a sort
of sick dread of the future, and of being consigned to
nothing else for life. The recollection of her full joys
as a sailor's daughter returned upon her as they had
scarcely done in her earlier years, and the longing for
the midshipmen who had been her playfellows, the
officers who had been kind to her, and the very sound
of the rough voices that would not talk of anything but
folly and pettiness. She yearned for change and the
outer world, or rather the outer sea, and yet she had
little reasonable hope, for she did not believe she had
any portion that would win any one to marry her, and
no one could take her for love, always shut up where
she was, never seeing any man except the old Abbé.

Then she began to wonder whether they had any right to keep her, and all the spirit of the British navy began to rise within her at the thought of captivity. In this mood she contrived to write a letter to her English uncle, and the next time there was a visit from one of the ex-pupils, she confided it to her to be posted.

Time went on, and she grew more and more anxious and impatient, as the possible time for an answer came, and no letter. There were only too many probabilities: her friend might have been unable to send the letter, or the very uncertain post might have miscarried, or Uncle and Aunt Darpent might not choose to reply, or, if they had done so, the Abbess might have suppressed the letter. She grew wild sometimes as she lay awake in her bed, above all when some rumour penetrated the convent walls that France had espoused the cause of a revolt in America, and was at war with England. She was sure there must be victories of the British navy, the institution which she loved beyond all others, and she was passionately grieved at being debarred from all knowledge. It accounted for her not having heard from her uncle, and she felt herself almost a prisoner.

Yet, after all, a change came at last. Sœur St. Hilaire came and announced that Mademoiselle de Bellaise and Mademoiselle Darpent were to prepare themselves to be fetched away from the convent by Madame la Marquise de Nidemerle. Their amazement and delight were great.

"Is there not a marriage for me—for us?" demanded Cécile, for leaving a convent without an intended marriage was an extraordinary thing.

"I believe there may be. I can hardly believe you would be summoned away otherwise," returned the

Sister. "Ah! my dear children, you will soon be in
the world. Forget not all that you have learned here."

In due time the carriage arrived. The young ladies
were summoned downstairs, they bade adieu to their
companions, and were received by the Marquise with
all her wonted fervour.

The full truth, which she confided to the Superior,
though she would never have thought of doing so to
the *jeunes filles*, was that Monsieur le Baron de Henisson, whom his own family had designated for Cécile,
had been travelling in England, and had become
touched with Anglo-mania and foolish ideas, "which
had not common sense," and he had absolutely refused
to give his hand to any young lady whom he had never
seen except through the grate of a convent, and insisted on having the opportunity of making some sort
of acquaintance with his bride. Ideas! as the lady
and the nun agreed, throwing up their hands and their
chins at the folly. This being the case, it was advisable to take Caroline at the same time, to serve as a
companion, and likewise because she had so small a
portion that it was unlikely that she could be suitably
disposed of in marriage unless some one free to act
for himself was struck with her beauty. Besides, not
only was it evident that she had no vocation for the
cloister, but it was probable that her Protestant uncle
might scruple at paying her dowry there. The nuns
were not sorry to be rid of her, for they had a strong
instinct that there was something in her that did not
bend to the discipline of the convent, and which might
break out at any time.

So, little understanding all this, she and Cécile were
packed into the coach with the stately marchioness, to
rattle over the paved streets of Paris.

The first person she met on descending at her aunt's house was Zélie, her wool showing whiter under the red and yellow turban, by which Madame la Marquise chose to make her negroes picturesque. Poor Zélie was in an ecstasy, though hardly able to believe that her own picaninny was the same as the tall, slender young demoiselle who threw her arms around her neck in a transport of joy and affection.

The marchioness interrupted the exchange of caresses and tender epithets by ushering both the girls into her own apartment, which was spread with materials, and where a dressmaker was already waiting to give her aid and judgment on what would be most becoming to the *jeunes filles*, yet not be too simple, nor seem to imitate the fashion of the "American Quack-ker" — a creature of whom Caroline heard for the first time. Zélie was allowed to hold the pins, while madame, her own woman, and the modiste consulted over the muslins, taffetas, and brocade, and measured and tried colours with their complexions, and debated vigorously and scientifically, and it was then that Caroline learnt that she was a true white Ribaumont, with the same pure pink-and-white complexion, and hair *blonde cendrée*, — a veritable blonde Anglaise, and that justice might be done to her uncommon cast of beauty.

Truth to tell, she was at first elated, and then pleased by the varieties of fine clothes, but ere long she was dreadfully tired of the discussions over her, and almost regretted her convent when she found she was not to be seen by the outer world till her dresses were finished, that she might burst on the beholders in full radiance.

However, Mélanie came to see them, and brought

her baby, for she stirred nowhere without him, and had an elegant scarf to support him slung round her neck. Such was the new fashion in compliance with Rousseau's teaching.

"Ah," said her mother, "how the world alters! I scarcely saw either of you before you were sent off to be nursed in the country. But then you were only girls! And this is a son!"

So the grandmother timidly took the child in her arms, and studied his charms as an absolute novelty; while the young Madame de Limours chattered away, and assured Cécile that she would find M. de Henisson entirely charming, and delightfully full of new ideas. He had even been at a fox-chase in England!

The Limours family were a good deal imbued with the new opinions, and Mélanie was urgent with her mother to bring the two young girls to her mother-in-law's reception that evening, when little of dress or gaiety was required, but all that was most distinguished was collected.

"There are new notions of what is distinguished," exclaimed Madame de Nidemerle. "To my mind, it is an assembly of mere roturiers ——"

"Ah! but that the roturiers should be there at all proves their genius, maman," replied Mélanie.

"Genius is seldom noble," said the mother, holding up her chin scornfully.

"So much the worse for the noble, as Monsieur mon Mari would say," laughed Mélanie. "Come, dear maman, be persuaded. We shall no doubt have the Henissons there."

"That renders it impossible, when these poor children have no clothes."

"Ah! dear mamma, depend upon it Alexis de He-

nisson is ten times more likely to admire her in her
simple pensionnaire's dress than in hoop and powder.
It is the way young girls go. I engage that you will
see Mademoiselle Necker in just such a dress!"

"The daughter of a Swiss banker! That she should
set the fashion!"

In spite of her disgust, the counsels of her daughter,
or perhaps reluctance to spend a solitary evening, pre-
vailed, and the two girls, in their convent white gala
dresses, with unpowdered hair only adorned by a
snood of ribbon — Caroline's blue, and Cécile's rose-
coloured — were allowed to go to the salon of Madame
la Comtesse de Limours.

As they walked in behind their chaperon, they saw
a dazzling scene of glistening brocade dresses, powdered heads, waving feathers, brilliant velvet coats,
while Mélanie and her mother-in-law came forward to
welcome them. There was little apparatus at the
party: one or two tables where *eau sucrée* and little
biscuits were provided, and pretty boxes of sweetmeats; but people came not to eat but to talk; and
there were seats arranged so as to make places for
conversation, and screens here and there, but the seats
were very uncompromising chairs, for nobody would
have thought of lounging in public, and there was no
provision in the way of entertainment except one
book of prints upon a stand, no piano, no attempt at
music.

Yet all was one buzz of conversation, or rather
one outcry, in the shrill French voices that have never
learnt that low tones are "an excellent thing in
woman," but loud as they were, had a certain grace
and refinement in their emphasised accents.

"Ah! my angel, they are *à ravir*," cried the elder

Madame de Limours. "Their simplicity is exquisite. Thou needst not have feared."

Then, when bows had been exchanged with the two Messieurs de Limours, one in crimson and gold, the other in the splendid blue uniform of the Body Guard, Mélanie said, "I will find you a companion"; and she brought them to a row of chairs, where some ladies and gentlemen were in eager conversation, and a girl, a little younger than themselves, very plainly dressed, not handsome, but with a wonderful pair of eyes, sat bolt upright upon a stool.

"Madame — Madame Necker," said Mélanie, "allow me to present to Mademoiselle Germaine my young sister and her cousin."

There was an exchange of courtesies, and Caroline and Cécile found themselves seated on either side of Germaine Necker and deserted by the sister.

Germaine did not pay much attention to them; she was listening with all her ears to a discussion that was going on upon some subject that seemed a mere bewilderment to the newcomers, nay, sometimes putting in her word, and, as it seemed to the two girls, obtaining real attention and interest, as if what she said was brilliant and to the purpose; but if she leant forward in the eagerness of speaking, her mother was sure to say, "Germaine, redressez-vous."

Cécile was soon tired of listening, and began to gaze round at the younger men, who were half-listening to the discourse, presently deciding that one with a feuille-morte and blue and silver coat, and light-coloured eyes with thick black lashes, must be Monsieur de Henisson.

Caroline, on the other hand, was struck by a figure in a plain long grey coat, with his brown hair coming over his ears and unpowdered, who seemed to be laying down the law in imperfect French, which had an English ring in her ears.

When, presently, a move was made, the elder Madame de Limours coming to present some one to him, Caroline eagerly asked Mademoiselle Necker if that gentleman was English.

"Eh, mademoiselle, you do not know the great English, or rather American, envoy, M. Franklin?"

"Ah! I have heard something. You will tell me, mademoiselle! Is there a war — a war with us, with England?"

"You are English, then, mademoiselle?"

"Yes, the daughter of an Admiral. I only came out of my convent to-day. I entreat you tell me."

"Ah! then you had not heard that the American-English, oppressed and taxed beyond all bearing, have risen against their tyrants, and have appealed to the French nation for aid. It is like the days of William Tell," she cried, as her eyes lit up with animation.

"They have rebelled?" said Caroline.

"If you call it rebellion to shake off an unjust yoke. The young Marquis de La Fayette did not think so. He left his home, and his young wife — whom I know — assisted him to make his escape and fight in the cause of liberty."

"My father would say it was in the cause of revolt," said Caroline.

"Injustice and oppression justify revolt," contended the young Swiss.

"But do I understand that there is a war on behalf of those miserable colonists?" exclaimed Caroline.

"Perhaps Leopold of Austria called it war on

behalf of miserable mountaineers," drily responded Germaine.

It was the old unanswerable question with two sides, and in after-years Caroline did not wonder that she had been unable to answer Germaine, when she identified her with Madame de Staël. And just then "*Germaine, redressez-vous*" broke in upon the conversation, and Madame de Nidemerle came up and resumed the care of her young ladies, to whom she considered Mélanie to be giving too much liberty to converse, and with a mere little roturière, a banker's daughter.

CHAPTER V

THIS was the first time that Caroline really knew of the American war of independence, or of the part that England or France took in it. She was on the alert to hear more; but this was not an easy thing for her to do, for the *jeune fille* was not supposed to know anything of politics, and newspapers, such as they were, were prohibited articles.

Indeed, her mind had plenty of more immediate occupation, for her brocades came home, and her hair was dressed, frizzled, added to, pomaded, powdered, and built up into a terrible structure, on which was planted a whole flower-garden of forget-me-nots and hyacinths, with white feathers above. It was complete before eight o'clock in the morning, and then she had to sit motionless in the powdering-closet, while her cousin and her aunt were under the hands of the friseur. Cécile wore a head-dress adorned with little fluttering doves, suspended upon wires, and her mother a still more imposing fabric, supposed to represent the landing of Æneas in the Bay of Carthage.

When all were drawn up in the salon, seated upon the great black gold chairs, to receive Madame de Henisson and her son, as well as a considerable

46

party, they were a grand spectacle, with the Limours
family, equally resplendent, added to their force.

Mélanie came in, baby and all, with a good deal of
merriment, and sat herself down between her sister
and cousin, admiring them critically, but all the time
chuckling to herself with a good deal of amusement,
the cause of which she chose to keep to herself. The
room began to fill, and Monsieur and Madame de
Nidemerle were occupied with the graces of their
reception. An old gentleman in a brown-and-gold
coat came near and began to talk to Mélanie. He
was one of those whom Caroline had met at Madame
de Limours', and when he began to talk to her, she
brightened up, and answered with animation. Moreover, she discovered what she wished so much to know
— the bearings of the case between France and England — and she showed a familiarity with naval affairs
and with practical geography which amused him much;
and her face was full of life, while Cécile sat, grave
and sedate, shy and stiff, as became a pensionnaire
on trial, while Madame de Henisson and Madame
de Nidemerle talked over her head, and the young
Henisson with the Anglo-mania wandered near, sometimes talking to other gentlemen, sometimes listening
to one or other of the conversations.

Mélanie de Limours seemed extremely diverted and
delighted with the whole evening, laughing over it
heartily in her pretty way, and declaring that little
Caroline had made a conquest, if not two — one being
of the old Vicomte de Noirmont, an ancient widower
and Chevalier de Saint Louis, who could do whatever
he pleased; and the other — no, she would not tell
who it was who was smitten, but she laughed the
more.

Madame de Nidemerle was a good deal excited by the notion of the Vicomte. It would be a magnificent *parti* for Caroline Darpent; and, after a few years of being an old man's darling, she would be free to amuse herself and wed whom she pleased. But it was good taste that the young lady should be wholly uninformed of her suitors; so nothing was said to Caroline. Indeed, the mother and her married daughter questioned whether, having made the impression by her *esprit*, she had not better be sent back to her convent till the preliminaries were arranged, so as to whet the ardour of the old gentleman, and to make her willing on any terms to return to the world. However, this plan was put out of the question by an outbreak of small-pox in the convent. The good nuns were of the party who held inoculation to be impious, and the deadly disease was raging amongst them with the utmost virulence, so that Caroline's return was impossible.

Mélanie and her mother were closeted for a long *tête-à-tête*, the upshot of which was that Caroline was to go back with her cousin and become a guest, with Zélie, in the Hôtel de Limours.

"You see," Madame de Nidemerle had said, "thanks to these ridiculous ideas of liberty of choice, here is that foolish young Henisson strangely attracted away from Cécile by the English air and English manners of Caroline, while Cécile remains the quiet little pensionnaire, with manners *comme il faut*, and knows what is becoming far too well to attempt to win him."

"I do not think Caroline intends anything; but one must allow that she is far prettier and in a more uncommon style than poor Cécile," said Mélanie.

"A great rosy-cheeked shepherdess, with no air,

only fit to associate with her father's sailors, after whom she pines."

"She really cares for little else."

"Would that she were among them again. I am in continual dread that the youth may be insensate enough to speak of love to her, and then who can guess what the effect would be! And when the good old Noirmont is on the point of proposing for her."

"There is no harm done yet."

"I think not! Her head is simply full of this war; but who can tell what may happen at any moment?"

"Well, mother, let me take her home; I will make my mother-in-law understand. We will undertake to keep her out of the way of M. de Henisson, and to let M. de Noirmont have every opportunity of being fascinated by her plump roses and her lively tongue."

And so it was settled, and Caroline found herself transferred to the Hôtel de Limours, a much more amusing abode than that of Nidemerle, and where, moreover, she had a room to herself, or only with Zélie on a pallet on the floor.

Mesdames de Limours were sufficiently infected with the new ideas to afford Caroline a good deal more liberty and sympathy than she had previously met with. The elder watched and philosophised, the younger laughed and was confidential. It would hardly have been in the nature of things that Mélanie, so very little the elder, should not, in gaiety of heart and self-importance, confide to Caroline all that she was not meant to confide, especially when M. de Henisson made his appearance on an evening when he was by no means expected, when the ladies had settled themselves down to listen to a poem upon the Gracchi, written by a candidate for the Academy, and were

E

devoting their fingers to *parfiler*, namely the unravelling of gold lace on trimmings or epaulettes, to be made up again into ornamental trifles. He came and hovered about, offering to hold a long piece of lace while Mademoiselle Darpent unravelled it; and in the meantime the elderly Viscount sat bending his grizzled eyebrows, and cynically criticising poor Caroline, even to the verge of impoliteness.

Mélanie was so much tickled that she could not help following Caroline to her room, and making merry over her two admirers. Poor Caroline's eyes grew round with horror.

"My cousin, you are in jest; M. de Henisson is to marry Cécile."

"If he will; but he has been in your country, my dear friend, and has ideas of his own."

"Impossible. His honour is engaged to my aunt and uncle."

"Only his mother's word! Come, my dear, you should be flattered."

"Flattered? To find myself the supplanter of my dear Cécile? Mélanie, what are you thinking of?"

"Very well, then, you must pay more attention to your other *pretendeurs*."

"Now I am more puzzled than ever, unless you simply want to tease me."

"You have, then, never observed the rapt looks of poor Monsieur de Noirmont?"

"He! Now I am sure it is a joke."

"See whether you think so when my father and mother fetch you to sign the contract of marriage."

"Impossible. Why, his face is the colour of *café au lait*, and puckered like an old sailor's who has faced wind and sun for forty years."

"Nevertheless he is visibly taken with you — all your *esprit*, my dear. He made inquiries of my belle-mère as to your connections and your *dot*."

"I have no *dot*, I am happy to say."

"Ah! that does not matter to him. He has I know not how many thousand livres de rente in Périgord, besides a pension as master of the Queen's lap-dogs, and he is a Chevalier de St. Louis! You would have *les grandes entrées*."

"What do I care for that? He is wrinkled like an old ape looking out of his fine waistcoat. I once had a monkey from Demerara exactly like him. Oh! Mélanie, it is impossible!"

"You will not find it so. And after all, as my mother says, you will soon be free, and a rich Viscountess."

"I will never believe that my aunt said anything so wicked."

Mélanie shrugged her shoulders.

"I shall write to my uncle in England. Ah, this war!"

Caroline began to weep bitterly.

"Oh cousin, dear cousin, cannot you help me?"

"I? All the girls I have ever known would be transported at such a prospect! Do you not know that it is absolutely shocking to think about love for one's *fiancé?* If my mother heard you, what would she say? Turning away from such an admirable *parti*, just to cross poor Cécile's marriage, and make her betrothed in love with you!"

"Never! never! You know that would be too horrible."

"I may know it, but my mother would never believe it, scarcely even my mother-in-law, unless you are a good child and quietly accept M. de Noirmont."

Wherewith Mélanie heard her son crying, and hurried away, leaving Caroline in tears of despair.

She wept herself to sleep in the perplexity between the choice of seeming to betray her cousin, or of allowing herself to be bestowed on the old man whom she regarded with all the horror of youth. However, she went to sleep, and with morning light began to regard all that Mélanie had talked of the night before as a sort of bad impossible dream.

And the morning's events drove the matter out of her head. All the bells all round were ringing for joy; those of the church close by almost deafened her. She generally went thither to Mass, with the elder Madame de Limours, for motherhood had dispensed Mélanie from going, and if the mother-in-law did not go, Zélie walked close behind her, and a footman a little further off.

Something was murmured of a victory, and the priest, as he took his position at the little side altar, called on his dear children to give thanks for a great naval victory over the English.

Caroline felt anything but thankful. Her heart was hot within her; she flatly disbelieved that the English *could* be beaten, even when she came home and found all the family in transports of delight. Captain Chandeau de la Clochetterie in the *Belle Poule* had actually beaten off the English ship *Arethusa* in the Channel, and forced Admiral Keppel to retreat with all his fleet. Nay, there were those who declared that all the fleet had been captured and carried into the harbour of Brest.

Poor Caroline! She wept angry tears, and begged

for a sight of the *Gazette*, out of which she got so
much comfort that she could not find the name of a
single British ship captured, or even sunk, which she
would have preferred!

"Yes," she cried with flashing eyes, "I had rather
sink with my father's ship, or be blown to atoms than
that he should strike his flag."

The ladies went out for a walk in the Tuileries Gardens, in the stiff paths, shut in by trees and statues,
Caroline prancing and dancing with excitement, ready
to snap contradictions off at all who did but mention
the navy.

Suddenly she saw Dr. Franklin's grey Quaker costume, as he talked to some stranger. There was no
holding her in. The two Mesdames de Limours were
scandalised by seeing her fly up to him, leaping over
a bed of pinks, and, clasping her hands on his arm,
cry out in English —

"Sir, sir, pardon me; but at least you will know
the truth and tell it to me. What is this? What has
happened to the English fleet?"

He looked down at the eager little flushed face,
amazed.

"Thou art English, child?"

"Oh! yes, yes; my father was a British Admiral.
I cannot hear the truth here. Tell me! Has harm
befallen our fleet? Have the French beaten us? Oh
no, I cannot believe it!"

"Be content, little patriot. The French know how
to blow their own trumpet."

"Then it is not true?"

"I might say I wish it were, but I have too much
British blood to care to see this nation triumph even
in our cause on the British element," said Franklin.

"Good, dear sir!" ejaculated Caroline.

"What happened was this. The *Licorne* and the *Belle Poule* frigates were attacked by the English *Arethusa*. The Unicorn gave in and surrendered, after the fashion of that fabulous animal, but the Fair Hen ruffled her feathers and wings and made such good defence that by the time she had got among the Breton rocks, the *Arethusa* was dismasted and well battered. There was a calm, and no other vessel could come to her aid, so —— "

"She did not yield."

"Oh no! She drew off and joined the rest of the fleet! And the *Belle Poule* came into Brest, and the Gallic cock has been crowing ever since, till it makes an honest man sick to hear him."

The two ladies de Limours came up, very much shocked, at the same moment. They could endure a good deal, but this, in full view of the promenaders in the Tuileries Gardens, was more than they could tolerate, and they had hurried round the devious paths, not taking the short cut like their charge.

"Monsieur le Docteur, I am desolated, I pray you to excuse her," began the elderly lady.

"She is a good little patriot, madame," said Franklin, in his halting French, not removing his broad-brimmed hat, but making an inclination that might pass for courtesy. "A good patriot, though not on my side of the question, and I honour her. Adieu, brave Anglaise."

The ladies, fairly capturing Caroline, bore her off between them, but could not chain her tongue, as she called out:

"Farewell, Dr. Franklin. Take all my thanks. You have told me the truth."

Madame de Limours tried all the way home to bring Caroline to a sense of the enormity of her proceeding; but Mélanie would do little but laugh at the patriotic English "Mattelotte," as she called her, "skipping over the pinks as if they had been waves," and gaining the applause of the great "Quackker."

And even Madame de Limours the elder allowed that it was the less harm, as he was in a manner English also, only it was to be hoped that no one had seen her, especially no one who would tell M. de Noirmont.

While Caroline went back, attending to very little that either said, only swelling with delight that the French should call it a victory to have the *Licorne* taken, and to have barely succeeded in beating off the *Arethusa*.

The *Belle Poule* might have been a turkey-cock for the triumph she made of it!

CHAPTER VI

CAROLINE's exasperation was to be increased to the last degree. The next night the whole family party went to the Opera — Gluck's opera of *Armida* — and there, in every box, from that of the Countess of Provence downwards, was to be seen what was called the Coiffure Belle Poule; namely, on the powdered expanse, raised a quarter of a yard above the ladies' heads, there tossed a sea of green gauze, upon which elevation appeared the best model of the *Belle Poule* that Parisian art could devise, in full sail, with the fleur-de-lys at her masthead, chasing the *Arethusa*, saucy no more, but going off with shattered masts, behind the ladies' back hair, where the Union Jack, or what was supposed to be such, trailed in disgrace.

The anger of eighteen years is a vehement matter. Caroline's eyes flashed lightnings as she looked from one box to another. She bit her lips, could hardly swallow down her fury, or keep from breaking in on Gluck's compositions, which might soothe Rinaldo, but were very far from soothing her.

Then she remembered with glee how very small the advantage had been over which they were exulting, though, in truth, the amiable Parisian public really believed it had been a magnificent victory.

"Thankful for small mercies!" She could not but quote the old Scottish saying. "We should have called it next thing to a defeat!"

As in fact "we" did.

"My dear child, do not talk so fast! It is not good taste," remonstrated Madame de Limours.

"If they would not triumph when there is no triumph," said Caroline. "Why, they could not even make a Union Jack properly. They mixed up all the crosses together; but that was a good thing, for it was *not* the English flag that they trailed in the dust."

"Literally in the dust," said Mélanie; at which they all laughed, thinking of the white clouds of powder at the back of the ladies' heads, and she began to talk gossip so vehemently that Caroline was silenced.

She meditated, however, and devised a revenge! How should she carry it out? It was of no use to talk! M. de Noirmont, whom she favoured with an outpouring of "the simple truth," only took it as her national spirit and another form of *esprit;* and indeed Madame de Nidemerle came to her daughter replete with delight at his having actually asked the young lady from her uncle. There would really be the brilliant marriage that had been held out to Mr. Darpent for his niece, without much real hope that it would be attainable, and moreover Caroline would be removed from being an obstacle in Cécile's way, and the tardy Baron de Henisson might at last proceed in the matter.

Mélanie rejoiced that the matter was broached while Caroline and Cécile were both out of hearing.

"It had better be arranged before she hears of it, dear mamma," she said. "If there seems to be no escape, she will be more likely to yield."

" *Comment ?* A well-brought-up girl refuse a marriage!"

"Ah, my dear mamma, you forget her original English breeding! She is so wild now about our victory, that she can think of nothing else."

After all, Mélanie was not quite straightforward. She durst not show her mother how much she sympathised with Caroline in her horror of the old monkey-faced Viscount, yet she sincerely wished to clear the way for her sister; and she gathered, before long, that she had only to sit still and connive at her cousin's own perfectly simple-hearted proceedings, to have the whole difficulty cleared up.

For Caroline's whole idea was to vindicate the honour of the British flag. She kept herself a good deal shut up in her room, and used to the utmost her opportunities of buying various chiffons. But even Mélanie was in consternation, when, at the next Opera, the huge calèche came off which had shrouded Caroline's head, and she walked into the box behind the two Mesdames de Limours, the two gentlemen being at a half-literary, half-political *soirée*. For on her head she bore, raised on a scaffold of powder and pomatum with other stiffenings, five English line-of-battle ships, beautifully and artistically constructed, each with a streamer bearing her name, and all taking the *Licorne* and a lugger into Plymouth harbour, which was denoted by an erection of silk and gauze, with the name over it, traced in beads!

In this way, holding her head aloft like a peacock, did Caroline Darpent march into the box and take her seat with the air of Britannia herself, regretting that she could not sit in the front place. For, after the first glance, Mélanie, who had generally given

way to her as a guest, took fright, and thought it
prudent to efface her as far as possible, suppressing
her own laughter, and growing very nervous as she
detected lorgnettes directed upon the party.

The elder Madame de Limours was rather blind,
and had not observed the full splendours of Caroline's
patriotic head-dress. In truth, its beauties were on
too minute a scale to attract attention in such light as
theatres then enjoyed, and there was a little sense of
disappointment. Something was lacking to the sensation that ought to have been produced.

However, between the acts, first one and then
another gentleman came into the box and performed
due acts of politeness to Madame de Limours, with
whom they were slightly acquainted, then evidently
studied the young lady's head-dress as closely as
politeness would permit, though they conversed on
casual subjects; but Mélanie's eyes began to grow
round with alarm.

"Unhappy child!" she whispered, as they went
away. "What have you done?"

"What do you mean? I hope they at least understand that I know what victory means."

"What could bring M. de Ratouville here?"

Meantime Madame de Limours the elder asked
complacently —

"He is no longer greatly connected with your husband, my dear?"

"No," returned Mélanie, under cover of the music;
"he dropped Charles for his friendship with the
Orléans party."

"You do not think he has any false suspicions of
Charles?"

"No, no. Our party is in favour now. But"—and

she shook her head at Caroline, with a meaning look
of anxiety, and by and by managed, during a great
burst of the orchestra, to say in her cousin's ear — "he
is said to be a spy of the police."

"Let him be," proudly replied Caroline. "I am not
ashamed of my colours."

But Mélanie remarked that M. de Noirmont did not
as usual visit their box, though he was visible in the
distance, apparently quite absorbed in the music of
Gluck. She was somewhat disturbed, and Caroline
felt a shade of vexation, for she would have liked a
tilt with him on her patriotism.

More, and probably stronger, opera-glasses began to
be directed towards the party, and while the elder
lady was wondering what was the attraction, M. de
Henisson came into the box, and, leaning over Mélanie,
said —

"Madame la Comtesse's carriage is in waiting. It
would be well to come away before the general departure."

Mélanie understood, and jumped up, laying her hand
on her mother-in-law's shoulder, and hinting to her
that there would be a final crush.

"But, my dear, I love the last chorus."

"Yes, yes, dear mother, but — but I must get home.
My baby —— " Mélanie coined the excuse.

"Ah, child, that new fashion! We knew better than
to let our infants be an inconvenience."

However she yielded, and M. de Henisson manœu-
vred them out, Mélanie pulling Caroline's calash as
far as possible over her head.

"You blind me!" cried Caroline.

"No, no; I conjure you, keep it on." gasped Mélanie,
as they made their way through the dark passages

with their pioneer; and as they emerged into the
lamplit hall they heard murmurs —

" It was the Limours party. That is the old lady."

And odd-looking men stood about, one of whom, as
they crossed the pavement to the carriage, contrived
to be pushed up against Caroline, and shoved back her
great hood, so that for a moment the English fleet
hove in view.

" There she is ! It is she ! The spy ! the traitor ! "
were the murmurs, growing to a growl and roar.

Madame de Limours was in the carriage, Caroline
turned on the step.

"No traitor ! I am English —— "

She did not finish the word. M. de Henisson fairly
threw her into the carriage after Mélanie, though not
in time to hinder a big lump of mud from falling on
her neck. He stood with half-drawn sword, exclaiming —

" Who dares find fault with a brave lady for defending her country's honour ? "

The mob of Paris was not what it became fifteen
years later. There was something that appealed to
their feelings in the notion of the gallant lady standing up for her country, and some of them even cried,
" Vive la belle ! " and though there was a counter cry
of " À bas les Anglais ! " the coachman was not hindered from driving off, with Mélanie almost in
hysterics between fright and diversion, Madame de
Limours feebly inquiring what was the matter, and
what it all meant, and Caroline chiefly solicitous that
the Parisian mud should not have touched the English
navy.

It was not till they had reached home, and were
fairly among the wax-lights of the salon, that Madame

de Limours fairly understood what the provocation had been.

"Look, mother, do you not see — Caroline's patriotism?" cried Mélanie, sinking into a chair, to laugh at her ease. "Look at her head."

Caroline, who had satisfied herself, by a glance at a mirror, that the British fleet was safe, had to sit upright in her chair while Madame de Limours, in her spectacles, looked her well over, with exclamations —

"Plymout! Ah! *malheureuse.* What have you done?"

"I have maintained the truth, and held up the honour of our flag," replied the undaunted young lady.

"Mélanie! how could you let her be so mad? That was the reason that Ratouville came in. What may she not have brought on us?"

"Whatever happens, I will bear the whole blame, madame! I have no fear for any one else."

"You do not know! There may be a *lettre de cachet* on its way for all of us."

"Oh no, mother," said Mélanie, "the days of the Bastille are over! It will only be a laughing matter"; and off she went again. "To see the puzzled, hesitating faces, when they began to aim their lorgnettes at her, much as if they had been pistols! and after all they did not half understand the point. You were too *fine* for them, Caroline, my dear. A walnut-shell boat would have answered the purpose quite as well as those beauteous miniature men-of-war."

"Surely you had no share in the concoction of this — this ——" Madame hesitated for a word.

"Oh no, my dear maman. Caroline can assure you that it was all her own doing."

" Yes, indeed. Of course it was my own. I would have no one's help but Zélie's," returned Caroline. "I let the coiffeur build up my head, but I changed all his ornaments afterwards. Do not fear, madame. I will explain that it is my own doing! and willingly go to the Bastille if they will."

" Well, child, go to bed now. Do not let *Monsieur mon Mari* see you in this trim."

Caroline was not sorry to obey, for seven ships, besides Plymouth harbour, were no trifle to carry upon her head, nor did she quite wish to encounter M. de Limours' satirical looks, which would be much more trying than the open condemnation such as she could defy.

She saw no more of any one that night, and dreamt that all the little ships were still on her head, and were firing at the enemy; but suddenly all turned into bonbons, and the smoke was a cloud of perfume, out of which came Franklin's voice, saying, " Cut off her hair, and put her into a 'Quackker' bonnet."

CHAPTER VII

DEFEAT

MÉLANIE came to her cousin's room betimes in the morning.

"Ah, my dear little cabbage," she began, "I fear they will never forgive you!"

"Who?"

"My father and mother-in-law. They say you must be sent straight off to your aunt at once, or we shall all be embroiled with the Court. Oh, my dear, my dear, when shall I see you again? You will not see this angel"—holding up her baby for a kiss, and with tears in her eyes.

Caroline joined in the passionate embrace, but still she was staunch, as became an Admiral's daughter.

"I am ready for the consequences," she said.

"It is all over Paris, my dear! M. de Limours heard that you stood in front of the box, crying, '*Vivent les Anglais; à bas le pavillon Français!*' That, of course, I told him you never did; but they say, too, that M. de Henisson kissed your hand, and dared any one to touch his *fiancée!*"

"M. de Henisson behaved only as any gentleman — any man — would to ladies in danger," said Caroline.

"We shall have my mother here in fury and despair about Cécile's marriage," said Mélanie. "Ah, ah! I hear wheels in the court! Depend upon it, it is she."

And so it proved to be! The whole party were summoned to the room where the elder Madame de Limours sat up in bed in her alcove, supported on laced pillows, and in an elaborate nightcap; and there stood Madame de Nidemerle, with her hand on the back of her chair, too angry to remain seated, with hot tears in her eyes.

" Miserable child!" was her cry. " What have you done ? "

" I have vindicated the honour of the English flag, that is all, madame," replied Caroline, whose blood was up, so that she made a little insulting curtsey.

" You have insulted the French nation, offended the Court, so that it is well if all of us do not spend the rest of our lives in the Bastille."

Some one murmured "No, no."

"Or in exile, at least, which would be as bad! And not content with that, she has overset two marriages — excellent marriages!" cried the lady, bursting into tears. "My daughter, my unnatural daughter, I believe you knew all about it. Here has the Vicomte been with your father this morning already to withdraw his offer for such a firebrand."

Caroline clapped her hands. " I knew it, the mean old fellow!" she muttered under her breath.

"Such a marriage, which would have given us all the lead. And as to Henisson, you did it on purpose to feed his Anglo-mania, mademoiselle — I know it too well — to attract him away from my poor Cécile —— "

"No, no, madame," broke in Caroline. " I never thought of any such thing."

" Then why did he come and play the hero of romance to your absurd exposition of nationality ? "

F

"He acted a manly part, as a gentleman would do," cried Caroline. "If he learnt only in England to stand by ladies in distress, so much the worse for France! I do not want to marry him, nor any Frenchman of the whole crew!"

"That is true, mother," ventured Mélanie. "My cousin sincerely wished to avoid hurting Cécile's prospects."

"It was your fault; you abetted her in it all."

"No, she did not," exclaimed Caroline. "All I did was unknown to her; indeed it was."

Madame de Nidemerle sniffed the air incredulously, but added —

"One thing is certain: back to the convent you go. Such a disloyal being shall not remain in my house, nor yours, madame."

"But the small-pox!" cried both the ladies de Limours at once.

"The small-pox is nearly over."

"In the most infectious stage!" exclaimed Madame de Limours. "No, she must go to the Ursulines. They would take her in till she can be sent to England."

Their conversation was interrupted, for M. de Limours came in with a very grave face, and, after greeting to the visitor, said —

"Mademoiselle Caroline, I fear your escapade has serious consequences. M. le Noir desires an interview with mademoiselle."

"The chief of police," sighed Mélanie. "Oh, Caroline, Caroline, what have you done?"

Still Caroline would not be frightened. Indeed, it is not certain that she did not enjoy having made such a commotion, and, at any rate, having disposed of her ancient suitor.

She held her head high, and declared herself ready
to see the great man ; but Mélanie and her aunt both
insisted on calling Zélie, and touching up her im-
promptu toilette, while she fidgeted, eager not to
keep him waiting, and to have it over.

When at length she was ready, M. de Limours
escorted her to the salon, accompanied by Mélanie,
who held her hand to give her the courage she did
not want. They found M. Charles de Limours and
M. de Nidemerle both in company with a military-
looking man, stiff in his uniform, and with a brown,
dry face.

"Pardon me," he said politely, when bows had been
exchanged, "I believe mademoiselle is English? "

"Certainly I am English. My father was Admiral
of the Red, and commanded the seventy-two gun
vessel *Corcyr*."

"Yet mademoiselle is the niece of Madame la
Marquise de Nidemerle? "

"Yes; my mother came from Guadaloupe."

"You have been at Paris — how long? "

"Five years. I sailed with my father till his death,
then I was sent to my uncle in England; but since that
time I have been here."

"In the convent of Ste. Lucie, outside the walls,"
put in M. de Nidemerle. "She has only left it for six
weeks, on account of the small-pox raging there, and
we are about to send her back at once."

"Will mademoiselle favour me with a sight of her
head-dress of last night?" politely asked the chief of
police.

Caroline was allowed to fetch it, and she brought
in from her toilette-table a tray on which she had
arranged her seven ships and her Plymouth harbour.

They were carefully and minutely examined by the
four gentlemen, and finally M. le Noir said —

"A marvellous work of art. Mademoiselle will forgive me for carrying them away."

"Since they are the only English ships that monsieur takes," said Caroline, with a curtsey, and twin-
kling eyes half downcast, though with a trembling
voice. She had been thinking over the retort, and
wondering whether she should have courage to utter it.

"Mademoiselle is a vehement partisan," replied M.
le Noir. "She cannot be surprised if his Majesty
objects to her further residence here. I have here"
— and he produced it — "an order for her immediate
leaving of the country."

Caroline's spirits rose at finding no one else was
to suffer, and she was ready with an answer.

"Thank you, monsieur. I shall be glad to find myself at home in my father's country."

"But — but," a cry arose from her kinsman, "can
she not have a little grace from his Majesty? How
can a young demoiselle be sent to England alone, and
in time of war?" said M. de Nidemerle.

"That has been thought of," returned M. le Noir.
"I gave, yesterday, their passports to an American
family of a merchant who desires to take them to
England. They will take charge of mademoiselle
until she can be returned to her family."

The matter had been done with much consideration
for those concerned — more, indeed, the ladies held,
than Caroline deserved, and they were heartily glad
to be free from so dangerous a patriot. No one even
shed a tear over her except Mélanie, for she was not
allowed even to see Cécile, though it was hard to say
how she could have perverted that young lady.

Zélie was to accompany her, and the party were to
be escorted, in honour of Caroline's presence, by two
gens d'armes as far as the borders of Flanders, whence
the Americans meant to embark in a neutral vessel.

One of the *gens d'armes* remained at the porte
cochère all night, which gave Caroline an odd sense
of consequence.   M. de Nidemerle went to see the
Americans, and brought back comfortable assurances
that Mrs. Rudyard was kind and friendly, and promised to watch over Miss Darpent like her own daughter.
The party went in two carriages, calling at the Hôtel
de Limours in early morning, when Mélanie attended
her to the bottom of the staircase, and parted from
her with showers of tears.

Caroline looked long at Paris, at the narrow streets,
the beautiful Seine, and the towers of Notre Dame,
little guessing what she escaped, or where her friends
would be in twelve years' time.

There is no need to describe her journey with
friends who showed themselves heartily kind, and a
good deal amused at the attention paid them by the
innkeepers in consequence of the attendance of Caroline's escort, who left them when they passed the
Flemish border.

At Ostend, an English brig, which had put in for
some slight repair, delighted the eyes of Caroline.
She was laughed at for expecting to take her passage in
her; but at the *table d'hôte* there appeared two or
three officers, whose blue coats and gold buttons were
exquisite joy to her.   Something soon passed between
Mr. Rudyard and the captain, and presently she
heard —

"Miss Darpent, Captain Aylmer desires to be presented to his countrywoman."

Her eyes sparkled. So did his.

"Miss Darpent! Can it be little Caroline?"

"Oh, George, George, is it you? Are you a commander?"

For her sake, Captain Aylmer offered a passage to England to Mr. and Mrs. Rudyard, and when they went on board the next morning, Caroline went up the side of the ship as if "her foot was on her native heath." All the crew were mustered to receive her, and the cheers in which they broke out to welcome their old Admiral's daughter, who had maintained the honour of the British flag, deafened the Flemings, who decided that she must be a princess in disguise.

A bower was constructed for her on deck, with the Union Jack suspended over it, and her three days' voyage to Portsmouth was a sort of ovation. Captain Aylmer obtained leave of absence to escort her to Walwyn, and there obtained the more hearty welcome for her from even Aunt Darpent, by his promise to come back for her and make her his own as soon as his present voyage was finished, and he was a post-captain.

And with this prospect, Mrs. Darpent could well accept the presence of the pretty bright girl, who accepted English habits and English church-going quite naturally, showed no perilous disposition to attract such of her cousins as were still at home, and was actually useful with her dainty convent cookery and exquisite needlework. Moreover, she fulfilled Mrs. Darpent's desires by teaching the two little girls, who had been added to the family shelter, French as well as English. And Mr. Darpent always had a story wherewith to raise a laugh among his friends when he related how his little Carry had maintained the honour of England.

PART II

THE RELEASE

CHAPTER I

A SUMMONS

Ye mariners of England !
That guard our native seas.

CAMPBELL.

IT was in a congenial place that Caroline was seated,
namely the cabin of the frigate *Oudenarde;* the narrow. odd-shaped space shared by the carriage of a gun,
which protruded from the porthole, while another
more manageable window gave her a view over the
green waters of Plymouth harbour, thickly dotted
with vessels of all sorts and sizes, from the seventy-
four gun ship down to the shore boat.

She was Caroline Darpent no longer, but Caroline
Aylmer. The kind lieutenant of the days of her childhood had come home full of honour from the Siege
of Gibraltar, and had employed his leisure on shore
in a courtship at Walwyn. Never was there greater
satisfaction at being again connected with the Royal
Navy. Squire Darpent, her uncle, jokingly averred
that R. N. was Captain Aylmer's chief recommenda-
tion; but there was old love and admiration between
him and the maiden of his choice, and there was enthusiasm enough within her, even after five happy years,
to be proud and gratified at his appointment to the
Oudenarde, though the vessel was put in commission
for the East Indian coast.

73

The drawbacks to her delight soon revealed themselves. Wives, if not prohibited, were decidedly discouraged articles on board, and Captain Aylmer would not hear of her going to Bombay, so as to be within reach, in the utter uncertainty of his whereabouts. She could only be with him while the ship was refitting, and there both had to suffer from the grievance of having had to leave their two little children under the charge of their grandmother, so that little Eustace would not have even a three-year-old's impression of his father's ship. Travelling was too expensive for him to be brought down for a day or two, and though his mother declared that he could be as happy and prosperous as she had been, her husband would not make his officers uncomfortable, nor expose the boy to the chances of picking up nautical language.

Caroline, as vehement as ever, had nearly quarrelled with him, being sure that nothing had done her any harm; but he only laughed at her indignation, though laughter was only the readiest way to stave off the manifestation of the pain of parting with his wife and little ones for five, it might be for seven, years.

In spite of not being able to teach Eustace the ropes, nor make him shout at the report of a cannon, the husband and wife were enjoying the sweetness of "last times," and prizing each fresh discovery of need of repairs that involved delay. Caroline sat at work, auguring that she should be able after all to finish the delicate embroidered muslin ruffles that her husband was to wear when he dined with the governor or the admiral, when she heard his step coming down to her, and, as she sprang up to meet him, he appeared with a large packet in his hand.

"Come by coach from Downford," he said. "Your

uncle sends it on from Walwyn. It looks like a despatch, but it is addressed to you."

"Yes, and they would have known where to write to you," said Caroline, as she cut round the large red seal with the quartered arms of Walwyn and Ribaumont. "No, this enclosure, 'Á Mistris Caroline Ailmère,' is from my French cousins; I have never heard of them since Mélanie wrote to congratulate me on my marriage."

"I remember the letter, telling you that you must be happy to belong to *la Marine*."

"Quite true, except at the partings. But see, this is a great business letter. Look at the curly twists and stiff writing!"

"You must read it, sweetheart. My French won't go beyond hailing a vessel."

"Here is something to read first, with M. de Limours' great red seal. Ah! this is a letter of explanation from him and another from Mélanie. My dear Mélanie! So my uncle is dead, and Cécile, poor Cécile! has nothing to hold her to the world since M. de Henisson was killed in America, and she is bent on taking the veil."

"That's not the purport of yonder packet. Look, without your compliments, don't tack even them. I ought to be on deck in five minutes —— "

"It seems there was an old Uncle de Mericourt — I never heard of him, — who lived on his plantation in Marie Galante, a Guadaloupe island, and now he is dead, and his property is to be divided between his two nieces or their representatives. That would be only myself and my two cousins, Mélanie and Cécile, Mesdames de Limours and de Henisson, and they want us to come to Paris to make the claim and assert our rights."

"Of course I cannot go — you might. How much is it?"

"I cannot quite make out, but Mélanie says 'the uncle, without being he of the Philippine islands' —— "

"What! have you an uncle there?"

"Oh, no! no! It is an allusion to *Gil Blas.*"

"Oh, go on. Never mind your French follies, stick to the point."

"He is thought to have made a good thing of the *cannelle* trade. Oh, I remember, that is cinnamon."

"Aye, Marie Galante was said to be a famous place for cinnamon trees."

"He lived like a hermit among his slaves, and spent no money, so much is expected; but all his debts are not yet called in, and M. de Limours thinks we ought to be at Paris to secure our share of the spoil. Here is a cordial invitation from Mélanie. Oh! they have taken the Nidemerle title. He is Marquis de Nidemerle now."

"You might go; I think you ought. It might make a great difference to the children. They should have some dependence besides my prize money."

"I wish I could take them with me. If it were not for leaving them, I would as soon go to Paris as anywhere else, while I mope my life away in your absence."

"Poor Carry! You should not be a sailor's wife."

"As if I would be anything else!"

"And you won't get into trouble again by putting the whole fleet upon your head."

"It is not the fashion now, they say. Besides, all that affair is forgotten."

"You will go under a different name, and things

seem to be changing.   Do not run any risk, my sweet
life."

"Not half so many as you do in those horrid East
Indies."

"Ah! remember that it is due to our children that
one of us should be careful."

So it was definitely settled that Mrs. Aylmer should
accept the invitation of her cousin, the Marquise de
Nidemerle, and repair to Paris to claim her share of
the West Indian inheritance, destiny so arranging it
that, while her husband went to the East, she would
go to the West.

Except for the children's sake, Caroline would have
been wholly glad of the distraction from the sorrow of
the parting.   She had been too much accustomed to a
roving life in her childhood to look forward with com-
placency to spending five or seven years as a sober
matron either with Uncle and Aunt Darpent at Walwyn, or with her mother-in-law at Downford, with no
particular interest at present except a boy of three,
and a girl of four, both their grandmother's treasures.
There would be plenty of time to devote herself to
being a mother to them after Mrs. Trimmer's most
approved system, when she should have secured their
fortune, and renewed her friendship with the cousins
whom she recollected with affection, increasing as she
was longer and longer separated from them.

Her husband had a few qualms as he bethought himself that Paris was a wicked place, as he had always
understood; but she declared that in all the years she
had lived there she had not seen any harm; but considering that she had spent six years in a convent, and
six weeks in the care of kindly and correct matrons as
a *jeune fille*, he was not greatly impressed by her experi-

ence; but he had full confidence in her principles if not in her discretion, and he thought that she was really less likely to act foolishly where she had to use judgment for self-protection, than if she were left to despairing impatience of the tedium of a monotonous life. She was very fond of, and obedient to his mother, but her uncle's wife always vexed her and impelled her to resistance. For at four-and-twenty years, Caroline Aylmer was still the same spirited and impulsive being she had been at seventeen, and if her husband loved her the better for these characteristics, and her Uncle Darpent was highly entertained by her, her aunt did not delight in these tokens of French extraction. The two homes which claimed her, at Walwyn, and at Downford, were not so far apart as to obviate friction. So he was not sorry that a few months of his absence should be spent in seeing something of the world, which would probably make it easier for her to settle down quietly for the remainder of the time, and he did not reckon on her absence lasting above half a year.

An old friend of her naval days, Harry Norton, was cruising in the Channel in a gun brig, and putting in at Plymouth from time to time for provisions; and he undertook to take her safely across to Havre, and see her farther on her journey to Paris, so soon as the *Oudenarde* had sailed.

CHAPTER II

When the wrong shall be right.
SCOTT.

COMMANDER NORTON did not lose sight of Mrs.
Aylmer till he had not only landed her at Havre, but
had arranged for her journey to Paris in company
with a deputy of the newly summoned *tiers état* of the
National Assembly, whose wife was accompanying
him, and who was glad to let the English lady share
their roomy *chaise de poste.* The said deputy, M. Normand, was a notary, who had had dealings enough with
England to be able to hold converse with the commander, and to promise every attention to the lady.
His wife was one of the well-educated, highly cultivated women of the middle class then numerous in
France. Captain Norton supped with them when
committing Mrs. Aylmer to their charge, and was well
pleased with all he saw of them.

Caroline had wept her first tears out when her
husband went out of sight in the pilot boat, and she
had been so long on the way that even Madame
Normand was not scandalised by her being able to
eat and speak by the time they came together. Indeed
the good lady herself was only just presentable after

79

the tears it had cost her to dispose of her daughter
en pension at a convent, but she was full of intense
enthusiasm, and Caroline, who had been living in a
world where port-admirals, post-captains, first and
second lieutenants, ship's carpenters, and boatswains
played the chief part, found herself awakened to the
new state of affairs in France, and the hopes that all
abuses were to be reformed, all unjust burdens removed, all invidious distinctions abolished. When
the carriage passed a hay-field, where a bailiff, or
mayhap a lay brother, was superintending the compulsory labour of the tenants for the lord of the soil,
Madame Normand triumphantly cried out that such
toils would soon be no more, and her husband quoted
the line

Sic vos non vobis, mellificatis apes.

When on entering the fresh Province of the "Ile de
France," their passports were *visé*, and their luggage
overhauled as if they were on the borders of a foreign
country; and when the *octroi* was demanded at the
gates of every city, the Normands submitted as a
matter of course, but sighed with envy and yet with
hope, when their fellow-traveller told them that she
could travel from Berwick to Land's End without any
such restrictions. Monsieur Normand knew it, but to
his wife it seemed too good to be true. He was a
cautious man, over-prudent, his wife said, and would
not let her talk freely in the inns; but on the roads,
between the avenues of poplars, and the vineyards,
or corn-fields, her discourse was free: now of the
liberties of Greece and Rome, soon to be rivalled in
France; now of the cruel exactions and injustice
suffered by her friends and acquaintances; now of

the horrid extravagance and dissipation imputed to
the Queen, and implicitly believed by nearly all the
country.

New times were coming in, and all would be liberty
and prosperity for every one. Nothing unpleasant
was there on the journey, not even the impertinence
of a postilion, or — as the deputy declared — even the
kicking of a horse, but madame believed it would be
set right by the *tiers état*.

"The coming of the *coquecigrues*," said her husband,
who liked to tease her.

There was a great sweetness and charm about her
which won Caroline's heart, and the two mothers in-
dulged in infantine anecdotes and comparisons of their
children, and made great friends of one another, before
the great Percheron horses were halted at the *barrières*
of Paris; and while altercations were going on over the
luggage and the *octroi*, Caroline saw a familiar face.
M. de Limours, or as he was now called, M. de Nidemerle, had brought his carriage to fetch her, and in it
she found Mélanie, as bright and charming as ever,
and they threw themselves into each other's arms with
tears of joy.

Caroline found the French side of her nature coming to the front, and her tears, always checked in
England, flowing almost as readily as those of her
cousins, especially when she met Cécile at the Hôtel
de Nidemerle, in her long nun-like veil of widowhood. It was the old quarters, for since her father's
death Madame de Nidemerle had repaired to the old
"Thrushes' Nest," as she said; and the Marquisate
being the higher title, it had been assumed by her
husband, who was properly Marquis de Nidemerle
Limours. Old Zélie, her wool turned white, received

G

her picaninny with rapture, and by and by the cousins sat round their dinner-table eagerly talking by
the light of the wax chandeliers. The party included
the boy whom Caroline had last seen hung in a scarf
round Mélanie's neck; and who was advanced to the
dignity of a velvet gold-laced coat, silk stockings, lace
cravat, hair powdered and tied in a queue, a tiny
sword, the title of Monsieur de Bellaise, and the possession of an Abbé for a tutor, — a clever-looking
young man in a silken *soutane*, with his *jabot* (broad
black bands) fringed with white, who sat at the bottom of the table, but joined in the conversation freely;
especially when M. de Nidemerle began to tease his
son about the little sword, which was a late acquisition,
and the little play in Berquin's *Magasin des Enfants*,
where the passionate boy is allowed to wear a sword
on condition of not drawing it. He does draw it, in a
fit of anger, and finds it a turkey feather.

It was a great amusement to declare that such a
catastrophe was in store for Gerard, for he was allowed
his Christian name, the first Bellaise so addressed for
at least a hundred years, symptom of the greater ease
and familiarity setting in with all classes. His sister,
Agathe, was a pensionnaire in the old convent of Ste.
Lucie, where her aunt boarded.

"I tried to keep her with me as long as I could,"
said Mélanie, "after the present fashion; but it was
too inconvenient (*cela me gênait trop*), so I placed her
with my sister, at least till we sail for Ste. Marie
Galante."

" Oh! do you think of going thither?"

"Certainly, my dear cousin. My husband thinks
that otherwise our affairs will never come to a good
conclusion."

" Yes, Mélanie is right. Only personal inspection
can bring those Creole lawyers to a division of the
sum due to us, or enable me to decide whether to sell
the property."

" And I should much like to see the old abode, of
which my mother told me so much, the palms and the
sugar-canes and the devoted slaves."

" Ah! mayhap they will be less devoted now, if the
general spirit has infected them," said the Abbé.
" Madame has a grand power in her hands."

" Emancipation ! Ah, to see all those poor negroes
kneeling at my feet, and to cry 'you are free!'" exclaimed Mélanie with clasped hands.

" The Government may take that out of our hands,"
said Monsieur de Nidemerle, " if matters proceed as I
hear whispered. I should like to sell the estate before
ruin becomes certain."

" But," cried Mélanie. " if we acted of our own free
will, these grateful blacks would love us, and serve us
willingly."

" It would be difficult for them not to love madame,"
said the Abbé with a bow. " They will think an angel
of freedom has appeared to them."

" Will you come with us, cousin ? " asked Mélanie ;
" it will be a distraction, and you are an experienced
traveller."

" Yes indeed, I should love the voyage and the
tropics, but I could not go so far from my children."

" Ah! you will think it over. If my sister would
join us, she would recover her spirits, and we should
be the most charming party in the world ! Consider
of it, sister. Would not our cousin induce you to
reconsider your decision ? "

" You are very good, sister, but I wish for no distraction. Devotion and the memory of my dear husband are enough for me." and she began to weep, and hurried from the table, attended by her sister.

M. de Nidemerle handed Caroline out, and as she recollected the manœuvres to prevent M. de Henisson from falling in love with herself, she wondered whether he had done much to inspire this devoted affection in the poor little Cécile, whose feelings had been apparently unstirred when last they met. But that might have been only decorum. Caroline might rejoice that her own courtship by George Aylmer had been unknown to those whom it would have scandalised. Yet their code was relaxed in some cases, though in others it was as strict as ever, and the uncertainties might create perplexities as she soon perceived.

"When is Félicité de Monfichet to be professed?" asked Mélanie.

"I cannot quite tell. It depends on when her uncle the Bishop can attend, or the relations of Madeleine de Torcy, who is a little saint, quite as eager to take the vows as Félicité is to avoid them," replied Cécile.

"I thought there were regulations to prevent people from being made nuns without a vocation," said Caroline.

"Ah! bah! there are ways of impressing a vocation, especially when one's uncle is a bishop," said M. de Nidemerle.

"And one's affections are ill placed," added his wife. "Affections! as if a young girl ought to have any. But it is all her parents' fault."

"Who is it, what is it?" asked Caroline eagerly.

"She is the daughter of Charlotte de Solivet — you remember her, Caroline. She had *la tête exaltée* even in the convent."

"She was one of 'les grandes.' I had a quarrel with her about the British flag."

"Ah! never mention your flag, you enemy that you were!" said Mélanie, shaking her head at her. "Yes, it was Solivet who appealed to Sœur St. Hilaire."

"She was married soon, I think. Was not she a kind of relation?"

"Far, far away, in the fiftieth degree, I believe. Yes, she married the Baron de Monfichet, and their heads were both turned with philosophers, and ency- clopedists, and I know not what, and they must needs keep their daughters at home, and give them an edu- cation after Madame de Genlis' system, with an Eng- lish governess, picked up I know not where, with all your English fashions. No care, no supervision, the poor girls left free to their games and walks with whom they would in the garden and avenue, and that when M. de Monfichet had filled his house with mis- erable roturiers, men of science, about whom Charlotte raved, but who had no notion of *les bienséances.*"

"Are you speaking of Beaudésert, *mon amie?*" said M. de Nidemerle. "A remarkably handsome, agreeable man, well-bred, and full of information; I was charmed with him, though, as to his ideas, they were too chimerical."

"It was all very well for you, but if it had been your daughter! Figure to yourself *la petite sotte* re- fusing M. le Duc de Drelincourt! There were tears, sobs, attacks of nerves. I know not what faintings, fevers, and even avowals that her heart was oc- cupied, and it would be a sin to accept one man when she preferred another. What well-brought-up demoiselle knew that hearts existed in our day?"

"Surely M. Beaudésert had not the presumption to address her?" exclaimed Cécile.

"What do I know? The wretch had the temerity to avow to monsieur, her father, that he was only waiting for her eighteenth year to declare his suit, when she would be old enough to decide, and his invention would be completed and accepted!"

"And what is he?" asked Caroline.

"*Bourgeois, mere bourgeois,*" said Mélanie. "You knew his family, M. l'Abbé, I believe?"

"His brother was in college with me, madame," replied the tutor. "Their father is a doctor of medicine at Rouen, a man clever and highly esteemed, as well as sincerely religious; his wife really devout."

"Ah, that might well be. I remember him at the *soirées* of the Monfichets."

"You came home in raptures with him," said M. de Nidemerle.

"Little knowing what was coming! Well, M. de Monfichet's brother, the Bishop of Charmilly, was called in, and he so spoke to Félicité that though she remained obstinate against the Duke of Drelincourt, she was alarmed at the crime of disobedience, and consented willingly to be sent to the convent, where she has made her novitiate, while the Duke takes her younger sister."

"Poor child," sighed Caroline; "and M. Beaudésert, what has become of him?"

"*Chassé,* of course," said Madame de Nidemerle.

"The Count de Rocheval, a Louisianian nobleman of large property," said the Abbé, "took him to New Orleans to act as tutor, and to study the natural science of the Mississippi, and perfect his invention."

"Let us hope he will console himself with an alligator," said Mélanie.

"Who knows what changes may be in store?" said Caroline.

"Not such as can compel us to sully our blood with *bourgeois* strain," said the Marquis.

"And à *propos*," cried his wife, "to-morrow the States-General go in procession to hear a sermon at the Church of St. Louis — Mademoiselle de Villy, my court sempstress, has promised us a window! You will come, my cousin? Happily, one can go *en bergère*."

Caroline willingly agreed.

"And thou, my sister? It is useless, I fear, to ask thee."

"Ah yes, a thousand thanks, dear Mélanie, but the Mother Abbess has convoked all the ladies who cling to her to hear a mass in our *chapelle*, and pray that this new order of things may be for the welfare, not the damage of France and of the Church."

So in effect was done by the Duchess of Ayen, her daughters, and many others of the pious women of France on the day of the opening of the States-General. We cannot help thinking of the righteous men who, Ezekiel foretold, should deliver their own souls, though they could not avert the sore judgments which generation after generation had been preparing. The scourges became in their case assuredly palms.

CHAPTER III

Thou many-headed monster thing,
Oh! who would wish to be thy king?
SCOTT.

WITH no forebodings did the lively party set forth in the great Nidemerle coach, the ladies with powdered curls under big hats, cocked up over one ear, and decorated with feathers, while their brocade, long-waisted bodices were kilted up over monstrous pockets, and coloured silk quilted skirts. Mélanie had put her cousin into one of her own chip hats, with green ribbons and green tipped feathers. The unfashionable cut of the rest of the dress did not signify, as they would be nearly squeezed to death by the crowd at Versailles. Mélanie showed her cousin that she carried in her pocket, not only her opera-glass, but a whole provision of more or less solid cakes and comfits known by various titles.

The road to Versailles was thronged, so that the four horses could make little way, and could only proceed in regular line behind another coach, creeping along in like manner; and streets and lanes were densely crowded with men and women of every degree below the aristocracy, some with looks of hope and joy, but others with scowls of ill-will that might seem

as auguries of the rage of the monster about to be
awakened. The trees were blossoming in the first
glories of summer, and the foliage was bright and delicate; but the multitude of carriages of all kinds, and
the troops of foot-passengers left little space for the
beauty of the morning.

They reached at length the tall stone houses of
Versailles, and proceeding at a foot's pace, and exchanging greetings with numerous gentlemen, they
reached the house where Mademoiselle Villy rented
a floor. She was, as Mélanie explained, a married
woman, though the title of madame was not given to
tradespeople in the days of the old régime; and though
not a regular dressmaker, she gained her livelihood as
a *couturière* by being ready to repair damages to the
toilettes of ladies who did not bring a maid to the
crowded palace, or who were only there for a few
hours.

M. de Nidemerle, who had ridden, was at the door
to receive them, as well as three other gentlemen.
The crowd, still polite by habit, made way for them
to pass, and the master of the house, whose livery
showed him to be valet to some gentleman at court,
led them up steep, narrow, not over-clean stairs, to
his wife's apartments, bare wainscoted rooms, but
with two windows with balconies, whence her stock-
in-trade had been removed, and whither she marshalled
Madame de Nidemerle, her cousin, and some other
select customers to chairs overhanging the street, especially the Vicomtesse de Champcéry, a quiet, pensive
woman, who belonged to the same window. Early as
it was, there was interest enough below, above, every-
where. Each window on the same level swarmed with
ladies in their hats and feathers, higher up were the

eager faces of countless *bourgeoises,* and the very roofs
and their parapets, even the chimneys, were filled with
spectators, while the street below was equally thronged
behind the soldiers, who stood keeping a line for the
procession.

There was a long time to wait, but there was too
much variety for weariness to set in. Mélanie was in
the midst of acquaintances, among whom she moved
from her own balcony to the next, introducing her
cousin, who found herself renewing an old convent
friendship; but the recognitions of the gentlemen in
the street, and watching for the procession, took up
most of the interest.

Caroline could not understand why so many nobles
were there. Why were they not peers in the procession?

Mélanie laughed. "Ah, my dear, the hosts there
would be! No; nobles used only to sit who were
peers of France, chosen out by the king. Now, heaven
knows how chosen!"

"Elected from their own order as deputies," said
Madame de Champcéry, "four hundred of them, four
hundred clergy also, and the same number of the *tiers
état.* Ah, may this not be a *bouleversement* of the state
when such hands meddle with it?"

"They will renew it!" cried Mélanie. "We shall
hear no more outcries for bread. Ah me, what a winter
we had last year! Who is that making signs?"

"That is the clever American, M. Morris."

"With a wooden leg?" asked Caroline; "but with
the air of a would-be man of fashion?"

"Ah yes," said Mélanie. "He does not resemble
your old friend Franklin, with whom, if I remember
right, you talked a little treason, my dear cousin.

He has friends among the Palais Royal clique, whom I do not love, and is always writing epigrams to them in English, which they don't understand."

"And therefore admire the more," said Madame de Champcéry.

Here there was an alarm that the procession was coming, but it was only that the mob were hailing M. Necker as he passed to take his place among the Ministry.

"He is to bring a panacea for all the woes of France," said Madame de Champcéry; "but I doubt whether human power can do that."

"Certainly not M. Necker, a mere banker, and not even a Frenchman," said Madame de Nidemerle.

"Who can?" asked Caroline.

"The finger of God," said Madame de Champcéry solemnly. "May it not be the finger of vengeance!"

But Mélanie chattered on. "His daughter — you remember Germaine Necker, cousin?"

"Ah, yes, and ' redressez-vous.' "

They all laughed, and Mélanie continued.

"Well, she is more magnificent than ever. An ambassadress, if you please. She has married the Baron de Staël, ambassador of the King of Sweden, and she has a salon and meddles with everything — literature, politics, society, and art."

"She is a very able woman," said Madame de Champcéry, "full of esprit."

"Of course, but she is frightful," cried Mélanie.

"Except her eyes —— "

"Eyes that transfix one and judge one, all at once. Oh! shelter me from those eyes! And she knows not how to dress herself."

"She will make a sensation by and by."

" What, with that face? "

" No, not that face. She has to see and weigh much, and outgrow the prepossessions of youth," said Madame de Champcéry.

"Ah! they are coming. Hear the shouts! hear the band!"

It was true this time. Along the street marched, four abreast, the procession of the States-General; first the *tiers état* or commons, in plain black suits, long white cravats, and black cloaks over one shoulder, in the dress of their order, in the time when it had been last convoked, in the days of Louis XIII., 1614.

In the long stream, Caroline looked for M. Normand; but presently Mélanie cried out, "Ah! ah! can that be le Comte de Mirabeau?" as there rolled along a gigantic figure, with a seamed and hideous face, of a strange keenness.

" Mirabeau, without doubt," said Madame de Champcéry. " He was rejected by the *noblesse*."

" Rightly! And so he degrades his rank! *Fi donc!*"

The black stream of commoners having flowed on, then came what filled Madame de Nidemerle with delight; the nobles in full cavalier array, with floating plumes, velvet cloaks, and coats rich with embroidery. She was in a rapture, kissing her hand to friends who bowed, and naming them to Caroline, and only indignant when she saw the red and bloated face of the Duke of Orleans, as he marched there instead of as a prince of the blood royal. Jewels and collars of St. Louis and of the St. Esprit glittered on their necks and shoulders. fleurs-de-lys were on their blue velvet backs; they made a gorgeous show. The bishops who followed were a less gay but equally grand spectacle, with their purple robes, surmounted

with white. richly trimmed with broad and beautiful
lace from the looms of Flanders, in contrast to the
plain black cassocks and white edged bands of the
curés who attended them. Several bishops, besides
the magnificent Metropolitan of Rheims, were pointed
out, Bishop de Montichet of Charmilly for one. "Ah!
there he is! Now Félicité will be professed!" said
Madame de Nidemerle.

"Poor girl," Caroline murmured to herself in English, as she looked at the dark, stern face, and thought
how hard resistance must have been, not wondering
that the child had yielded.

"Ah! there's the Bishop of Autun," as a small figure limped by in the procession. "My husband says
he is the cleverest man in France! but how lame he
is."

"That was from carelessness in the cottage where
he was nursed," said Madame de Champcéry, "you
know he is really the eldest son of the Count de
Talleyrand Périgord, but he was put out of the suc-
cession and compelled to enter religion on account of
his infirmity."

"Nevertheless he is making his way both in pleasure and in politics," laughed Madame de Nidemerle;
at which Madame de Champcéry shook her head and
said, "There may be excuses for him, in the manner
in which he has been treated."

Caroline, often in after-life, thought of those words,
and the little halting form, when the name of Talleyrand came before her.

Now, however, all were absorbed in watching the
march of the King himself, with his court preceding
him, the Prince of Condé and the young Duke of
Enghien, and next, the Counts of Provence and Artois,

his brothers, immediately before him. All like him in their robes of blue, sprinkled with fleurs-de-lys. Ecstatic cries of *" Vive le Roi!"* broke from the populace, while all the ladies in the windows rose and waved their handkerchiefs; Mélanie shed tears of enthusiasm.

"Ah!" said Madame de Champcéry, "this is but the beginning. Pray that this may not be the first stage in a general overthrow."

CHAPTER IV

THE OTHER SIDE OF THE QUESTION

There was a lady loved a swine.

Old Song.

Excitements came thickly upon the Hôtel de Nidemerle. Only the day after the opening of the States-General, an invitation arrived from the Mother Prioress of Ste. Lucie to Madame de Nidemerle to be present at the profession of Mesdemoiselles de Torcy and de Monfichet, with the further intimation that she should be happy to receive Madame Aylmer, though unhappily that old pensionnaire had not continued in the bosom of the Church Catholic.

Before, however, the appointed day, Caroline had found that in the hurry of parting at the *barrière*, she had carried off a scarf of Madame Normand's, which she wished to restore. She had her address, and desired to take the parcel herself. Mélanie demurred a little, but after all, Caroline was only of *bourgeois* degree, and moreover was ready to send for a *fiacre* on her own account, since the streets were in such a state of dirt that no lady could attempt walking in them, hardly a gentleman in his silk stockings. So Mélanie lent her own sedan-chair, and a lackey to keep watch over the bearers and the lady's dignity.

It was a splendid affair, with a marquis's coronet on the top, the family arms quartered on the back, and Paul and Virginie under a very conventional palm-tree making love, and another representing Virginie lying drowned, and Paul tearing his hair. The inside was daintily lined and cushioned with blue satin, and there Caroline seated herself, smiling over the wonderful notions of palm-trees and tropical scenery.

Once or twice, when they jostled against some cart or loaded horse, she heard growls about aristocrats, but she arrived safely at the doorway of the passage of an enormously tall house, with stories projecting one over the other, and the lackey, who looked very scornful all the while, inquired of the concierge for Madame Normand, and was answered "*Au troisième* — second down to the left." Up went Caroline, up stone stairs, a good deal dirtier than the Versailles sempstress', and by and by the footman found the door, and knocked. It was opened by Madame Normand herself, who cried out with joy at the sight of her travelling companion, and admitted her into an odd little anteroom, then into a more spacious chamber, where the bed was in an alcove partly shrouded with curtains, and over the little stove Madame Normand seemed to have been cooking a little mess of some kind. She had a large white cap over her hair, and a short linen wrapper over her stuff petticoat, not exactly the trim in which English ladies were wont to attend to their housekeeping avocations; but she was not in the least disconcerted, as she sprang to welcome Madame Aylmer, and while a pull here and a twitch there made her not only presentable but coquettish, she explained that this was their only room, but that she made a point of having some *goûter* ready for her husband, in case he failed to breakfast or dine or sup with some of his friends at his club. Caroline wondered what she lived on herself, but knew already that much less would suffice a little spare French-woman than an Englishwoman.

The little bright-eyed woman was as full of enthusiasm as ever, and could talk of nothing but the ceremony they had both enjoyed. "One saw what it was to be truly great," she said, "when the *tiers état* appeared in their ground. Simplicity in contrast to the feathers, and velvet, and frippery of the nobles. And did you see their faces?"

"No, I was much too high up."

"I was better off than you could be in your noble company. There one only sees *de haut en bas*. I was almost on a level! and — *pardonnez moi*, madame — you, thank heaven, are not noble."

"Oh no, as I told you, we are of the middle class, gentlefolks, but not what you call *gentilshommes*."

"Yes, yes. So it will be no impoliteness to tell you that after the *esprit*, the intellect, the fixed purpose that I read in the faces of the *tiers état*, the nobles looked to me either faded and effete, or else puffed up with pride, mere pegs on which to display their fine clothes."

Caroline laughed. "Ah! you looked with prejudiced eyes, madame. There is no want of *esprit* among the *noblesse*."

"*Esprit* that is wasted in fireworks of conversation."

"And there is sense of the need of great reforms."

Madame Normand laughed. "How is it with them when it touches their own domestic relations? They can foster the *bourgeois* in their families, treat him as an equal, enjoy the fruit of his labours, take to them-

H

selves credit for the charm he imparts into their
society, but let him lift up his eyes to one of their
daughters born in the purple! Ah! bah! *Roturier* —
vilain — *traître* — that is all that is good for him! If
he escape in this new reign a *lettre de cachet*, he must
be exiled, and she, *la pauvrette*, is immured in a convent, which is even worse, since it is for life."

"You remind me of a case of which I have heard."

"Ah! is it possible you should have heard of my
cousin, Henri Beaudésert and his Félicité, *le pauvre
garçon?*"

"Is he your cousin? I am to go to see the young
lady professed next Sunday."

"Alas! then the immolation is to be completed."

"Tell me, oh tell me all. Would that the poor girl
could be saved!"

"There is no hope. She did actually write to me
and say she had appealed to the Archbishop of Paris,
but her letter must have been suppressed, for we have
heard no more since the governess left her a year ago."

Then Madame Normand went on to say how she
had been brought up in the Beaudésert family, and
had known her cousin Henri like a brother. He was
very clever and brilliant, and had studied philosophy
and chemistry at the best schools, and carried his
researches further than his teachers and text-books.
He had made the acquaintance of Franklin, Laplace,
and Volta, and had marked out electricity with all
the vehemence of new research and discovery. He
had perceived how to render the occult and marvellous
powers practical for the safety of ships as well as of
houses, and had hoped to cause the means of safety by
conducting away the lightning, available for the safety
of ships and of houses, to be adopted by the French

navy.   It was a time when men of science were caressed by the more intellectual nobles of France, and
philosophy was the fashion.   Monsieur de Monfichet
had sufficient knowledge and insight to appreciate the
marvels that Henri Beaudésert made known to him.
He was connected with the naval service, and hoped
to get the system adopted by government; and while
going through the endless formalities requisite for the
presentation of the scheme, the young man had been
domesticated in his château, and lived on equal terms
with his family.

Of course, not only was Beaudésert too much in
advance of his period to be successful, but France had
too many political tempests working up for the slightest attention to be spared for physical tempests, and
the discoverer had the usual fate of his kind, waiting
and watching in vain for an answer to his statements,
or permission to demonstrate his plans.   His patron
had become weary of him, and had been derided for
putting forward projects so absurd, told that the idea
of guiding the lightning was impious and sacrilegious,
and even threatened with denunciation as an enemy
who would destroy the fleet.

Just then occurred the resistance of his daughter to
the proposed marriage.   Under the English governess,
Miss Fernley, Félicité had been allowed English freedom in the château and the gardens; Beaudésert had
even been encouraged by her mother to instruct her in
natural science.   They had read, built castles, bota-
nised together, and Henri, when certain of his invention, and hopeful of the brilliance of success, had
trusted to such a future as would justify the crown-
ing of his love and hopes.

He had not indeed spoken openly to the girl herself, but Miss Fernley had been his confidante throughout. She was of mature age, and serious, even stern, aspect, but her heart was full of romance. She expected unheard-of results from Beaudésert's invention, and was herself no insignificant conductor of the almost equally perilous sparks from one young heart to the other; and Félicité thoroughly understood the attentions paid to her.

Then came the fatal disappointment, when the unfortunate inventor was treated with contumely proportioned to the disgrace into which his project had brought his patron, and aggravated by the discovery of the presumptuous attachment to a *fille de qualité*, a maiden, moreover, who was not to be shaken in her constancy, and who avowed the doctrine, so preposterous in the eyes of French parents, that it would be an absolute sin to give her hand to one man while her heart belonged to another. Beaudésert narrowly escaped arrest; but the days of Cardinal de Richelieu were over, and the King himself had been interested by some of the experiments, so that it was intimated to the audacious inventor and lover that the only safe course would be to accept the proposals of the Count de Percheval, who inhabited Louisiana, then technically belonging to Spain, though settled by France.

At Havre he and Miss Fernley had met, her conduct, " infamous " as Madame de Monfichet called it, having been discovered, and her passport forced upon her. She was able to bring him an account of the persecution that poor Félicité had undergone, and how her uncle, the Bishop of Charmilly, had forced on her conscience that disobedience was a sin, and tried to make her believe that love for an impious philosopher

was a greater one. This imputation she had entirely
rejected, for, as the Normands well knew, Madame
Beaudésert had been herself *dévote*, with a tinge of
Jansenism, and had brought up her children so as to
be free from either scepticism or immorality.

Félicité, a girl of unusual spirit and resolution, was
not to be shaken in her determination to refuse to
marry the Duke de Drelincourt, or any one else, and
she had charged Miss Fernley with a message to that
effect. She was permitting herself to become a novice
at Ste. Lucie, but she had given Miss Fernley a letter
of protest to be sent to the Archbishop of Paris, and
had charged her with messages of constancy to Henri
Beaudésert. The governess had sufficient connection
with the household to be able to send her Henri's
vows of undying affection, but there all intercourse
had ceased, a little more than a year ago. Once in
the convent, nothing more could be heard by the Normands of the poor girl; they could only conclude that
her letter to the Archbishop had failed; and they only
knew that Beaudésert was making his way at New
Orleans, but heeded nothing of the successes that he
could not share with Félicité, though still he hoped
against hope.

All Caroline could do, sympathising as she was
with all her heart, was to promise to bring Madame
Normand a full account of the coming ceremony, which
would be so melancholy in her eyes.

CHAPTER V

I hold you as a thing ensky'd and sainted.
Measure for Measure.

Much moved by Madame Normand's history, Caroline Aylmer set forth very early in the morning with her cousin to witness poor Félicité's profession, Mélanie chattering all the way about her regret that it was not the novitiate that was to begin; that was a ceremony "*à ravir*," when the candidate appeared as a bride, all in white, with jewels and orange flowers. "I wish this was the same," said Caroline, "then the vows would not be irrevocable."

"Well that they are," returned Madame de Nidemerle, "you would not see her disgrace her family!"

"You know I am not noble."

"Ah! you English, you are droll — you who are almost a Ribaumont, and whose husband would be noble here — you, too, wish to see her married to a mere physician."

"Come, Mélanie, do not scold me, I feel already as if I were going to school! Those old streets are quite unchanged, but how empty they are! Only little girls, with the droll little babies rolled up in white caps."

"It is a disease! All the elders throng to stand round the clubs to hear what is the news from the States-General! Ah! the little wretches!"

For one or two bigger boys had come out of their rickety doors and were shouting "*A bas les aristocrates.*" The coachmen struck at them with his whip, but they skipped out of reach, laughed and yelled the louder.

These, however, were soon left behind, and the familiar outlines of houses and walls and trees made Caroline feel as if she were going to school again, as she caught glimpses of the Seine from time to time, and remembered how she had longed to follow it down to her own dear sea and liberty. Arriving in due time, after rolling into the outer court, the two ladies were ushered up a stair into a side building where Caroline had never been before, and which was appropriated to ladies in retreat, or boarding in the convent after the not infrequent custom alike of the devout, of widows under temporary retirement, and of persons wishing for a respectable shelter.

Madame de Henisson was at present the only occupant of a fairly spacious but bare apartment, holding no more than the absolutely needful furniture of tables and chairs and a shelf with a very few books of devotion. Her writing-desk and embroidery frame were on the table, and there were prints from the lives of the saints on the walls, and there was a door half open in the alcove, showing a little oratory with a crucifix and holy-water stoup. In the alcove was the bed and a few toilette necessaries, and there were three windows, one looking into the cloister, the others into the walled garden, the river beyond, the place where Caroline remembered both games with her companions and solitary pinings. It was deserted just now, and nuns and lay sisters were rushing about the cloister in the last agony of preparation for the ceremony.

Madame de Henisson embraced her sister and cousin, and the little Agathe was in her mother's arms in a moment. She was a dark bright-eyed child, arrayed in the old costume of "les rouges," but it was a shock to hear that there were only two other pensionnaires, both orphans. "Home education was the fashion — with what results you see!" said Mélanie, waving her hands towards the cloister, when Agathe eagerly narrated the gossip of the schoolroom, how "*cette* Monfichet had been detected trying to write letters, and how she had had *des convulsions,* and how she had set her lips like that!" said Agathe, screwing up her rosy lips, "and vowed that she would never be really a nun, for no one could make her break her previous vow!"

"Oh! hush, Agathe. It was frightful. Little girls should not talk of such things," cried her aunt. "Tell us of Madeleine de Torcy."

"Ah! exactly, she is a saint! She learns to make her vows. She prays before the shrine till the thread of her chaplet is quite worn through," said Agathe, but as if she thought the saint the least interesting of the two. "She wants her name in religion to be her own, but the Mother insists that she should be called de Ste. Françoise de Rome — but Félicité will not choose a name. She declares that she will never answer to any name but her own, for she hopes that felicity may be hers some time or other, and Sœur St. Hilaire says —— "

"Agathe, *mon enfant,* how do you pick up all these stories? We never did, did we, cousin?"

"Ah! where there are so few, discipline is relaxed," said Madame de Henisson, "but that is the lesson bell, it is time that we took our places."

" Yes, or we shall find all absorbed by the de Torcys
and de Monfichets," said Mélanie, springing up.
"Embrace me, my child, and run to your companions." Agathe disappeared, and Cécile ushered her
sister and cousin to the chapel, where straw-bottomed
chairs were placed in the narrow ante-chapel behind
the *grille* — a screen of carved open work in wood,
representing vines with grapes and tendrils, through
whose interstices the spectators were to look. One
side was appropriated to the pensionnaires, but as
they were so few, there was the more room for visitors, though the Monfichet and Torcy families nearly
engrossed the space on the other side. Caroline found
herself seated in her old place, with the same cork-
screw tendril she knew so well in front of her, but its
last coils were gone, so that she had a much improved
view into the choir. She observed that this was not
the only broken bit of the woodwork, and that the
touches of gilding on the grapes were peeling off —
indeed, in spite of all being decked for a gala day,
there was a general look of disrepair, and Cécile told
her that the bad harvests had made the revenues very
scanty, and the nuns had almost starved themselves
in their endeavours to supply the crowds of hungry
beings who pressed to their gates in last winter's terrible famine, and the present season did not promise
great improvement. No one thought of silence in
church, till a table was placed outside the choir with
the robes of a professed nun on it — a white hood,
black scapular, a girdle and a veil, together with a
vessel of holy water, and the aspersion. Then in
filed the nuns, fewer in number than Caroline remembered them, for their numbers had scarcely been re-
cruited since her days, each bearing a lighted candle.

Then, with attendant priests, came the Bishop of Charmilly, a dark-browed man, whom, plainly, it would have been very hard to resist. Mass was said as far as the Gospel, and then the Bishop seated himself in the large chair made ready for him, the Prioress likewise sitting. The two closely veiled novices in white were led forward by the mistress of the novices. They knelt before the Bishop in his robes and mitre. He demanded what they asked, and one voice was quite audible. Caroline looked anxiously, and believed that the lips of the other maiden moved. They went back to their places, and all sat still while a sermon was preached from a tribune at the side, after which the pure sweet voices of the choir of nuns were raised in the "Veni Creator," all kneeling in their stalls. It was beautiful and solemn, except for the knowledge that one of the two was a sacrifice, not to heaven but to the world, and that in her case the hymn was a mockery, as were the versicles and responses that followed.

And next came the vows, when the two maidens were led forward, and the profession of perpetual seclusion and obedience to the Mother of the Order was rehearsed aloud outside the *grille*. The voice of Madeleine was clear and distinct; the other voice trembled — nay, the Bishop paused as though to force it to be more precisely uttered; but there was more and more faltering. It was almost, as it seemed to Caroline, a protest instead of a vow; but it was allowed to pass, and the novices then were led to the table where they were to sign their profession. It was then that Caroline could first really see them. One face, in its deep solemnity and joyfulness, was good to see; it so entirely expressed dedication and hope. The other would have been as white as the veil, if the complexion had not been so *brunette* that the skin, though deadly pale, was sallow. The same dark contracted eyebrows seen in the father and uncle were there, and the lips had the same set look; but the pen was put into the hand, and a scrawl was made with shaking fingers. Therewith the dedicated maidens were to die to the world, and accordingly each was laid down under a large black velvet pall, with six large wax candles arranged around it, as at a funeral, while the priests and nuns intoned the Litany of the Saints. The sobs of the de Torcys were violent, even Madame de Monfichet shed tears, and the weeping of the young Duchess became hysterical, so that the "*De Profundis*" could hardly be heard.

When this was over, the Bishop said in Latin, "Arise, thou that sleepest, from the dead," and the palls were lifted, Madeleine rising up with a look of rapturous joy; but there was a shriek from the nuns, for Félicité lay perfectly white and motionless. There was a case on record when a votaress had actually been found to have expired under the pall, and the cry "*Elle est morte!*" could not be suppressed. Her mother shrieked, "Oh! I have killed her! You have killed her! My child! my child!" And the Duchess de Drelincourt fell back in such convulsive agony that she had to be removed between her father and husband, hardly hearing the verdict of the crowding sisters, "*Elle s'est trouvée mal.*" Caroline caught the sad murmur, "Ah! it is not death!" while the long heavy eyelashes were lifted for a moment, then sank again.

"Remove her, lest she cause another scandal," hastily ordered the Bishop, and poor Félicité was carried off between two lay sisters. Caroline would have given worlds to rush after her and rescue her, but was glad to see that kind-hearted Sœur Maria de L'Annonciation, whom gossip declared to have had a love-story of her own, had followed in her wake.

With a countenance almost recalling the pictured face of St. Catherine, Madeleine, or rather Sœur Françoise de Rome, was being clothed one by one in the mystic garments of a professed sister, even to the black veil. Some one came and whispered to the Bishop that his niece was sufficiently revived to go through this portion of the ceremony, but he replied, with a glance towards the spectators, "No, no; it would only create a fresh scandal. In these days it is undesirable. All has been done that is really essential."

Of course he meant the irrevocable vow, which cut the sister off from life and the world. The sisters and Madeleine were solemnly exchanging the kiss of peace, which was absolute joy and peace to the new sister, whose features beamed with a sort of intoxication of bliss. Now all was fulfilled! The desire of her heart from her cradle had been the dedication of herself, which was now accomplished. She could feel herself the spouse of Christ, a mystic resemblance of the Holy Church, His Bride, and it was to her a foretaste of the fulness of the life everlasting.

Alas! neither she nor Félicité de Monfichet guessed how much was to come before that final severance of soul and body, which one had thought to forestall, and the other hoped was actually accomplished.

Afterwards, in the parlour, there was a refection of the delicate sweetmeats and dainty confections of the nuns, presided over by the Prioress and her chaplain

as hosts, where the Bishop was as gracious and lively
as his saturnine nature permitted. Mesdames de
Montfichet and Drelincourt seemed to have quite recovered their spirits, and the de Torcys were uni-
versally complimented on the angelic demeanour of
their daughter. Still the conversation was not much
unlike that of any salon, and Caroline wondered what
her mother-in-law would think of her Sunday.

She asked Cécile afterwards how the precautions
against admitting a sister without a vocation had been
overcome.

Cécile shrugged her shoulders. "Oh! Monseigneur
de Charmilly undertook to examine her on that head!"

"Moreover," added Mélanie, "Madame la Prieure
could not afford to dispense with her *dot*."

"Ah!" sighed Caroline, "I have seen how what is
most holy can be most perverted."

"*Chut!*" exclaimed Cécile, "we must not have your
Protestant talk in these walls. You surely know
better who grew up here."

"What I know is what made our ancestors Protestants," responded Caroline.

"Yet what could be more holy and devout than our
sweet Madeleine?"

"All the worse that the semblance of such devotion
should be used as the means of coercion!"

And all unconvinced Caroline rolled away in the
great coach.

CHAPTER VI

THE BASTILLE

And such a yell was there,
As if men fought upon the earth,
And fiends in upper air.
SCOTT — Marmion.

CAROLINE was eager to fulfil her promise of going to
tell Madame Normand of the ceremony which had to
her been so sad, but there were difficulties in the way.
Mélanie claimed her for various engagements, chiefly
to old convent friends; though it was wonderful to her
how these were fulfilled, in so restless and even perilous a condition were the streets. Sometimes all was
quiet, and looked exactly as Paris had done eight years
ago; at others, stalls were taken in, sinister-looking
people thronged the streets, patriots with unpowdered
hair stood on chairs haranguing motley assemblages,
and now and then the livery servants were pelted and
there was the cry "*A bas les aristocrates.*" Yet somehow or other it seemed a mere necessity for society to
meet, play at cards, and exchange compliments and
conversation just as if nothing perilous was in progress. Ladies would arrive declaring they were half
dead with the horrors of their journey, and then, after
a sip of *eau sucrée*, would be eagerly discussing the

110

last *coiffure à la Grecque*, or the exquisite cashmere shawl they had last seen, or, if more political in mind, the resignation of the incorruptible Necker, which daunted the hopes of many; while others were only anxious to put down these dangerous invasions of their privileges, and return to the good old times, when there were employments about court for every one, and pensions abounded. There was much that was very amusing, but Caroline Aylmer was too English to be greatly delighted with all that she saw and heard. She had seen her aunt's public toilette, but that was a decorous affair, to wile away the time during the lengthy artistic operations of the hairdresser; but to find a lady sitting with her feet in hot water, surrounded by her cavaliers, struck her as remarkable, to say the least of it; but Mélanie only laughed, and declared that the fashion of simple hairdressing was to blame, since it left no better opportunities.

" You would not do so, cousin ? "

" Oh, I ! but I am behind the times, quite devoted to old grandmother's etiquette, they tell me."

" I am very glad of it ! "

" What would you say if I took you to see Madame Delacour sitting in her bath, as my husband found her, with M. Morris and half-a-dozen gentlemen round her ? "

" Impossible ! "

" Ah, there was milk in the water to make it opaque! Ah !" as Caroline made a gesture of disgust, "that was a little too strong. She is not of my society, but the gentlemen haunt her at all hours! And your Englishman, Morris, with the one leg—— "

" Don't call him an Englishman, Mélanie ! He is an American. If English, then a traitor."

"All the same in language and manners, is it not? He can open his '*petits soins*' to the ladies, administer soup to them in bed, write verses to them. He gives himself the airs of an *élégant!*"

"Rebel that he is! I saw him making his court to Madame de La Fayette, who received him very coolly."

"Oh! Madame de La Fayette was *née* de Noailles, and the family are all devout and correct to the last degree. But have you seen him with Madame de Staël — you remember her — Germaine Necker?"

"Oh yes. She defended the Americans. But has not she gone with her father?"

"No, indeed! She is Madame l'Ambassadrice of Sweden, and has a grand salon, where all the political and literary people meet. I will take you there some evening! As for the other days, I hear she is to be seen with her women wiping her feet, and the Bishop of Autun wielding a warming-pan for her bed! Ah! your English ideas are disturbed."

"We brought the same from our convent."

"One modifies a great deal. Convent manners will not do in the world, *mon chou.*"

"You would not allow such things."

"No, but I am discreet, though maybe you would not think so!"

It was true. Mélanie's habits were those of her mother, and of a large proportion of the Parisian ladies, entirely beyond the reach of censure; and Caroline felt safe to enjoy and describe all that her cousin promoted.

To enjoy, for there was a wonderful amount of enjoyment in lighter, surface ways, and likewise in the hopeful state of people's minds, as they looked forward to a great renovation of the country, and a loosening

of these bonds of oppression which had certainly grown
intolerable.

There were street cries and street mobs, but these
were almost matters of course, and the ladies visited
in spite of them. Madame Normand made a call on
Mrs. Aylmer one day when she was out; and Caroline,
knowing how anxious she must be to hear of poor
Félicité's profession, and of Cécile's message that the
poor girl had been very ill but was recovering, in spite
of herself, decided on borrowing the sedan-chair, and
making a second visit.

The streets were remarkably, nay, ominously quiet
as she was carried through them; and she found Madame Normand alone, but in a vehement state of excitement, scarcely able even to think of Félicité.

"The troops are coming to Versailles!" she exclaimed, "the people are rising. Camille Desmoulins
has declared that there is preparing a St. Bartholomew
of patriots."

"You don't believe that, my dear lady?"

"How do I know? Royalty is capable of any
atrocity."

"If you could only see the bright, tender Queen, —
the good-natured King——"

"Pardon me! You are deceived. Frivolity makes
the taste for blood! Hark!"

The street resounded with shouts of "arms and
bread," and an endless stream of dark, fierce-faced men,
with green branches in their hats, and wild gesticulating women in white caps, some with streaming hair,
came trampling past, carrying with them in the current
men of a better class, but with the same green badge,
all bawling at the top of their lungs. In the midst
were carried — what Madame Normand greeted with

I

a shriek — two heads veiled in crape — alas! the pre-
cursors of flesh-and-blood heads, for these were the
busts of the Duke of Orleans and Necker, as her husband, rushing upstairs the next moment, told her. He
was out of breath, dusty, dishevelled, and his hat wore
the green badge.

He bowed with instinctive courtesy to the guest as
he said, "I have sent in your chair into the back court.
You cannot go back in it. I wonder you came here
safely, while," — then recovering his politeness, "I rejoice that we have the honour of seeing madame here."

"Is there danger?" asked both ladies together.

"None, except in the streets. The people are plun-
dering the bakers' shops on their way to demand arms
at the Hôtel de Ville."

"They do look half-starved. Ah! see the woman
with the child in her arms. She is a living skeleton
of fury," cried Madame Normand.

"And oh! the man with a red handkerchief and
projecting teeth. He looks wolfish," exclaimed Caroline. "What are they yelling?"

"It is a change. I must go out and see," began M.
Normand.

His wife, however, held him fast, and Caroline
joined her entreaties, and while he was trying to tear
himself from them, a fellow-provincial deputy tumbled, rather than entered, into the room, hatless, his
coat torn, and altogether knocked about.

"Ah! it is terrible," he cried. "Your Parisian
mobs are atrocious! This is the way I have been
treated for want of Desmoulins' precious green-leaf
badge."

"What are they crying?" exclaimed all, too eager
to give him commiseration.

"To the Bastille!" replied the deputy. "There is a report that the guns there are levelled upon the town. I joined the electors at the Hôtel de Ville in assuring the mob that there was no such intention, but a fever has seized them; they will hear nothing; and see how they have treated me."

"Hark! What was that? Was it thunder?" said Madame Normand.

"Ah, no!" said Caroline. "It was a cannon shot. I know the sound. Oh! the howls — they are far more terrible!"

"De Launay must be hard pressed," exclaimed the deputy.

"I must go and see," declared M. Normand, seizing his hat.

"No! no! I entreat you," burst out his wife, throwing her arms round him. "I shall die if you go! What could you do? Hark to the horrible sounds. It is like the sea in a tempest."

"Worse," said Caroline, awe-stricken.

"My dear, let me go. Remember, the mob would not hurt me. I am on their side, no defender of tyranny."

"No one is safe! See what they have done to Monsieur Gracey."

Attention being turned to M. Gracey, his host led him off to repair the damages he had suffered, and there was a sort of lull, though presently the outcries rose louder and louder, but still, as Mrs. Aylmer bade her companion remark, without the sound of musketry, whence they argued that there could be no fighting; yet to her ears the human roars of rage and exultation, all indistinct in themselves, yet forming one terrible volume of wild frantic yells, were almost more frightful than the more regulated volley.

The gentlemen could no longer be withheld, though they promised not to run into any danger, and advised Mrs. Aylmer to wait till all was quieted down, as indeed she was obliged to do, for her chairmen, having hid the emblazoned chair as best they might, had disguised their liveries, and mingled with the mob.

She and Madame Normand waited together, the latter divided between fits of anxiety for her husband, and of exultation for the storming of the stronghold of oppression.

"I can't understand," said Caroline. "The Bastille is like our Tower of London, is it not? Everybody would grieve if that were stormed."

"That is your English constitution. It is not an engine of oppression."

"I don't know. Henry VIII. cut off his wives' heads there, and I have seen the spikes where the Jacobite nobles' heads used to hang."

"You have seen?"

"Yes, my husband took me. Nobody would go to London without going to see the Tower and the Lions."

"Your constitution," again said Madame Normand. "You are free."

As the horrible cries arose again she had a fresh fit of terror for her husband; but such anxieties came again and again, for they had a long time, half the day in fact, to wait before intelligence came to them. All was still for a time, the neighbourhood quite deserted, and they found themselves very hungry. Madame Normand looked out in search of the *concierge*, who might send a boy out to a shop, but the *concierge* had shut up his box and was gone, and there was nothing for it but to wait.

By and by their patience, or impatience, was re-

warded, for in came the two deputies, who had looked
on at a safe distance, but were greatly shocked at what
had passed before their eyes. Not for the sake of the
Bastille itself, though they confessed that its days of
being a grim fastness of tyranny had ended long ago.
Only two prisoners had been found within the cells,
one a restless, impecunious Englishman, and one a
poor, worn-out old wretch, who was frightened out of
the few senses remaining to him by the wild plaudits
of the mob, and only begged to be taken back to the
cell, which had been his home and refuge for half
a lifetime.

But De Launay had been induced by two officers of
the National Guard to surrender to the mob, who had
poured in in fury, and in spite of the personal efforts
of the officers, had murdered and trampled on him,
and now were parading his bleeding head through the
town, with the two former captives dragged unwillingly to swell the triumph in the rear.

M. Gracey, who knew something of the De Launay
family, was overcome at such treatment of a good and
honourable man, though he durst not manifest his
feeling in the streets; but he threw himself into a
chair, hid his face on the table, and wept and sobbed.

"It is well there are none to betray you, my friend,"
said M. Normand.

"Weep for the instrument of foul tyranny?" cried
Madame Normand; "as well weep for the stones they
hurl from the battlements."

"The stones are not living men with a sense of
duty," returned M. Normand. "Pull down the dun-
geon, that is well, but to slay the brave men who
defended it was a crime."

"A crime! Ah, bah! why should they be brave

in the cause of oppression?" declared the lady, still exalted.

"Ah! madame," returned Gracey, "I augur ill for a revolt inaugurated by dishonourable bloodshed."

"Bah! as though victories were to be won with rose-water!" declaimed madame. "Did Junius Brutus at Collatinus expel the Tarquins without a drop of blood?"

Her tirade was interrupted by the cries that betokened the approach of the mob, and she sprang out to the balcony, followed by her husband and Caroline. Gracey, who had had enough of such sights, remained within the room.

The Marseillaise had not yet been brought to Paris, but the people were never at a loss for songs and choruses reflecting the feeling of the day, and one of these fell on the ear, as, after the inevitable advanced guard of children and dogs, came the people, walking in better order than on their previous way, waving branches of trees, with boughs in their hats and singing. Some carried the pikes and weapons captured in the Bastille and Hôtel de Ville; some had loaves of bread at the end of their sticks, and there was the usual proportion of fishwomen mingled with the grim dwellers in the slums, and the slender, youthful enthusiasts who careered along, transported with their achievements. In the midst were the prisoners, one, the Englishman, gesticulating as if infected with French frenzy; the other poor fellow dragged along between two big *poissardes*, who held him up, half-dead and wholly unconscious of the situation.

Then, accentuated by the cocked hat, thrust upon the grizzled hair, was borne the head of poor De Launay, those of his major and lieutenant, and of the *Prévôt des Marchands*.

Caroline recoiled from the ghastly spectacle, and turned back into the room. Perhaps Normand himself would fain have done so, but he knew that the least manifestation of disgust was dangerous, so he remained; and his wife was in a state of exaltation far above horror, and added her voice to the cries of " *Vive la nation! A bas la tyrannie.*" She came in, trembling and shedding tears of joy. She had seen the first-fruits of the reaction against the oppressions under which France had groaned for centuries, and she was transported with joy. Indeed the feeling was one that all the moderate, indeed half Europe, shared, excepting those who pitied the defenders. The Bastille was to them the emblem of despotism; multitudes had there been unjustly immured, and it was well that it should be overthrown.

The streets were quiet enough after the triumphal procession had passed by, and Caroline was anxious to get home, and to know how her cousins had fared. The July days were long, and it was still light, but her chairmen had disappeared, and the sedan remained in a dark outhouse. The streets were thought impassable for ladies, and she was scarcely shod for even her English feet to attempt a passage; but the *concierge* had returned, and a *fiacre* was with some delay procured, in which she was taken home. M. Normand insisted on escorting her. She found Mélanie much terrified by the procession, and the reports which had reached her, and Monsieur de Nidemerle about to send the chairmen to fetch her home. Only on inquiry they were not to be found. It was thought that they had been put to shame by their friends for having acted as beasts of burthen to a *vilaine aristocrate*.

CHAPTER VII

With thee, my bark, I'll quickly go
Athwart the foaming brine,
Nor care what land thou bring'st me to
So not again to mine.

BYRON.

AFTER the overthrow of the Bastille, society became much the same as before. There were important discussions. now and then alarms of mobs, cries of "*A la lanterne*," when an unpopular aristocrat was met in the streets: sometimes even a murder, and reports came in of risings of peasants against the seigneurs. and attacks on their châteaux; but the streets were in general fairly quiet, and visits, theatricals, and talk, political and frivolous, filled the salons as usual. Eating, drinking, talking, marrying and giving in marriage, engrossed the world, as in the days before the Flood came and took them all away.

Captain Aylmer's mother had some connection with the family of Lady Gower, the English ambassadress. She had left her letters of introduction, and, when possible, was a visitor at the Embassy, attending the English service whenever she could. in duteous obedience to her husband and mother-in-law, whose orders she felt she had almost transgressed by witnessing the

120

profession of the two nuns: but that was a *spectacle*.
She was always made welcome at Lady Gower's salon,
and was often much amused at the sentimental little
semi-flirtation that M. Gouverneur Morris carried on
with the great lady, and which was plainly diplomatic
management and amusement on her part if it was
vanity upon his. Through the Embassy was conducted her correspondence with England and with her
husband, and as the novelty of this passed, she began
more and more to live on the expectation of these,
though even Mrs. Aylmer's were few and far between.
Her husband's were uncertain, but they were journals
and very delightful.

Letters came also from the West Indies, which decided Monsieur and Madame de Nidemerle on going
out to Ste. Marie Galante to obtain possession of their
property, and adapt it to the new circumstances that
might befall them. Mélanie had a picture of island
life in her mind, compounded of her mother's childhood, of Coralie's talk, and of Paul and Virginie, and
she looked forward to palm-trees, humming-birds,
cocoa-nuts, and obsequious slaves, to whom she should
proclaim freedom. She wanted to take out, not only
her children, but her sister and cousin. Cécile, however, would not hear of leaving her convent, and Caroline could not go so far from her children. She would
have delighted in the voyage, and she had real, vivid
recollections of more than one island; but there was a
stronger force connected with the downs of Downford,
and she resolved on remaining where she could hear
of her little ones, and get letters from her husband
more easily than in a French island.

For all agreed in declaring that she must not go
home as yet. If she could not go out to Guadaloupe

she must remain at Paris, within reach of communication and of notaries, and pursue her claims, if she
hoped to secure her share of the property. To remain
in the Hôtel de Nidemerle without the protection of
the master thereof did not seem to her possible, and
she therefore decided on joining Madame de Henisson
in boarding at the convent of Ste. Lucie. There she
would have full liberty, as well as protection, and the
nuns had become too poor to venture any objection to
a Protestant who could pay them. Besides, was she
not almost a child of the convent? So it was decided.
The two children of the Nidemerles were to accompany
them, under the tutorship of the Abbé, and the care of
a *bonne*, and they also decided on taking with them
their negro servant, offering Zélie also a passage with
them.

Zélie, however, having once recovered her dear
Mamselle Caroline, was resolved never to part with
her again. Her own kith and kin had long been forgotten, and there was nothing in the world that she
loved so well. Her wool was grey, under her scarlet, gold-edged turban, but she was still an effective
femme de chambre, and Caroline was glad to retain the
familiar nurse of her childhood.

Another precious possession was left with her.
Mélanie called her into her room one evening, and,
after locking the doors, opened a doubly fastened cabinet. She took out a casket, rich with ivory and gold,
with the Ribaumont arms engraven upon a shield on
the lid. "There," she said, unlocking it, and display-
ing the bed of velvet, "do you know them?"

"The pearls of Ribaumont. Oh!"

"Here is all their history, on this yellow paper,
written out by our great-grandmother, Madame Mar-

guerite de Ribaumont Bellaise, who had this casket
made."

"I shall love to read it. The story was a yarn — I
mean *une historiette* — of my dear father on board
ship. I do not think my uncle cared for it in the
same way."

"You must read it. There are two, if not three,
veritable romances in it. One night we caused M. de
St. Pierre to read it aloud in the salon, and I assure
you there was no one who was not plunged in
tears."

"After all, Mélanie, they are not so beautiful as I
expected. I have seen finer pearls. That pendant
which my father gave me in memory of them has
larger pearls, and not so yellow. This one, too, is half
broken."

"Bah! You are not worthy to have the charge of
them."

"No, no, Mélanie, I honour them all the more. Of
course King Edward would not wear his best pearls
on his helmet in a night attack, and this yellow pearl
must have been the one that Eustacie sent as a token
to her husband. You see it hangs apart from the
rest."

"You know the history better than I do, my
dear."

"I think my father knew it by heart. He could
remember his great aunt, Naomi Fellowes, who had
been in France, and had seen the pearls. Oh, yes, I
honour and love them, and delight in the sight of
them. Do you mean to take them with you, or leave
them at the Château de Nidemerle, or with your
banker?"

"Best no. My husband thinks that no place here

may be safe from those frightful mobs, though Anjou is better than most parts of France, and bankers may be robbed at any moment. So we mean to take all our valuables with us to the West Indies — plate, jewels, and all — but this, an heirloom of the Ribaumonts, should, he thinks, be put out of the way of danger, and therefore that it had better be committed to you, where it will be safe in England, even should our vessel founder. Ah! then we should be all together. None would have the misery of surviving the rest." Wherewith Mélanie burst into tears, being already in a terrible fright about the voyage.

"Oh! that is folly, my dear Mélanie. Vessels are not always foundering. You will have a delightful voyage, and see the porpoises, and the flying-fish, and only be grieved to come to the end of it. If only I were going with you!"

"Dear Caroline, come with us. Then I should not be nearly so much frightened if I had you with me."

"I wish I could, but it is impossible without orders from my husband; nor could I leave my children at such a distance. If I had the little things with me it would be a different matter, but I feel day by day as if my boy were drawing me home. I hear him in my sleep cry 'Mamma, mamma!' I shall not bring myself to stay long after you are gone."

"What, return contentedly to the little provincial town and the belles-mères. I ask their pardon, one is an aunt ——!"

"But my mother-in-law is the one I love, and the uncle. Indeed, though if there were no one else, my son and daughter would be enough. These politics of Paris, and still worse, these gaieties; oh! they make me sick!"

"And as for me, I shall pine till I see Paris once more."

Caroline was safely installed in the convent before the Nidemerles departed; for in fact they almost stripped their hotel, carrying with them their handsomest articles of furniture, tapestries, and carpets — a perfect ship load — as well as all their black servants, evidently reckoning on a considerable stay, for perhaps M. de Nidemerle understood the signs of the times better than his wife, and doubted how it would fare with the nobles, who had already stripped themselves of much of their power and privilege.

Cécile and Caroline drove out of Paris with Mélanie, and her cavalcade of carriages, servants, and baggage, on the way to Nantes. Murmurs and distrust of emigrants had not yet begun, especially on the Breton road, and they went on unmolested as far as the first stage, where they were supposed to dine at the pretty old trellised inn of the Ermine, in a large room with a tiled floor and bow window. Supposed to dine, for every one, even the boy, was too much overcome to eat. It would have seemed a disgraceful want of sensibility to be able to swallow, and Caroline, with her English appetite, was quite ashamed of being hungry, and the Abbé, no relation to any one, only swallowed soup surreptitiously. Then, in perfect convulsions of grief, Mélanie was detached by her husband from her sister's embrace, and lifted into the carriage. Then followed her daughter, crying piteously, but as much from alarm at her mother's state as from the sorrow of separating from her aunt, and her brother and father were full of passionate tears and embraces. The *bonne* and the Abbé followed, the grand old-fashioned *berline* was closed, and dashed off with its six horses; white handkerchiefs were waved from the windows, the lackeys, white and black, hung on behind, all, and the ensuing chaise with the rest of the servants, disappeared in a cloud of dust, and Madame de Henisson, in a dead faint, remained to be tended by her *femme de chambre* and Mrs. Aylmer till she could be recovered sufficiently to return to Ste. Lucie.

CHAPTER VIII

" I wish that I were dead, but I'm not like to die."
Despair it was come, and she thought it was content ;
She thought it was content, and yet her cheek grew pale,
And she drooped like a lily bent down by the hail.

LADY ANNE LINDSAY.

THE rooms in the convent of Ste. Lucie were not an
undesirable residence, especially since the numbers
both of nuns and of pensionnaires had so much diminished. They were bare, but neither English nor French
society was lavish of furniture, and Mrs. Aylmer did
not miss it. Her rooms were in a building reaching
along one side of the cloistered quadrangle, to which
the main entrance was through the gateway, but
which had another door leading to the outer world.
These rooms were in fact over the offices of the convent — the stores of wood for fuel, and the stable
where lived the donkey, and the two cows which
gave milk to the inmates, also the old man who took
care of them, but who was carefully locked out of the
garden, where the lay sisters did the work. There
was a high boundary wall and thick hedge between
the garden and the field where the three animals dis-
ported themselves, and which led down to the Seine.
The flour, wood, and other articles used in the convent

127

were, as Caroline soon learnt, brought by water and
carried in by this mode of access, which she had never
been allowed to suspect in her pensionnaire days. The
long passage into which her rooms opened led to two
narrow stone staircases, one terminating in a door
towards the highroad, the other opening into the field
bordered by the river with the little landing-place;
and it was indescribable what a sense of liberty this
gave her, though she might not often avail herself of
it. To know that she need not always walk in the
garden as in old times, nor always have a carriage up
through the great gateway, made her feel that she was
really no pensionnaire but an English sailor's wife!

She had two rooms; Cécile also had two, and they
dined and supped together; but devotion occupied
Cécile through many hours of the day, as she shared
in most of the regular hours of the nuns, and had
besides vowed a *neuvaine* for the safety of her sister's
voyage. Caroline had written a solemn pledge to her
very Protestant aunt and mother-in-law, and—what
she regarded even more—promised her husband to
abstain from the Roman Catholic services, which they
dreaded the more as she had been habituated to them
in her youth. She had thus a great deal of solitude
to dispose of, and she sometimes felt as though it were
wicked of her not to pray likewise to the same amount
for her husband and cousins, and she tried, but could
not fix her attention; moreover, she had been diligently taught to put no faith in "vain repetitions."
She had been to the ambassador's chapel on Sunday
when in Paris, but it was too far off to go at present
except when she slept at the Embassy, where Lady
Gower made her kindly welcome. Visitors now and
then came to her, and she could return their visits

when she liked, but she did not often like, for the
tumults in Paris were becoming alarming.

Her life was very dull, chiefly occupied by the long
letters always in hand to her husband, and by her interest in poor Félicité — or rather Sœur Philomène.
The girl was obliged to attend all the devotions of
the sisterhood, but at other times she wandered apart
in the garden, a lovely figure in her black dress and
white veil and scapulary.

She had been very ill after her forced profession,
and had not long been recovered enough to be out of
doors again, which, perhaps, prevented her from being
employed in any of the many avocations of the sisters,
in curious contrast to Sœur Françoise de Rome, whom
Caroline met merrily bearing a great pan of milk,
looking as happy as the day was long, or if she were
walking in the garden alone, with her beads in her
hands, there was on her soft sweet face a rapt look
of meditation, as though the rosary was not to her
a mechanical arrangement for soulless forms, but a
real implement for aiding devout aspiration.

But poor Sœur Philomène sat drooping on the garden seats, and once Caroline found her hanging over
a young lilac just coming into blossom; and as it
seemed watering it with her tears, though her veil
hung so much forward that it was not easy to be certain. However, the impulse to comfort or at least
to sympathise, was so strong that the warm-hearted
Englishwoman could not help going towards her and
gently saying, "My poor child!"

Félicité sprang up in terror, and then, as she perceived the large hat and blue dress, she exclaimed,
"Ah! you are *mondaine*, you are Protestant, madame,
you can pity me."

K

" I pity you from my heart, indeed I do, my dear.
I have heard your story from Madame Normand."

" You will then excuse these vain, vain tears.   I
know they are wicked; but oh! how to check them
when I saw and smelt that sweet lilac.   It is only
two years ago that he — that Henri — was showing
me all its beauties, and dwelling on the wisdom shown
in the grace of the blossom.   I had a flower of it in my
Livre d'Heures, but they found it and took it away.
They said it was sinful to cherish what reminded me
of a disobedient, self-willed attachment, and oh! if
they knew of my weeping now ——— ! "   And the weeping became, not louder, but more overpowering, all the
more because the poor young nun thought it absolutely
wicked.

" No, no, I do not think it wicked," said Caroline.
" Never fear!   I am sure it does you good; I will
not betray you."

Presently the bell for vespers made Sœur Philomène start up and hurry into the chapel in fear of
penance, drawing her veil over her red eyes, though
these were too frequent a sight to excite more than
a sigh of blame to her for being unable even yet to
accomplish " detachment " from the world or from her
sinful passion.

Was it sinful?   Nuns, uncle, and confessor all
taught her that it was so, having begun, they said, in
indiscretion and disobedience, and being now absolutely
guilty in a professed nun.

But Félicité, who, after that first day, had learnt to
seek out Mrs. Aylmer, and confide in her, often speaking in English, was torn to pieces between her real
and her fictitious conscience.   She could not think
there had been indiscretion in the intercourse which

had been overlooked by the governess and sanctioned by her parents.

"My father used to be delighted when I repeated my scientific lessons to him. He was charmed when I explained the letters on botany of Jean Jacques Rousseau which I read with Monsieur Beaudésert."

"Ah! but —— "

"I know what you would say, but there never was a word between us. I knew nothing till there was the great *éclat* and they fell on my dear Miss Fernley and on me. Then I knew how it was, and that he loved me, and that I had been loving him all the time; and Miss Fernley said I was right, and that was the way things were done in your happy England, and it would be a crime and a falsehood to let myself be married to any one else when I loved no one but that one. And now he is gone, they have sent him away to those dreadful swamps and marshes among the crocodiles, where every one dies of fever or gets killed by your Indians."

Caroline could reassure her as to the perils of Louisiana, and much more was gradually told as to the persecution the poor girl had undergone at her home, till she had accepted the residence in the convent as a refuge. The last message that Miss Fernley conveyed to her had advised her to submit to this arrangement, which would give her peace and pledge her to nothing. Henri Beaudésert bade her be patient, trust to him, and await better times, when he hoped to be able to rise to a level where he might meet the nobility. "'Patience, hope, and trust,' those, he said, were to be our watchwords, and they are engraven for ever on my poor heart, faithless as I have been."

Then came the history of the silent inducements

of the sisters, and the active denunciations of Monseigneur de Charmilly, who had half cajoled, half frightened her into consenting to the novitiate, when the marriage with her sister had been arranged, and at the end of the year had returned on her with heavy denunciations, all the stronger for having already accepted the dedication from which she wished to retreat, for the sake of an unholy love for one of those philosophers who were working the ruin of France, godless, unholy men. What did he know? He had heard reports that the wretch had forgotten her, and was linking himself in marriage with a Creole heretic.

Félicité avowed that this had staggered her. She was giving up all hopes of marriage, and profession would shelter her from further torment on that subject, so she had given a sort of consent. Only afterwards came the *arrière-pensée* that she ought to have demanded evidence, whether she could have obtained it or not; and now Caroline was able, whether wisely or not, to assure her that Beaudésert was far from forgetting her! Alas! alas!

"But," cried the girl eagerly, "I never uttered the vow. I protested first, but no one heeded my protest, I believe it was intercepted, I was utterly desolate, no one pitied me, I yielded and let myself be led forward, but I only moved my lips. Monseigneur, my uncle, took it for granted that I spoke. I think he knew that it might be dangerous to press me to extremity, and I was so faint, I should have been able to scream perhaps, but hardly to speak. No, I have made no real vows, they were treated as made when the habit was given to me; I do not feel myself bound, not within, not in my conscience. ' Patience, hope, and trust,' he said. Perhaps the time will come that I

can appeal," and she clasped her hands with a look
of fervour.

" Appeal ? " said Caroline, " to whom ? "

" To the Bishops ! Nay, to the Pope himself. The
Holy Father could never consent to a reluctant sacrifice. He would not have the lamb driven struggling
to the altar. God would have willing offerings like
Sœur Françoise, not those whose hearts are elsewhere, and to whom every observance is misery
because she feels it wicked mockery and hypocrisy."

" Cannot you pray that God will deliver you from
this bondage and captivity ? "

" Eh ! But that would be wicked."

" Surely not. God will hear us in any trouble, and
this is a real one. Only ask Him to help you, and He
will find the way."

That was the tenor of the conversations which Mrs.
Aylmer held almost by stealth with Félicité, often
going back to the happy days in the château garden,
and the lessons on botany or electricity, or dwelling
on the details of the struggle, and sometimes on the
question how far she was bound. The poor girl was
conscientious and religious at heart, and the sense of
hypocrisy in her obligatory devotions was an additional misery to her. Caroline's training had been so
far Catholic that she did not esteem them all, as her
Protestant friends at home would have done, as additional sins, but she tried to persuade the maiden
that such prayers might be mentally turned to her
own case.

" But how ? how ? How could I be helped ? "

" God can find out a way."

" This is an iron cage — an adamant cage."

"Oh! hush! hush! Nothing is impossible with Him."

"My own word. The holy vows."

"You have said that you never really made them."

"Do not talk in that way. It would be impiety in any one else."

"You are not like any one else."

"Oh! I know it cannot be. It is no use to pray."

"Don't! don't!" cried Caroline, "prayer is sure to bring blessings in some way. He could make you happy and content here."

"I don't want to be content. That would be forgetting Henri and all the joy I could ever have in my life."

"Or again, God could deliver you out of all these troubles."

"Death! Oh!" as she wrung her hands, "I have asked for death again and again, and He will not let me die! Think! I am not nineteen, and I shall go on as Sister Philomène in this hateful black and white, within these weary walls for fifty — sixty years! What do I know? Oh, if I had let them kill me — but they told me he was married!" — with a fierce gesture.

"But while you are alive, your prayers can still do him good."

"You! Protestant as you are, you say that."

"I — of course I do. My father taught me that my prayers would hover round to guard our ship, and they can call the angels down to guard your Henri in America. I trust mine are helping to keep my husband safe, and my little ones."

That seemed a softening thought, and the discussion was renewed several times, sometimes in one mood,

sometimes in another, either despairing or resigned;
all was poured out to Caroline, as the only person
who could listen and sympathise without blaming.
For even la Mère de l'Annonciation, though she pitied
with all her heart, could not but censure the repinings,
and preach patience and submission, with forgetfulness
of M. Beaudésert, who, in the good nun's opinion, was
nothing better than a heretic or an atheist.

Time and consolation had a certain effect. Félicité
ceased to weep half the night, and in chapel she took
her part in the avocations of the convent, and ceased
to hang so much upon her friend, who, though sometimes a little wearied with the perpetual lamentations,
still missed the excitement in the dulness of her life.

She had another interest on certain days. The
sisters of Ste. Lucie had established a connection with
a monastery lower down the Seine, and all their country provisions were brought from thence to their own
little landing-place, a very important convenience, as
it spared both the *octroi* and the transit through hungry Paris, where the populace might have permitted
nothing to arrive at its destination. Caroline found
her way through the field of *marguerites* and *espe-
rances* to the banks of the river, and there witnessed
the handing out of sacks, faggots, and bags of charcoal, cheeses also, and other commodities by the stout
Norman peasant, the porter, and the strong-armed lay
sister who helped him. One face struck her as anything but Norman — more ruddy, more freckled, and
set in reddish hair, turning grey, and the tone was
not quite French, though the language was. She had
a sense of recognition, and, on the other hand, though
all the men looked with wonder at the unwonted spectacle of a lady, this face had a puzzled look of scrutiny,

and at last a familiar, "Yo ho," made her exclaim,
"Irish Denny!" while at the same moment he broke
out with, "By the powers, little missy! Ye won't
report me, miss?"

"Whom should I report you to, Denny?" she
exclaimed, laughing. "I am sorry you are a deserter
all the same."

"Ah, and thin, Miss Caroline, it never was the same
aboard since your father — heavens be his bed! — went
to glory. Captain Smith, the nagnor, he *was* a tyrant
and no mistake, and when he gave me twenty dozen
lashes just for nothing at all, and the food was not
what a respectable pig would look at twice, what
should hinder me from swimming off to Bill Burton's
boat — an honest man-of-war's-man that carried on a
little free trade with the Frenchies — me that was
pressed at the first in Cork harbour, and had no call
to serve King George first nor last?"

"Then how came you here?"

"Ye see, miss, or ma'am, for some one tell'd me you
were married to young Mr. Aylmer — and a good offi-
cer he was, bless him — I could pick up the French
lingo faster nor some of them, and then I found I
could practise my religion in these parts, and there
was a little colleen whose black eyes just made my
heart no better nor tinder."

"So you married her and settled down here, and are
as good as a Frenchman?"

"You've hit it, ma'am; only I'd never fire a shot
against the old flag that the Admiral sailed under.
I've got a sweet little house not far from Rouen, the
very moral of my mother's cot in ould Ireland; and I
have a chance of serving the good fathers and the holy
mothers, to make up for the days I could have no re-

ligion, and small blame to me! And you be one of
them, ma'am, as your blessed mother was? "

"Well, I don't quite know that, Denny, but at any
rate I am living here, with the good mothers, while
my husband is on the East Indian station, till I can
hear about some property in Ste. Marie Galante."

Deserter as he was, there was something so attractive in Irish Denny, and the very sound of his brogue
was so pleasant as at least an echo of English, that
Caroline could not help going down to the landing-
place whenever the boat was coming in, and having a
conversation with him. She even constructed a little
hood for the little gossoon, whom she soon understood
to be the pride of his heart, and a ball, which made
him declare that he perceived she knew what it was
to be a mother. Altogether it was a great enlivenment
in her rather dreary convent life.

"Oh had I but known of that passage," sighed
Félicité under her breath, "before I was professed!
And yet what good would it have done? His relations could not have sheltered me, and now, and now!
Yes, I know it was no genuine vow; but no one, nothing can absolve me save His Holiness." And again
she wept hopelessly.

CHAPTER IX

Force should be right ; or rather, right and wrong,
Between whose endless jar justice resides,
Should lose their names, and so should justice too.
Then everything includes itself in power,
Power into will, will into appetite ;
And appetite, an universal wolf,
So doubly seconded by will and power,
Must make perforce an universal prey,
And last eat up itself.

Troilus and Cressida.

LETTERS were slow in coming either from the west or east. Western ones came first, as Captain Aylmer's, besides having a longer passage, went first to England, as he never knew how soon his wife might be there; whereas, thus far, there was direct communication between Guadaloupe and Paris. When tidings came of the travellers, there was very prosperous news of the arrival. The charm of the place enchanted Madame de Nidemerle, who felt at home there directly, and was sure she could never be happy anywhere else.

Her husband, however, wrote in more anxiety. The islands were in a restless state. Rumours arose that all citizens were to vote for representatives to express their will to the National Assembly. This notice had

138

created a great jealousy, since the mulattoes or half-caste races, who were not slaves, claimed the same rights as the pure whites, and this was resisted and resented by those who had so long been masters. The tenure of property was insecure, commerce began to be threatened, even the slaves had scented freedom, and there was little chance of being able to sell the estate, or even to realise such an increase as previously.

The next despatches described the family as comfortably settled down at Ste. Marie Galante, Gaspard perfectly happy with boat and fishing-rod, and his mother recurring to the habits no doubt ingrained in her ancestry, for the gentle apathy and ease of the climate had descended on her as well as on Agathe ; and the Abbé, finding them easy-going, indolent scholars, was dividing his time between natural history and teaching the negroes. It was quite possible to live on the estate in peace and plenty, and Monsieur de Nidemerle thought it would be better to remain there, and retain possession while the storm seemed to be brewing in France, and it might be safer to escape the outburst which he foresaw.

As to being able to send a share of the value of the estate to his dear cousin Caroline, he could give her no hopes — not even of remittances until affairs both there and at home should be more settled. He could only send her papers fully establishing her claim, if that could be of any use to her, and he advised her to take them and see them registered by the notary and put in his possession.

With these papers Mrs. Aylmer started for Paris in a *fiacre*. She had decided that there was little use in lingering in Paris, and she was longing to be at home with her children. The streets were fairly quiet, but the notary's clerk wore a red cap of liberty on his head, looking at her insolently; and he called out to his master, " *Citoyen*, here is a *citoyenne* to see you."

Mrs. Aylmer had no title to be forfeited, but she looked as if she had, and that was quite enough to lead to insult. The notary durst not make his bow till the door was shut between him and his clerk. He could only confirm what Monsieur de Nidemerle had said. There was very little hope of her obtaining any proceeds from the Nidemerle property. He would take care of the duplicate papers which had been sent to him, but he advised her to place another set in security elsewhere if she could. " Alas! would anything be long their own ? " the old man said, lowering his voice.

He threw his tricoloured scarf around him before he durst conduct her to her carriage, and he looked almost reluctant to repeat her order to be driven to the British Embassy; but though England's unpopularity had broken out again, the driver, who had taken her there before, and knew that he would be regaled by the servants, made no objection, and promised to return for her the next day, for she was to spend the Sunday there.

She was received as usual very kindly, and told that she was just in time, for a packet from England had just been brought by a messenger, and there was a letter for her. There was none from her husband. She had heard from him too lately to expect another letter for some time, but there was one from her mother-in-law, saying that both the children had been ill with whooping-cough, and that the little boy was not recovering favourably, that he was very fretful and pining, and often asked for " mamma."

" My little son ! My dear little Eustace, I must go home. Property, what is that to me ? My boy, my boy, I must get back to him ! " Such was Caroline's cry, impetuous as ever, and her hosts were quite ready to forward her departure.

Lord Gower thought that every English person, not detained by absolute duty, would be better away. It was only a week since the royal family, after a terrible night of alarms, had been dragged into Paris from Versailles amid cries of " Here come the baker, baker's wife, and little baker's boy," by the frenzied crowd, who fancied that the court devoured all the food, and that an ebullition of loyalty on the part of the Guards meant a plot to master the people, and deprive them of the liberties from which they expected so much, perhaps to butcher them. The Marquis de La Fayette had found himself utterly incapable of restraining them or even of protecting the life of the Queen, being, in fact, as was well said of him, in a position too great for his abilities. Lord Gower had seen the King, who was practically a captive in the Tuileries, but endured his situation with a passive resignation that looked like stolidity. Poor man, he was probably perfectly aware, though his loyalty would not avow it, that on him were being visited a long course of ancestral crimes.

That more and worse was to come was to be apprehended, and the ambassador said that he should have advised Mrs. Aylmer's departure if she had no pressing call. He could undertake for her passport, but Paris was hardly in a favourable condition for departing through the streets, for emigrants were beginning to be interrupted and watched with jealousy ; and in the headless heedless state of the mobs even her claim to Englishry might not protect her from alarms, if nothing worse.

If she could go without encountering large towns or disaffected seaports, it might be all the safer, though no one could tell what would be the humours from day to day. Caroline thought of her smuggling friend, the deserter, and declared that she thought she could make her way without encountering much danger. The danger of a river boat, and uncertain passage in November, seemed like nothing to her. So before she took leave, Lord Gower was able to provide her with a passport in all due form, fit to serve her if she did pass through Paris, Rouen, or Havre, the last two places being what she could not probably avoid. She would gladly have gone to see the Normands, but they had quitted Paris. M. Normand's voice had not been heard in the National Assembly, and this disappointment had considerably cooled his lady's ardour in the cause, and made her endure that he should be recalled by provincial business ; besides that she had had enough of mobs, whom she had found not to be quite the humane and enlightened assemblies that her imagination had painted them.

Impatiently Caroline waited at Ste. Lucie for the next convoy of wood, rejoicing that it was sure to be a large one for the approach of winter. It was a shock to her kind entertainers to hear she was going, but the Mother Prioress, a shrewd woman of the world, thought she was prudent. Evil times were apparently coming, and one who had no duties to detain her would be better at a distance. Cécile too agreed that the call was certainly to the country of husband and children.

"Come with me, Cécile," she entreated. "There is a chapel in our town not far off, and some Catholic

families, and you could pray there whenever you
would, and you would be safe with me from all
these dreadful men and their stories. You would
so love my little ones ——"

"Alas, they would only remind me of my babe that
only lived an hour," said Cécile, beginning to weep.

"Indeed they would be life to you. You love
Agathe and Gaspard; I know you would love my
Mary and Eustace."

But Madame de Henisson was unpersuadable; only
she promised to remember her cousin's offer if things
became worse, or the privileges of the nunnery were
invaded.

To Félicité it was a blow. "You are the only person to whom I could speak, the only one who has any
feeling for me, or who has given me hope. Oh, madame, how can I live without you?"

"Yet you have not been much with me of late."

"No, but I knew you were here! I could look up
at your window."

"Look still, Félicité dear. Recollect what I said
that nobody is ever devoid of some loophole where
they may see the light. There is no storm that does
not come to an end somehow, sooner or later."

"Ah, often down in the depths."

"But, as my father used to say, there is hope; the
best of hopes even there."

"Oh, why cannot I keep you to hearten me!"

"My mother-in-law once told me, when I did not
understand it, that a song of joy is delightful, but
when one is able to sing a psalm instead of a song it
is even sweeter and better."[1]

[1] The thought is from an American book quite modern, *An
Old Maid's Diary*, but it is worthy to be remembered.

"I do not understand. Our eternal psalms weary me! Yes, there are translations in our breviaries, but they do not help me."

"Ah, they will by and by. I felt it when my husband went away. Think and try."

"If you could always be with me!"

Such was Félicité's moan, not to be silenced all the time that the boat, *La Demoiselle*, was waited for.

When at length with early morning she saw, from what a lively nun called her *fenêtre mondaine*, the mast of the ship, it had a tricoloured flag flying, and when she made her way down to the landing-place, to her dismay, the name painted on the stern was *La jeune citoyenne*. Was all her hope lost? No, a hearty voice called out, "All right! The top of the morning to ye, my lady."

"The same to you, Denny; I was frightened lest it should not be your boat."

"Bless you, ma'am, the spalpeens down the river would have been after sinking or burning the boat if I had not flattered them by changing the name of her just by means of blarney, as the holy ladies would have been ill off for their firewood."

He spoke confidentially in tone, though there was no one who could understand the language, his two assistants having no smattering of English.

Caroline ventured to ask, "And suppose I asked you for a passage on your return, would you have me, Denny?"

"And is it yourself, Miss Caroline, as would honour me by sailing under my flag? Then it's I that shall be the proud man."

It was then arranged, partly then and partly later in the day, that when all the stores for the nunnery had been landed, and the vessel made as clean as was in the nature of herself or her crew, Mrs. Aylmer should be taken on board with her luggage, Denny undertaking to transport her as far as Rouen, and to provide for her further journey, if possible, to Havre. Beyond this he could not go, being afraid of being recognised by British crews as a deserter; and at present England and France were at peace, so that there would be no difficulty in making the voyage. He advised, however, that she should wear over the travelling dress which she called a riding-habit or *amazone*, a Norman peasant cap, kerchief, and apron, so as not to attract the attention of the people on the banks, who might very well suppose her to be a girl returning from service in Paris.

A lay sister, who had come from Normandy, was able, in the course of the day, to make up the needful dress, the high white cap, and the white apron; the coloured neckerchief was supplied from Caroline's own wardrobe; the lay sister dressed her abundant light hair, observing, however, that a real *Normande* would have cut it off and sold it. Such tresses were worth — oh, so much, so much!

Caroline looked so pretty when her toilette was complete that the sisters were delighted, and could not cease from admiring her; and little Sœur Françoise de Rome fairly danced about her in childish ecstasy.

The maiden did not wish for change, she was perfectly content; and yet a little change, a little costume were a refreshment to her, enjoyed because of her absolute self-surrender to the spiritual life in which she found her happiness. Caroline often remembered that face of glee and the form full of joyous

L

action under the black veil. Cécile wept, as she always did, but Caroline bade her remember that if things looked dark in France, there were always cousins in England who would gladly welcome her.

The Mother Prioress inquired about the Roman Catholic chapels and facilities for worship in England, but Caroline could not tell her much, though she knew that one existed, and was spoken of with undefined dread at Downford, as though some day it might be a centre to explode and blow every one up, or light fires to burn all the Protestants up.

"Who knows what times are coming," said the Mother, "or whither our poor maidens of the Church may be driven to seek a refuge?"

"Always write to me, if I can help you," said Caroline.

And amid general weeping, she took leave, with Zélie stowed below only to show herself when they were quite safe from spectators. It was a half-decked boat, with shelter at the stern with no real accommodation, but the sailor's daughter did not care for this as she was only to be on board one night, and the evenings were still warm.

CHAPTER X

La Jeune Citoyenne was not by any means a disagreeable mode of conveyance. Denny, who could quite depend on the two men and boy who formed his crew, had done what he called, in his comical mixture of French, Irish, and sailor's English, "*bien swabbé le deck vraiment ílégant*," and borrowed a chair where madame might sit in comfort. Her goods were packed in the space where the fuel had been, and space was left where Zélie could be curled up whenever it was expedient that her black face should not be observed.

There Caroline sat enthroned, while the *canot* or barge smoothly dropped down the gentle current of the Seine, on a still warm day of early November, decidedly breathing St. Martin's Little Summer. Denny ventured to put up a somewhat ragged and dirty brown sail — a contrast to the brand-new tricolour overhead — a rather trying flag to Caroline to sail under. At places where care was required Denny himself took the helm, and in case of need the oars were used by the two stout Normans; but usually two persons were at liberty, and either the Irishman or his mate sedulously attended upon their

147

passenger, telling her the names of the villages and châteaux that they passed, or of the numerous convents whose grounds came down to the water. There was the forest of St. Germain with one grand peep of the château in its park, not looked at with much goodwill by the mate, who was attending to the sail, but by no means unwilling to talk to the lady.

"Eh!" he said, as the morning sun touched the tops of the trees, and revealed a few deer grazing upon the green sward, "there will soon be an end, they say, of all those enclosures, and the laws that punish a poor man for even touching one of those beasts that the gentlemen foster on our crops for their own pleasure."

All the spirit of the old poacher, *braconnier* or Norman complaining of forest laws, was in the man, and it was plain that he, like his kind, would soon be devastating the preserves of all kinds of game.

Through the towns it was thought needful for Zélie to disappear; indeed the men regarded her with a certain amount of awe, and saw her eat and drink and speak much as they would have looked on at a monkey's performance.

No obstruction was met with, but it was not possible to continue the journey in the dark, so the *canot* had to be moored in the twilight in a village, where Denny undertook for the reception that madame might have from Mère Nanon, an old *paysanne* whom he had known for many years, and whose eggs and butter he was wont to call for on his upward voyages for Ste. Lucie, secretly, for fear the steward should find out the trade, think she was growing too prosperous, and come down on her with some exaction.

She lived close to the banks, and Denny assisted the lady to walk over a slippery board, and then over

some stepping-stones through the quaking banks. She
enjoyed this, and tripped over gaily, but poor Zélie
stood quaking on the end of the plank, afraid to put
out a foot, in spite of her mistress's encouragement.
"Pray help her, Denny, she is old and unused to such
places, my good old nurse."

"Come on thin, in the name of the saints, my dear.
There's nothing to hurt yer barring a frog or two, and
maybe you are used to worse nor that — a crocodile
or two! There — your foot there — and I've got a
good grip of the black hand of ye — leap now — and
ye'll be as safe as if ye were in Our Lady's Church."

Then, having safely landed the negress, he bade the
two "come up aisy now," and they proceeded slowly,
while he sprang up a rough path, leading beneath a
chestnut tree to a low hovel, in front of which an old
woman sat spinning. What passed between them was
in the rapidest possible French, which Caroline could
not half understand, but it ended in the old lady, resplendent in white cap and long gold ear-rings, coming
down with the lowest of curtsies and outstretched
hands to welcome her, and assure her that "all was at
her service. Ah oui! Any friend of ce bon Denis!
Yes, and even la noire. Had she not heard that there
were such beyond the sea, for whom our good priest
had collected our alms on Sundays? Ah! but was
she indeed a good Christian?" as Zélie fell on her
knees before a little shrine containing a small image
of Our Lady.

Nothing more was needed; Mère Manon sprang to
her and embraced her, and was astonished to hear her
respond in very fair French. "Ah! even she speaks
French!"

Caroline, whom she perfectly understood to be a

lady in spite of the disguise, was installed in a wicker-chair, in a room that might be described as "*assez propre*," but which was very inferior to the dwellings of the labourers on the Walwyn estate, having nothing in it save the chair, a spinning-wheel, a table, a bench, and a sort of dresser with a few articles of crockery upon it. There was a turf fire, small but bright, and Mère Manon hastened to cook an omelette over it, withstanding all her visitor's entreaties and demonstrations of having brought food with her, and showing truly polite hospitality. There were only brown bowls and beechen trenchers for the table, and the coarsest brown bread; but not only was there omelette, but there was a *pot au feu* over the hearth, savoury with all sorts of vegetables, and with certain bones in it, in which Caroline detected the leg and breast of a pheasant.

"Ah! they did not fear to show such things now," the hostess said, nodding at Denny. "The neighbours had risen on Colas, the Garde Champêtre, so that he had barely escaped with his life, and she believed he had made his way to the town and endeavoured to escape suspicion of his former trade by pretending to be a *sans-culotte outré*."

At the moment there was a knock at the door, and a little, unkempt, ragged child looked in. "*De grace*, Mère Manon, we have nothing to eat, my mother is so white — so weak. She will die, and the neighbours all beat me from the door."

"She is the poor child of the Garde Champêtre," explained Mère Manon. "The neighbours spite the family because of the injuries they have suffered from the father, and they are almost starved."

The poor child did not go away without food or

money; Mère Manon was plainly one who did good to all parties alike when in distress. "She might have come from the county of Cork," said Denny.

Her bed, reminding Caroline of the berth of a ship, was not inviting, and sleep on the bench was preferable; though it was with aching limbs that the very early summons was obeyed, and with a draught of milk and piece of rye bread seasoned with a thousand thanks, and the blessings of the good old woman, Caroline embarked once more, and in the foggy close of the November day, saw the steeples of Rouen rise before her.

Denny rejoiced in the heavy mist which would enable him to make his way to the wharf without remarks on his passengers. When safely moored there, Caroline was advised to keep out of sight below, while Denny made his way to M. Normand's with a note that she gave him, and tried to ascertain whether it was safe for her to land.

It seemed an interminable time before he came back, and mistress and maid tormented themselves with all kinds of conjectures, such as that he had been arrested and sent to prison, or that M. Normand was afraid to notice them; but at length the plash of his oars was heard, and he soon came on board, bringing a horn lantern with him. "Monsieur was waiting at the end of the street," he said. "He thought madame had better land, and in her dress as a lady, and he would undertake for her further progress."

It was welcome news, and as well as she could, in the scanty space and scantier light, she threw on a cloak, took off the conspicuous apron, and assumed the large hat and feathers, the least remarkable head-gear of the time. She murmured her thanks and put a coin into the hands of the crew, descended the side of the little vessel with practised agility, and was rowed below a lamp suspended from a beam projecting over the water. Such a lantern hung at intervals along the streets and at the crossings, but all was very dark, except around them, and a little light pouring down from the upper windows of the tall houses which nearly met over the narrow streets; and the dirt could only be guessed at through sounds of splashing under each step, as Caroline clung to her friend's arm as they made their way up the town, to the porte cochère of a handsome old house, where a light hung over the entrance, and Madame Normand came flying down the stairs to embrace her with "effusion," as if she had been the oldest of friends.

Soon Mrs. Aylmer, apologising for her riding-habit, was seated at supper, being hospitably and affectionately entertained, and exchanging tidings and advice. Normandy was as yet not in a dangerous state, and not indisposed towards the English, and communication was open; so M. Normand advised that, as Caroline's passport was in full order, she should go to Havre in her own person, as an English lady, and there embark in a packet. He would send to Havre to ascertain the day when such a vessel would cross, and in the meantime she would become his guest, her luggage being brought up in early morning from *La Jeune Citoyenne*.

Madame was in transports of welcome, and Caroline, who was very tired after her bad night and early rising at Mère Manon's, was conducted to the guest-chamber, a huge place, like a salon except for the great bed, hung with richly embroidered silk. Madame Normand hovered about assisting her to undress,

and assuring her that she had enough to tell and to
hear to last a day, no, a year of that dear Henri and
his Félicité.

Caroline was too much tired out to remember at
first who was *ce cher Henri*, but when the name of
Beaudésert was added she almost wakened to interest.
Madame Normand, however, had the discretion to say
she would wait till her friend had rested, and Caroline
sank among her pillows with a feeling of repose, and
of being so far on her way to her little son.

Denny and one of his men brought up her boxes in
the morning, and rather to her hosts' surprise she
insisted on going down to see and pay and thank him.
He was glad of the arrangement, for he said, "I'd
have been proud to have taken you to Havre, ma'am,
but maybe it is safer not. The English sailors may
any time be about there, and an old man-of-war's-man
might know me, and be dirty enough to inform on
me."

"They could not take you here."

"Not they, blessings on St. Denis, that is my pathron
as well as this country's, though they have disowned
him now, the spalpeens! But it might make it the
worse for me if I were took in the free trade — not
that I would heed it a moment if it was for you,
ma'am, or the holy ladies up at Ste. Lucy's. You are
after writing a line to them?"

"Yes, if you will take one when you go down again
to Ste. Lucie."

"Then might I be so bold as to ask you to tell them
that if ever Dennis Molony can do them a turn, they
might walk on his head, and he would hold it all as
the greatest honour of his life — that he would lay
down and glad if it was to help one of them from the

villain rogues that are casting ugly looks on the holy places."

"I will tell them, Denny, with all my heart, in the letter I am going to send back by you as a surer hand than the post. I will unseal and add your message to Madame de Henisson, who will deliver it safely to the Mother Prioress. Will you wait here while I write it?"

Denny was glad to do so. "The blessings of Our Lady be on you, ma'am dear! You have as understanding a heart as if you were born a Catholic, like one of us, and I'll never cease praying that heavens may be your bed, and St. Peter may wink at you as you goes by, Protestant though you be!"

Caroline was almost ready to tell Denny that she believed that she had been baptized by a Roman Catholic priest, but she shrank from the controversy that this confession might involve with the faithful Irishman. and contented herself with adding to her letter to Cécile his ardent offers of assistance, saying that she thought him wholly sound-hearted and to be depended upon. She was not without thoughts of Félicité as she wrote, though she had little hope of release for the poor child, whose conscience and family would bind her, even if the doors of her convent were broken open.

Madame Normand, as soon as her numerous household occupations were finished, and her husband gone after a late breakfast to his bureau, came to sit with her guest and discuss the affairs of the unfortunate lovers with her. She had heard from Henri de Beaudésert, who seemed to be prospering well in the United States. His count had scientific friends there to whom he had been recommended, and he had had

the good fortune to find some valuable ore in one of
the hills bounding Georgia, and had been installed
there as manager of the mining which was being
commenced.

"Alas!" he said, "if one most beloved were only
here, I should be quite happy. Nothing would be
wanting to me. Ah! my dear cousin, do not tell me
that I am insensate in still cherishing hope. You tell
me that the good English lady who witnessed the
cruel ceremony of her profession says that she fal-
tered and fainted and scarcely uttered the vows. Can
it be that she is not thus bound? Strange *bouleverse-
ments* are, by all accounts, happening at home. How
will it be with convents and enforced vows? I often
ask myself, and keep life in my heart, for Félicité
will ever be wanting to me."

Tears sprang to Caroline's eyes as she listened, and
recollected how poor Félicité was longing on her side
in her convent; and she related the conversations she
had held.

"Ah! they will be brought together," cried Madame
Normand; "the impossible must come to pass."

CHAPTER XI

Grief dwells in France and England
  For many a noble son;
Yet louder than the sorrow,
  "'Thy will, O Lord, be done."
                          A. A. PROCTER.

THERE was no difficulty in accomplishing Mrs.
Aylmer's journey to Havre and embarkation in an
English packet, which conveyed her safely to Portsmouth; here her husband was of course known, and
money could be obtained for her homeward journey,
which was taken partly by coach and afterwards by
post-chaise to Downford.

Through the Dorsetshire chalk-hills she drove,
sometimes sticking fast in the deeply rutted mud,
sometimes feeling bound to walk up the hills to
ease the toiling horses, while Zélie groaned and
sighed at the damp cold. At last they were in sight
of the old town, a county town with a street of handsome old residences, some still occasionally used by
the gentry in the winter when they did not desire to
be isolated by snow or mud from all intercourse with
society. Captain Aylmer had inherited one of these,
probably an old monastery, though altered and freshly

faced with freestone quoins and sash windows; and it
was his home when on shore as well as his mother's,
though, even now that a nursery had been added to
it, it was much too large. Welcome to Caroline was
the sight of the row of poplar trees in front; and at
the sound of the carriage the big door flew open, and
on the steps appeared first a little girl in a round cap,
white frock, and blue sash, with outspread arms; then
a sweet-faced old lady in a big white cap going round
under the chin, a black silk gown, and white apron,
and beside her a tiny boy, dressed like his sister,
and a bevy of servants behind, headed by the old one-
armed sailor butler.

The little Nancy or Annora was instantly in her
mother's arms, then came grandmamma's kiss and
the stoop to lift up the boy, who, shy and frightened,
retreated behind his grandmother's skirts and showed
symptoms of crying, all the more because there was
a general exclamation of "Oh! Eustace, Eustace! it
is mamma. Oh! don't be a bad boy."

So hungry felt her bosom and arms for the child
that Caroline too might almost have cried at this
rejection by her boy, but the sight of poor Zélie's
black face awakened a screaming fit on the part of
each child; only Nancy clung to her mother and the
boy to his grandmother. The negress, who had
known such demonstrations before, was quite ready to
efface herself in the kitchen; while the children, with
the boy still sobbing, were taken into the parlour.
Caroline made another attempt to embrace him, but
he hid his face on his grandmother's shoulder, though
his sister's little voice assured him.

"Why, baby, it is mamma at last."

"You have been talking all day of mamma coming

home," added the grandmother. "Won't you look at her?" but as he kept his rather peaked and pale face turned resolutely away, "Ah! never mind, we must take our time."

"Ah!" said Caroline, quite in tears, "that's what comes of running away from one's children."

"Never mind, it will all be right soon," said grand-mamma, settling herself, with the little Eustace on her lap, but still turning his back to the stranger fondling and being fondled by his flaxen-haired sister.

"Have you any letters from George?" was, of course, the question.

"Not since the last I sent you — from Bombay — on the 5th of June."

By this time the little legs were getting restless, and the dark eyes peeped round for one moment, and then were turned rapidly back again as soon as they caught the eager glances bent on them.

"The 5th! Oh! when did you send them? Can I have missed any?"

Eustace began a hard studying stare.

"Papa wrote me a little letter in great big writing," put in Nancy. "All mine! I have got it in my red box."

The kiss with which this was received brought master down from grandmamma's knee to run across and try to push his sister aside, but the mother was only too happy to gather them both together into her bosom. "Now I am really come home," she said. "Nobody wanting but papa. And oh! tell me about him."

"I will get my letter," said the proud Nancy, but alas! a run to the nursery brought her down in alarm and dismay, crying, "Nasty black woman in the nursery."

Then came the soothing assurance that " Poor dear Zélie was very good, and had been mother's nana," and Caroline herself had to lead the child up to the old woman, and make her submit to the kiss with a trembling recoil; but the boy was by no means to be brought. He put his hands before his face, screamed, and kicked, and grandmamma advised that the battle should be given up during the weary hours of evening.

Indeed he screamed in his sleep, and when the elder Mrs. Aylmer bent over him, piteously declared that " Mamma had come home with a black face."

Nurse was for scolding and slapping him, but grandmamma carried him off to her own bed.

In such domestic troubles, and in the exchange of tidings about the absent father, passed the evening hours, and very happy, peaceful, and restful was the ensuing Sunday when Caroline joined again in the services she had learnt to love and had so often missed. True, she was in a narrow pew, and had to look up at a tall carved sentry-box; but she was between her little girl and that dear grandmother, and she heard the familiar words praying for those that travel by land and water.

And in the walks to and fro, after exchange of greetings with many and old congratulating acquaintance, though the streets with the shuttered shop windows might be dull, there was a wonderful sense of rest in the free, fearless walk home through the broad, clean, open way bordered with closely clipped trees, without dread either of mud below, or the far worse dread of a truculent mob, yelling for the downfall of somebody or something. Mrs. Aylmer would hardly believe her when she said that no lady could attempt to set foot in the Paris streets.

To her surprise and delight, the first sight on her return to the house was Master Eustace, enthroned and grinning in Zélie's arms, pinching her black cheek, and playing with her coral necklace.

After the convent life, spent on the outside of services in which she was forbidden to share, Mrs. Aylmer's Sunday was lively as well as restful to her; and there were the children — not permitted, young as they were, to be boisterous — but delighted to exhibit to her the Noah's ark, their father's grand parting present, to say some of Watts' hymns, and Nancy could even repeat the four first answers in the Church Catechism. Then came out the big many-pictured Bible, inherited from several generations, and eager little tongues, stumbling one over the other, explained about "naughty Cain," or "poor, poor Joseph in the pit, and his cruel brothers."

It was home, it was rest; and there was ample pleasure too the next day, when the unpacking took place and the French toys that Caroline had secured a good while before her return were unfolded, — the unfailing doll, the delight of every generation, and the great curly white poodle. While against the future times appeared the dissected map of the world, an invention, it was said, of the poor King for his children. For grandmamma there was a beautiful soft cashmere shawl; the like, only in bright colours, for Aunt Darpent.

"Please, please, give grandmamma the blue and pink," entreated Nancy, "with all the yellow and red curlyworlies. It is so much the prettiest."

"No, no, my love, grandmamma never wears bright things," said Mrs. Aylmer.

"Oh do — do — grandmamma; I do love you, and

I can't bear Aunt Darpent," was Nancy's cry; and
Eustace responded with "Nasty Aunt Darpent, ugly
up in her face."

At that moment a tremendous knocking at the front
door resounded through the house, and the children,
rushing to the window, proclaimed: "Uncle Darpent
— making a funny face — poking his whip up. Oh,
and that's Aunt Darpent in the red riding-habit."

Down, of course, went the two ladies, sending the
children off to the nursery to be made presentable,
and the ladies took off their aprons, and arranged
their hair before the glass. Each was smothered in a
big wide-bordered cap, but Mrs. Aylmer wore powder,
and Caroline followed the prevailing French fashion
and showed her light-brown tresses, with one long
lovelock on her shoulder. Her dress, too, was much
more scanty, and clung more closely than what the
other ladies wore; and she saw and felt that this was
what first struck the eye of Mrs. Darpent as they
entered the parlour, curtseying as they did so, but
being received with embraces and the voluble explanation that the roads were impassable for the chaise,
and so Mrs. Darpent had ridden over on a pillion on
Dobbin.

"The only beast that would bear her weight," said
her husband, laughing, "and he was near enough to
protesting on Hardclimb Hill. It is another question
how we are to get him home."

"That is all your uncle's jokes; you know him,
niece Caroline," said Mrs. Darpent, who in these
years had grown in massiveness in proportion to the
diminution of her husband's weight. Not that he
looked unwell; he was active and wiry, but to Caroline's mind the French extraction showed itself more

M

than when he was younger. In that he approved himself as a relative, with his black brows, bright keen eyes, and brown skin, alert movements, and with his hair drawn back into a queue. His greeting was, however, as English as possible.

"Well, Caroline, my dear, how goes it with you? I'm right glad to see you back from foreign parts, with your head on your shoulders."

"I am rejoiced that you are returned again," chimed in Mrs. Darpent, who had highly disapproved of Caroline's journey, and intimated the same to her and her husband before she went, and afterwards croaked continually.

"I hope you obtained your purpose," she added drily, in a tone that evidently expressed quite a different hope, so that Caroline was sorry not to be able to disappoint her with truth, and only said lightly, "We expect to know more when the affairs of the colonies are arranged."

"Ah! I knew nothing was to be gained by your expedition. And how does the poor little boy?"

This was answered by the opening of the door, and the appearance of the children, very prim and shy, the girl "bridling" and curtseying, the boy bowing, but at once running up to his grandmother, and laying his face in her lap.

Grunt went Mrs. Darpent. "That's always the way with spoilt children, I never allowed mine in such bad manners."

It was an old sore that Captain Aylmer had chosen to leave his children with his mother instead of with their great-aunt. Caroline thought she remembered battles with bashfulness in which Mrs. Darpent had not come off the conqueror.

" Poor little man! he has not been well," suggested the mother.

" What could you expect from children left without a mother's care for six months ? "

" Come, come, that's over now. Come here, Nancy, come, Eustace! You all know where to look in my pockets," called out the uncle, holding out his arms to the children, who both ran up to him, and were taken on his two knees, where they dived into his big waistcoat pockets.

" I hope you succeeded in your object, Caroline," proceeded Mrs. Darpent.

" I cannot say our affairs have come to any satisfactory conclusion," returned Caroline; " they say it is impossible while the affairs of all the colonies remain so unsettled."

" Ah! probably all would have gone just as well as if you had remained at home. Only then you would have lost your Paris gaiety."

" I did not see much gaiety," said Caroline; " people were too anxious."

"Oh! they'll have the devil to pay, now they have once begun to give vent to their abuses," said Mr. Darpent, while his little great-niece, patting him, exclaimed —

" Don't say naughty words, Uncle Darpent."

" Quite right, little pussy cat," he said, laughing, " but that old gentleman has had his will among them secretly for so many years, no wonder he is bursting out at last. Our forefathers did well to come away, eh, Carry ? "

" And I wonder any one should hanker after going back again," said his wife; " but excitement has its charms for you all."

" Bred in the bone," laughed Mr. Darpent.

Caroline could not help defending herself.

"Captain Aylmer wished me to go to Paris for the sake of the children, and Monsieur de Nidemerle and the lawyer advised me to wait to hear from Ste. Marie Galante. Indeed I came home as soon as I could, and I was far from the world after my cousins went."

" In a nunnery," sniffed Mrs. Darpent, with infinite scorn in the sound, " but that was your doing, Mr. Darpent, letting the poor child go there long ago."

"Indeed! I thought it was some one else who insisted on my taking her to France."

" As if I had known what they meant to do with her, or would have consented, had I been there."

" You might have gone with me, and studied the situation," observed her husband.

"I! 'tis not my way to leave my poor children to pine themselves to thread papers, and get the manners of bears in my absence. I'm a true born Englishwoman, and don't run after French habits or Popish customs."

So the wrangling went on, whenever the husband tried to avert the point of his wife's arrows. Caroline knew that it was the usual style of conversation, and that they loved each other heartily all the time, but it jarred on her as a disagreeable novelty after being habituated to French graces of conversation. Yet she was sorry when her uncle jumped up, declaring that he must go and see that his horse was fed, while Mrs. Aylmer regretted that he had not put it up in her stable, though she feared that there might be damp. And Mrs. Darpent declared with a cough that she did not come sponging on her neighbours.

The uncle's presence had been a protection, for as

soon as he was gone his lady proceeded to inspect
Caroline closely, and express her disapproval of the
French fashions, which had begun to imitate the classi-
cal, and were as far as possible removed from the days
of hoop and powder; and she did not scruple to call
them "vastly improper."

The hair, too, was unpowdered, and only of the
natural height, though covered by a big white cap.   It
was a shocking sight to the two ladies, both of them,
all the more because the young traveller laughed
heartily at their consternation, and declared that she
could not have gone about otherwise. "Every one at
Paris was trying to look like a Greek statue.   And
depend upon it, it would be the same in London."

"Well, I have seen a picture in a number of the
Lady's Magazine," owned Mrs. Darpent. "Naomi borrowed it and brought it to me, but I thought it was
only the fine fashionable good-for-nought ladies that
made themselves such a spectacle. Bless me! what
are we coming to. No powder! It is quite indecent.
You did not let her show herself in church that figure,
dear madam?"

"Really, I was so glad to have her go to church
with me again that I scarcely saw what she had on
under her shepherdess hat."

"I don't know what we shall come to without
powder! and with all those Popish ways."

"They are throwing off their Popish ways, more's
the pity," said Caroline.

"One hears most dreadful things of their doings.
What is it?   They hang you up to the lamp-post as
soon as look at you, don't they?   And Caroline chose
to stay and see it all."

"It is not the lamp-post," explained Caroline, "it

is the chains by which the lights are hung across the
streets. But I never saw it, oh no!"

"No wonder! Poor blinded Papists!"

To get into the lady's understanding that Popery
and the outrages of the Revolution were unconnected,
was quite past any one's power, and she ended by
drawing Mrs. Aylmer apart, and advising her to take
care that her niece did not prove a firebrand in Downford; between her Popish ways and all those French
democraws that had been infecting her, there was no
knowing the mischief she might do. To look at her
was enough!

At the early dinner, with Mrs. Darpent present,
there was enough gossip of the neighbourhood to keep
tolerable peace, but Mrs. Darpent remained thankful
that she had no son at home, since both were so
dangerously fond of Cousin Caroline as to be easily
misled by her novelties.

CHAPTER XII

> Ye abbeys and ye arches,
> Ye old cathedrals dear,
> The hearts that love you tremble
> And your enemies have cheer.
> BISHOP CLEVELAND COXE.

ANXIETIES could not but press upon the sister-hood of Ste. Lucie. The decree of the National Assembly, confiscating all Church property, left the Prioress in doubt how her daughters could live; and she had many consultations with the chaplain, the Abbé de Pont de Loire, over the future. They hoped that better times would come before a purchaser would offer himself for the convent, but in the meantime life was hard. Their revenues did not come in, their last pupil had been recalled by her relatives, the dowry of the nuns was unpaid, and the chief dependence was on Madame de Henisson's payment for her board, since the friendly old family notary continued to pay her, though he insisted on her signing herself Cécile Chenonçeau instead of by the title which had been abolished. Some of the nuns were reclaimed by their relations and departed. One or two wept bitterly, but some could not help betraying pleasure in the

167

change of scene and the prospect of living with their families, but all vowing to observe their hours of devotion and return with better times.

The Prioress desired her two youngest sisters to write and ask to be taken away. Félicité, otherwise Sœur Philomène, obeyed, but received no answer, and there was reason to believe that the Monfichets had repaired to their estate in Burgundy, if they had not actually crossed the border, as the Duke and Duchess of Drelincourt had certainly done.

When Madeleine de Torcy, or Sœur de Françoise de Rome, received the same orders, she clasped her hands, and entreated almost in the words of Ruth, " Entreat me not to leave thee, dear mother, let me cling to the Church, which is mine, and to my Heavenly Spouse, from whom nothing can divide my heart."

"But, my child, it is for your good! Think how hard we are all pressed for very maintenance."

"Ah! but I love fasting — privation is angel's meat to me — I need barely a crust or a morsel of chickweed!"

However, the Prioress insisted on her writing, though she looked almost ethereal in her transparent beauty, her blue eyes shining with adoration. She obeyed, but after some delay Madame de Torcy wrote back word that the family were suspected, living under surveillance, and that she thought her daughter safer at Ste. Lucie, and prayed her to attempt no further communication at present, for her own sake or her parents. The present letter had been conveyed out of the house at Lyons in safety by a private hand.

The chapel looked piteously empty, the chant of the offices was very thin, though Sœur Françoise's voice pealed out with wondrous beauty among the few wor-

shippers. Only the little wiry Prioress was left, with
old Mère de St. Hilaire, kindly old Mère Marie de
l'Annonciation, and Mère Dominique du Chapelet,
who was paralysed and almost helpless, though she
was daily supported into the chapel by sisters Marie
and Françoise; and she was so blind and imbecile that
she never missed the voices of the full choir. The
glorious, ecstatic chant of Sœur Françoise alone penetrated her deafened ear, and chimed in with her understanding.

Winter came, and fuel was scarce. The poor nuns
huddled together for warmth, and began to burn the
less needful of their woodwork, Sœur Françoise running backwards and forwards with loads, and making
merry little jests, as she tried to wield the axe with
fingers blue with cold.

"Ah! naughty child," said the Prioress, "where
should we be without you to keep up our spirits?" as
she came in with her veil full of chips.

"No one knows how sweet is a little licensed mischief," she cried. "Come along, Sœur Philomène, we
shall get down the door at last, and make it serve us
all the evening!"

The oath was at first not administered to chaplains
of convents, but they were forbidden to admit any out-
siders to the services, and when villagers were caught
repairing to the chapel they were beaten and ill-used.
By and by the Abbé was denounced for having min-
istered to a sick woman, and though not taken, he
only appeared now and then, by some secret passage.

Worse news was yet to come. The oath to the constitution was imposed upon the priesthood, and with
few exceptions, was refused. The faithful clergy were
proscribed, and those who were not arrested, or would

not fly, lurked in forests, or in obscure cottages. One of these was the Abbé de Pont de Loire, and the sisters lost their morning masses, and were reduced to their own chants at the "Hours," except when now and then the chaplain stole in under cloud of night, and departed in the darkness of the morning.

"It is like the Church of the Catacombs," cried Sister Françoise, with her eyes shining with joyous enthusiasm.

Cécile de Henisson was just returning from one of these morning rites, when she was startled by seeing a male figure in the passage leading to her room. In much alarm she hesitated for an instant whether to fly, or to accost him; but at once he spoke, removing his slouched hat, bowing and speaking in a hasty whisper but with much courtesy, "Pardon, madame, could you give me the favour of a room and an ear to speak to you? Madame Aylmer," he said in easy French, though with an accent, "will have told you of me."

"Dennis from Ireland. Oh yes."

"Chut, madame, take me where no one can hear," said Denny, looking round with scared anxious eyes.

Cécile obeyed by taking him into her sitting-room, and there he ventured to speak. "Madame, the good Mrs. Aylmer bade me do all I could in case you needed any matter of help, and I swore upon my patron's head that he walked with under his arm from Montmartre that I would never fail you."

"Yes, yes. What is the danger?"

"Madame, sure as the holy Virgin reigns in heaven, the rogues are coming this very night to sack this blessed place, because they say, the spalpeens! (this was in Irish) that 'tis no better than a nest of super-

stitious aristocrats, grown fat on the poor, and that
you opened the chapel to outside worshippers. They
think the holy man, the Abbé, is hidden somewhere
here."

"The monsters, he is not!"

"That's neither here nor there. They will have their
will of the holy place as I have seen — bad luck to
them — and the worse for those as are not safe out of
their way."

Cécile clasped her hands. "Oh! good man, good
man, what can we do? Has Heaven sent you to protect us?"

"Well, my lady, it is little the like of me can do;
but if you, and maybe two or three of the holy
mothers could be at the quay by the water-side by
twilight I would take you off in my boat, as I did
Mrs. Aylmer, and the saints would see what might
come next."

There was no hesitation in the gratitude with which
such an offer was accepted, and Cécile only asked for
time in which to fetch the Prioress, making Denny
lock the doors behind her till she should return, since
her maid had latterly become so impertinent that it
was not certain whether the spirit of the times might
not have infected her.

The nuns were about to eat the scanty breakfast of
dry bread which Cécile had of late shared with them,
and they had been waiting for her. She went up to
the Prioress, and with her hand on her shoulder entreated her to come with her. "You have ill news, my
daughter," said the Prioress, looking at her blanched
face.

"Ill news, reverend mother, but with a hope of
safety. Will you come with me?"

The Prioress was a quick, shrewd, practical woman, by no means helpless, and she had so far expected some such emergency as to have been gradually putting valuables into a rapidly portable form; and when, after breathless whispers from Madame de Henisson, she stood before Denny, she looked the least dismayed of the two, as indeed the offer of the Irishman came as a relief.

Quickly she disposed of his proposals and her own thanks, and desired to know how many he would have room for in his boat. He could readily take four, but when he found that there were seven women in need of a rescue, he looked grave. The flood had begun to rush heavily with the winter rains, and a heavy load might even swamp the boat. To take them at twice to a little shelter by the river-side would be possible so as to be out of the immediate reach of the mob, but how to go farther with such a freight he knew not. Could any of the good ladies find some other asylum? They must take all the warm clothing they could, and, if there were means, that which did not look like religious. Cécile could only offer all her wardrobe.

Denny hurried away to make ready his boat as secretly as he could, and the Prioress to use the short hours of daylight in preparing her nuns for the flight, while Madame de Henisson looked out her stores of secular garments. She wept a good deal as she did so, trembling at every sound, and grieving at the coming desecration and desolation of the house that had been her venerated dwelling for so many years of her life.

One by one the nuns came to her to be dressed for their voyage. Félicité had a bright face and eager eye, as if the opening of the cage was welcome; and she laughed as she looked at herself in the glass, with

a handkerchief tied over her cap; and poor old Mothers
de St. Hilaire, and de l'Annonciation came hand in
hand, and crying, "Ah! the change, the change, Mère
St. Hilaire had hoped Ste. Lucie was her home for life,
never, never to leave it except for the cemetery, but
the.will of the Lord be done."

Mère de l'Annonciation murmured, "Ah! it was
hard to bow my will, but I had done so perforce once,
and now — too late — too late — all that I loved is
gone. Save for obedience I would throw me down
before the Altar and let the mob work their will of
my poor old withered heart."

But the Prioress did not come, nor Sœur Françoise,
but Cécile reflected that the lay sisters might be pro-
viding for them.

Every moment was a terrible one. Ears were
alert for sounds of evil, for who could tell that the
mob might not precipitate the attack; though Dennis
declared that he had obtained intelligence that they
would wait for certain demagogues from Paris, who
were attending a meeting of the Jacobins. A cock
could not crow nor a hen cluck without provoking a
suppressed scream and cry of "There they are!"

However, each carrying a tiny bundle, the seven
nuns and two lay sisters all assembled at three o'clock
for the last time in their denuded chapel, and with
shaking, sobbing voices sung their vesper chant, end-
ing with the "De Profundis." It was a dark, cloudy
day, of overcast sky, and fog rising from the river, all
the better for their embarkation. They could hardly
see one another, and by no means with recognition in
their unwonted dresses. Cécile, who was weeping
piteously, only knew by the clear young voice that it
was Félicité who guided her steps.

In thick white mist, and gathering darkness, she heard a lowered voice say, "Blessing on the fog the saints have sent us! Come, madame, you are as safe as if you were in Our Lady's arms." Those two big hands did not feel exactly like Our Lady's, nor the serge-clad arms that lifted her, she knew not where, up and then down, while another voice, in better French, bade her sit down and arrange herself as well as she could. Sitting was needful, for it was impossible to stand in the tiny hole, barely illuminated by a dark lantern. Félicité tumbled down with more volition, and was presently followed by two or three more helpless bundles; but immediately after the voice of Denny asked whether they were all settled. "*Rangez vous, mères saintes et reverendes,*" and therewith the lantern was put out.

They did not feel very saintly or reverend, being in some doubt which limbs belonged to which mother, and some one burst into a choked peal of hysterical laughter provoked by the Irish tone.

The atmosphere was choking, and though the vessel was felt to be moving off, it was very slowly, for great precautions were needed in the fog. Scarcely anything was to be heard but the low splash of the muffled oars and the stifled weeping of the poor ladies. Hours seemed to them to have passed before the voices above grew louder, and presently Denny said from the opening, "All clear, *mesdames — mes saintes dames,* I mean. You can come up and stretch your legs a bit."

The poor ladies were so much cramped that they could hardly obey the welcome summons. Félicité was the first to scramble to her feet within reach of the helping hand, and she helped to push up the

others, till they all could see by the light of a nearly
full moon, rising in the distance, the one black mast
before them, the steersman at the rudder, the path
of light on the waters, and the low meadows lying
around. Trees rose behind them, but they were out
of sight of their own priory. Denny busied himself
in finding seats for them, for the elder nuns could
scarcely stand at first. Then it was not till they were
on deck that there was a cry —

"Where is the Mother Prioress?"

"Where is Mère Dominique?"

"And oh, where is Sœur Françoise?"

"Down below, in another cabin? Oh where?"
exclaimed Félicité.

"The reverend mothers refused to come," said
Denny. "Ah! I would have taken them if it had
swamped the *Jeune Citoyenne*. Yes, I would, madame, but they would not come. She's a fine captain, the reverend mother, keeping to her ship to
the last."

"Go back, put back and save them, I command
you," cried Mère de l'Annonciation. "Not a step
farther will I go without the reverend mother."

The sailor suppressed a little laugh, and Mère
de St. Hilaire exclaimed, "Ah, now I know what our
dear mother meant when she confided you all to me,
my sisters. Yes, and put this blessed reliquary into
my hands, and the key!"

"And she would not let me dress her," cried
Madame de Henisson. "She said a cloak would
suffice."

"She is a martyr, a willing martyr," declared
Mère de l'Annonciation. "Eh! and the poor
child!"

"Weeping and wailing loud arose," but "the clamorous woes of every simple nun" were checked by a peremptory sign from Denny, who proceeded to say, "Not so bad as that, my good ladies, the lay sister had good hope of keeping her and the poor crippled sister with the young one safe in the gardener's cottage. That poor lady could scarcely have lived in the hold there."

"That is true," they could not but sigh.

"I would have stayed with Mère Dominique," murmured Mère de l'Annonciation. "Oh, would that I were there!"

"I thought the young sister with the fair face was here," said Denny. "Nay, that is the dark one in the white kerchief. Where is she? One, two, three, four, five ——"

"Ah!" burst out the lay sister Bonami, "she thrust me forward in her place, the angel, I knew not that she came not with me!"

There was no help for it. The Prioress, with the helpless Dominique, and the youthful Françoise had been left behind, of their own free will! Putting back to rescue them was an utter impossibility. Not only was the convent two miles behind them and against the stream, but it was probably already in the possession of the sans-culottes. The hour was about seven, as Denny knew by the rising of the moon, by the light of which he meant to continue his course while the night favoured him.

At this time actual personal violence to women was not common among the peasant mobs who threw themselves on the châteaux and convents in blind revenge for past exactions, and there was hope that the nuns might elude their assailants; but all the fugitives fell

on their knees to recite their prayers, and Denny
chimed in with all his heart and soul, infinitely invigorated by knowing of a precious relic that he had on
board, and vowing that if better days came, *La Jeune
Citoyenne* should become *Ste. Lucie.*

N

CHAPTER XIII

She raised her eyes in mournful mood,
Wilton himself before her stood,
And joy unwonted and surprise,
Gave their strange wildness to his eyes.

SCOTT.

IN undertaking to protect the escape of the nuns of Ste. Lucie, Dennis Molony had a far more difficult and perilous task than when he had assisted the journey of Mrs. Aylmer more than a year previously.

The Revolution was rushing on to its most terrible crisis. The captivity of the royal family had begun, and the fear of interference on their behalf from foreign sovereigns and from emigrant nobility impelled the people to madness, lest all that had been gained should be rent from them by force of arms. Every one who endeavoured to leave the country, however helpless and innocent, was supposed to be a traitor, and excited furious distrust; and the oppressions which, unfortunately, religious houses had exercised in some cases, together with the refusal of the clergy to accept the oath to the constitution, and the general reaction against all authority, spiritual as well as temporal, had made all ecclesiastical personages especially obnoxious, and those who assisted them scarcely

less so. Besides this, Caroline Aylmer was a hardy
personage, experienced in vicissitudes of land and
water travelling, and able to take care of herself and
give hardly any extra trouble; whereas of these poor
things, even Madame de Henisson had never walked
except in well-appointed gardens, Félicité de Monfichet had never gone beyond a few woodland paths
with her governess, or the village green on a fête day,
and as to the two nuns, Mère de l'Annonciation's experiences were of salons thirty-five years previously,
and Mère St. Hilaire had only spent a single year outside the convent since she left her foster-parent's cottage at five years old. Sister Bonami was a village
girl, and could go out bravely enough.

"Blessings on them," Denny muttered to his mate,
"it is like having to do for a set of tame pigs that
have been petted up in a hovel, turned loose among
the wild sangliers that roamed the forest before the
peasant folk set upon them, that *are* the boars themselves, bad luck to them!"

His mate was a Norman smuggler whom he had
known long enough to rely upon, and who had been
employed before in transporting fugitives across the
Channel. The *Gabelle* had made many a man of worth
a smuggler, and Jaques le Boux was no exception;
but he agreed with Denny that he should much prefer
a cargo of obstreperous pigs to these meek and mournful ladies. They sat, shivered, and sighed as they told
their chaplets on deck, or heaped themselves up below
without a word of complaint. They never seemed to
be hungry, and accepted all varieties of distresses as
divine favours; and yet it was almost impossible to
know how to deal with them. If he wanted them to
lie hid in a reed bed while he went to get them food,

and to walk across a bend of the stream to meet Jaques and the boat beyond the wiry revolutionary *barrière* that lay in the loop, he found them so utterly unused to walking and so ill shod that he could hardly get them over paths meant for heavy sabots, instead of delicate slippers. Poor things, their feet were cut and bruised even to bleeding, and their terrors were perpetual. Not a fish could leap, not a duck flap her wings, not a frog croak, without eliciting a suppressed scream, and making them grasp one another, or almost fall upon him or upon Sœur Bonami, whose arms must have been black and blue from the pinches they gave her. Mère St. Hilaire and Félicité were the boldest, and kept up the others, for Madame de Henisson was the most timid, and Mère de l'Annonciation was so much exhausted at the end of the first mile that she begged to be left to her fate. Félicité and Sœur Bonami dragged her on almost by force, for she rejected with a cry of horror the assistance of "*ce gros matelot*," as she called him; it would have been profane, and contrary to her vows, and then she began to apologise lest she should have hurt his feelings.

After endless disasters, and much more delay than was advisable, and having seen no one more dangerous than a little girl leading out a cow to browse on the banks, they arrived by daylight, all drenched with early dews, and with the remnants of shoes scarce holding to their feet, at good Dame Manon's, where Denny had decided on hiding his charge for the daylight hours while he reconnoitred Rouen. Dame Manon was as faithful a Catholic as himself, and as ready to think it an honour and a blessing to receive persecuted nuns. She stood at her door with hands clasped, and a torrent of exclamations of pity and

horror as they tottered and limped forward. She
drew them into the hovel, and garrulously mourned
that she had nothing better to set before them than
the contents of her *pot au feu.* Then as she saw the
bleeding, blistered feet, her exclamations redoubled.
"Ah," said Mère St. Hilaire quaintly, as she held up
her foot, "I never half understood the merits of the
sisters *Discacées.*"

"Ah! but the merits are even greater when you
are suffering through wicked men!" said the good
hostess, who was making ready quickly to heat some
water to wash the poor feet. What next was to be
done? Sabots must be procured, but the purchase of
five pairs in the village a mile off would excite suspicion. The Prioress had thrust on Mère St. Hilaire a
bag which was found to contain plenty of money, so
that there was no difficulty on that score, and it was
decided that pairs of sabots should be bought by
Manon, Denny, and Sœur Bonami in different shops,
in the course of the day.

Denny could reach Rouen far more promptly on
foot than in his loaded barge, and the nuns were
helped up to the hayloft over the cottage, where they
might be safely out of the way of possible incursions
of the neighbours. It was close, but not warm; however, the good ladies were glad to lie there at rest,
while Sœur Bonami, who had easily become a thorough
peasant woman in appearance, could go on errands
and assist Manon. Félicité would fain have done the
same. The liberty she had regained, such as it was,
seemed to make her feet tingle to be on the move;
and she sat by the slit between the planks of the frail
door, drinking in the charm of the open meadow, the
stubble field, the gliding river and the ducks that

sailed upon it. After years of convent walls the
sight was delightful to her, though the wide space
made the elder nuns feel themselves utterly desolate
and forlorn, as if they were out in the cold. Towards
evening the sabots were all brought in triumphantly,
but when the poor ladies tried them on there was a
new difficulty, for they hurt the bruised and tender
feet as much or more than did the stones and stubble
fields. However, when once embarked again, they
would not need to wear them for some time; and
Denny had arranged that there should be shelter for
the next day at a sort of boat-house near his own cottage, and that they should pass through Rouen at
night, when a friend of his, who had often winked at
his contraband loads, would be in charge of the office
that observed the passage through the wharves. In
those anxious times of emigration and relaxed, uncertain law, the merciful, as well as the interested, often
shut their eyes.

So, plunging through the mire and swamps of the
reed beds, with many a little suppressed shriek, the
fugitives re-embarked, and floated down the river,
resting as best they could on deck, or in the tiny pre-
cincts of the hold which the elder nuns preferred as
being less cold. There they lay, all that night, and
when they halted the next day, under the loosely
thatched roof of reeds, they were visited by Denny's
trim little kindly French wife, who brought them
milk and apples, and kneeling before Mère St. Hilaire
asked her blessing.

Another day of close concealment, and then they
came to Rouen; but Félicité was only allowed a
glimpse at the steeples rising up in the dark before she
was peremptorily bidden to seek the hold, where she

sat as near the opening as she could and gasped for breath in the stifling atmosphere.

She heard loud voices, as the barge ceased to move. Then there was a laugh.

"Furniture from an old convent, is it? Oh, I will take your word, Denny! I need not search! No perilous articles, eh?"

Those were the most distinct voices that she caught as there she sat crouched together, with a sense that there was no solitude around, and an occasional flash of light as the *Jeune Citoyenne* slowly moved on and on; and at last, after she had once or twice stiffly fallen asleep and wakened, cramped, aching, and longing to stretch herself, upon some little movement of the kind, Denny's head was put over the opening, and his voice whispered, "The reverend mothers might come up if they are awake."

Félicité communicated the intelligence, but the reverend mothers were much too chilly to think of profiting by it; and when she tried to stand up she found her limbs hardly able to move, and would have fallen but for the hand that was held out to her, and which pulled her up, almost by main strength, for she almost sank upon the deck before she could reach her seat upon a coil of rope. The tardy dawn was beginning, paling the eastern sky, and whitening the banks of fog. The morning star was shining on the horizon. She had never seen it, and it brought the recollection of Henri Beaudésert's explanations about the planets, and why the evening star could also be the harbinger of the sun. She had thrown back her muffling kerchief, so as to breathe better and enjoy the spectacle; but she started on perceiving that the mate was standing near looking at her, and the lantern was shining on his face. No: was it the mate? It was certainly his dark-blue garments and red fisher cap, but whose face was that? Was imagination playing her a trick? She shut her eyes. The face was turned away to attend to the rudder, but the figure, the gesture, was the same. though the gentleman's garb had been exchanged for the sailor's. She was shocked at her own momentary idea, showing herself false to her vows, and a burning blush spread over her face. She lifted her hand to draw her kerchief forward; but in that instant the look had returned, and on either side there was recognition. a momentary ecstasy, though he never stirred from the heavy beam which formed the helm. and she hid blushes and wonder behind her hands. Though each had had such an effect on the life of the other, yet in point of fact they had neither of them ever spoken a word of direct love, and it was more than three years since their separation. The one exclamation, "Mademoiselle!" broke from Beaudésert. She answered with a kind of shudder, caused by. as she would have called it, *un serrement de cœur;* but nothing more was uttered, for Denny was helping Sister Bonami out of the cabin, and for a professed nun to converse with a stranger man was an impossible idea, all the more so as honour bound them to their rules when beyond their cloister and the supervision of their Prioress. However, in spite of all perplexities and scruples, Félicité could not help having an undefined sense of protection and well-being, as from behind the sail she looked across at the firm, well-knit figure and bright, dark eyes of the helmsman.

It was Madame de Henisson who, on coming on deck when the sun was first on the horizon, remarked —

" You have a new assistant, Maître Denis."

"Truly, madame is right. If I may confide it to her, he is a gentleman under the same need of a foreign tour, a bit of a trip to England, as herself, so I let him come with me as my mate, and let him take a hand at the steering when I saw that he knew the river and the ropes."

Madame de Henisson, being a free woman, unbound by any vows, followed her instinct of courteous sympathy, and bows were exchanged with the stranger; but in the midst she exclaimed, " Pardon me, monsieur, I have met you before, though I do not recognise you at once."

" At Monsieur le Comte de Monfichet's, madame," he replied, with another bow, " where I had the honour to act as tutor."

" Ah !" she exclaimed, with a little scream of dismay, as she recollected all the passages that had served to bring Sœur Philomène here as a nun ; but recalling herself, she resolved to try to ascertain whether he had come with any vain revolutionary scheme of recapturing the lady of his affections. " I thought you were in America, sir," she said, coldly; but Félicité was sitting near, with her face turned to the river, and it was to her listening ears that he spoke.

" It is true, madame, that I was there for a time, and I had the good fortune to discover a vein of tin ore. It was decided to send me to England to obtain Cornish miners to pursue the discovery, and at the same time I was to proceed to France to see my friends and realise the property to which I am entitled. I found, however, much confusion as to inheritances. I learnt that the refusal of the clergy to take the oaths had led to much violence towards convents. I

made anxious inquiries of the bargemen, who I knew
supplied the convents on the river, and perhaps im-
prudently, for I was warned that I was about to be
denounced as an emigrant. Going down to the wharf
to arrange for escaping in one of the barges of these
good fellows, I encountered Maître Denis, who undertook to substitute me for his mate, provided I could
assist in the escape of certain ladies from Ste. Lucie.
Imagine, madame, what was my joy!"

"And you will take care of us, monsieur," exclaimed
Cécile, too much relieved to find herself with a male
protector of something like her own rank and culti-
vation to be able to dwell on the intricacies and com-
plications of the escort.

"I would give my life, madame, rather than that
any harm should touch you or any of your companions."

Félicité drank in the assurance, and the tender
trembling of voice with which the last sentence was
pronounced. She too felt safe; and though she was
soon ordered down to lie close while passing Elbœuf,
it was with a heart throbbing with delight. Madame
de Henisson, gentle as she was, was a woman of the
world, and she squeezed Félicité's hand, saying, "We
will not mention names, my friend, it might distress
our good mothers, and they might think there was a
scandal, though all was accident and we must have
his protection. I shall only tell them that I had known
him before."

Félicité was content to have it so. She had too confused and agitated a heart to endure that her conduct
should be watched by Mères de St. Hilaire and de
l'Annonciation; but she could not help being amused
when she heard madame's communication being re-

ceived by the two old ladies curled up in the hold,
with inquiries whether she was sure that their new
friend was "*bon Catholique*," to which she returned an
unhesitating assurance. The Prioress had been a very
careful woman, and neither of them had been aware
of the name of Sœur Philomène's lover, so that Beaudésert's presence was not a disclosure to them. Indeed, Madame de Henisson was a determined chaperon.
She impressed on Beaudésert from the first that it was
due to the reputation of Mademoiselle de Montfichet
that nothing should give colour to any report that she
had eloped under his care. As to the future, when the
journey was over, and they could have recourse to ad-
visers — the countess waved her hands, she could give
no opinion; but for the present nothing must give umbrage to Mère St. Hilaire.

He submitted, he could not help it; and so did
Félicité, all the more readily that she was dreadfully
ashamed of her own bliss, and sense of liberty and
hope. Sometimes she felt guilty and like a recreant,
and was ready to hide her face for ever; at others she
was comforted by recollecting Mrs. Aylmer's assurance
that prayer would be answered either by content or
by freedom. So contending feelings absolutely made
her shrink from Henri Beaudésert, and had he not
been able to recollect that first glance and blush, his
spirits and hopes would have sunk still lower than
they did, as the tardy barge moved down the widening
river.

Havre was not all that it became under Napoleon,
and in the later times of commerce, *entente cordiale*
and travelling; but it was a recognised harbour, and
Denny thought it safer not to enter it, since there
always might be officials on the watch to prevent

emigration. He succeeded in obtaining the use of a
rough country cart, which had often been employed
in the transport of contraband goods, and in this the
nuns and Madame de Henisson were packed. They
were at a loss to decide which was worse, this or
walking in sabots. Félicité decided in favour of the
wooden shoes, and trudged along by the side of the
lay sisters, invigorated by the sight of the figure who
was leading the donkey which drew the sisters.

They reached the haven at last, a rude little fishing-
village where, however, the church had not been disturbed, and was full of votive offerings of little ships
and anchors, and queer paintings of wrecks, out of all
perspective. There the people still prayed, and their
priest not being " *assermenté*," lurked in hiding —
sometimes in a smuggler's cave among barrels of salt,
sometimes in one cottage, sometimes in another, or in
the woods and cattle-sheds, coming from time to time
in early morning to give them a mass. Here the nuns
were sheltered and honoured, and could worship unmolested, while Denny and Beaudésert hovered about
making arrangements for their transport in a smuggling vessel.

Sœur Bonami, having taken no vows, and being well
able to earn her own living, decided on remaining
where she was. She could not bear the sight of the
sea, to which the dear mothers were about to com-
mit themselves. And it must be confessed that they
often envied her and longed to be with her, before *La
Bonne Margot* put into the harbour of Wareham.

CHAPTER XIV

DISCIPLINE *VERSUS* CHIVALRY

Must I be better than the rest,
And harbour justice in my breast.
                              GAY.

A RUBBER of whist was in full progress at Mrs. Aylmer's. Card-parties in rotation took place at the houses of the society of the town, always for sixpenny points, and the rector, the doctor, old Mrs. Aylmer, and Mistress Penelope Swan, were all absorbed round one green baize table, while "young madam," as Mrs. George Aylmer was commonly termed, the doctor's son, the rector's pupil, two old maids, and the widow of the last rector made up a round game, much more merry than that of their elders, though in a hushed way. Though it was high summer, the candles were lighted in the tall silver candlesticks that Captain Aylmer had taken in a Spanish vessel. They were very tall, and perhaps had been altar lights; but the ladies had no such suspicion, and used them quite innocently.

Suddenly there was a rattle of wheels outside. The round-game players looked up.

"That sounds like a coach!" said the widow.

"Like *the* mail," said the pupil. "It is its time."

"It never stops here."

189

"It *is* stopping!"

"Are you expecting any one?"

"Oh! if it should be the captain!" cried Caroline, jumping up and clasping her hands, upsetting a whole deal of cards; thus first disturbing the whist players, one of whom, as in a dream, murmured a reproof to the young people for making so much noise. Caroline had flown to the door, when it was opened by Bond, the one-legged old sailor butler. "Young madam," quoth he, "here is an out-of-the-way crew asking for you. Shall I have 'em in?"

"News of the captain? Oh!" she cried, as at the same moment there advanced upon her four black-robed, black-veiled figures; and she had a glimpse of Denny in the background before she was enfolded in the embrace of Madame de Henisson, who threw herself upon her, sobbing, "Ah! my cousin, at last."

Cécile habitually dressed as a widow, and no sooner had the nuns set foot on English ground than they had resumed their hoods and veils, so that their aspect was sufficiently startling to a sober-minded English card-party, whose French, if it existed at all, had long been in abeyance. The pupil, indeed, was at first inclined to suspect a masquerade, and communicated his opinion to the doctor's son; but a word or two from Cécile had assured Caroline that they were refugees from Ste. Lucie, fleeing from the mob, who after sufferings *affreuses* had ventured to make their way to her, their dear friend.

Caroline knew their faces, and was specially glad to recognise Félicité; and a few words from her explained the situation, as far as she knew it. Pity for French emigrants was strong in the nation at the time, and a murmur of "poor creatures" went round, as the worn, haggard features were partially disclosed. Only the pupil murmured, "What old witches!" and the doctor's son answered, "The young one is passable enough," while the most romantic of the old maids felt a sense of bathos at the wrinkled old yellow faces of the two elderly nuns, Mère St. Hilaire's still so shrewd and French in spite of exhaustion. She had hardly explained something about the dreadful voyage, and the diligence, when Bond opened a chink of the door, and signalled to young madam to come and speak to him, looking so peremptory that she could not but obey; but happily catching sight of Zélie, she sent her in to help the strangers and serve as an interpreter.

"Ma'am, I've got him! I'd swear to him, for all his French toggery. He is Molony, the filthy great Irishman what deserted from the *Tiger* in Swanage Bay — has the impudence to show his ugly face here again. But I have locked him into the servants' hall for the present; and come to know whether it's your pleasure that I go for Dick Brown the constable to-night, or keep him here till morning, when Dick is more like to be sober. He can't be at none of his tricks there, ma'am."

"Dennis Molony! Why, Bond, he was my best friend in getting away from France! Depend upon it, he only ventured here to take care of these poor ladies, who have been driven away by those horrid Jacobins. I would not have a hair of his head touched, the generous fellow."

"All very fine, ma'am, as generous as you please, but that doesn't hinder him from being a deserter and a traitor to his flag," grimly returned Bond.

"I tell you, Bond, I will not have him touched,"

she said with a stamp of her foot. "No, nor my husband, the captain, would not either. I am going to see him. Have you given him anything to eat? No! Then go and fetch some bread and meat and a mug of ale directly."

The man-of-war's-man went off muttering, "a deserter, a deserter for all that."

Caroline could waste no more time on Bond nor any one else. She darted into the hall to see his prisoner. "Oh, Denny, how well you have done! You have brought my poor dear friends all safe!"

"And it was time, ma'am, when the murdering folk at Paris were coming out to make an end of the holy place, just like black Cromwell's men. So I brought them down in my boat — all that would come — for the Lady Prioress gave us the slip, and so did that pretty-faced young one, having a turn for being a martyr, no doubt."

"Oh! you have done a great deal, Denny; but it is not safe for you to be here!"

"Well, ma'am, I could not let the poor ladies come all alone by the stage, not knowing a word of the English tongue, and all of them kilt with the sickness at sea, and nothing to steer by but a bit of a scrap of paper with your address on it. I could not but see them in harbour, and if I swing for it, it is a holy work."

"You shall not do that, dear good Denny, but I am afraid Bond knows you."

"The boatswain aboard the *Tiger*, and no better than a tiger he was himself on the rough side of him."

"I have said all I can to him. He is a good old fellow, but he has terrible notions of discipline and faithfulness to his flag, and I don't know what he may think his duty. So as soon as you have rested and had some food, I think it would be wiser not to stay."

"Never you fear, dear lady, it's not the first time I have made fools of a gauger or a man-of-war's-man."

"Bond is busy enough now," as the cook came in with some cold meat and bread, her eyes extended with dread of that awful person, a smuggler who had turned Frenchman.

Promising to return, Caroline went where she was almost equally needed, to the parlour, where such ladies as had a smattering of boarding-school French were trying to understand Félicité, who had an equal amount of English; and Zélie was standing by Mrs. Aylmer, and translating her offers of refreshment as Bond set down on the table the dainty little supper prepared for the card-party — all in a nest of dishes fitting into a hexagon shape.

The most Protestant of the old maids had departed with the rector to escort her; the most patriotic stayed behind, vainly trying to understand Madame de Henisson.

Mrs. Aylmer was doing the honours with her best endeavours, but utterly confused by the polite bows and thanks of her unexpected guests, as well as by Zélie's interpretations.

"The holy mothers thank madame, but they will have no chick — it is *jour maigre* — meagre day — madame."

West Indian French done into broken English was not very explicable, and Caroline found the meagre day a strange puzzle to her mother-in-law.

"Do persuade the poor lady to pick a bit of friar's chicken, or here's a nice veal cutlet. I am sure they

o

want something to support them. Meagre, why they
are quite lean."

"*Jour maigre* — it is a fast-day. But you need not
fear, dear mother," she added in French, "friar's
chicken is without any meat. You can safely eat it;
but, indeed, it is rest more than food that they want."
She added in English, " May I send Molly to prepare
the blue and the red rooms for them ? "

" Poor things, they must stay here. And one is
your cousin? "

" Yes, Madame de Henisson — let me present you,"
said Caroline, remembering due forms. "*Ma belle
Mère Cécile;*" then, "These are my dear old mistresses, Mère de St. Hilaire, Mère Marie de l'Annonciation, my dear friend, Sœur Philomène."

There was a general curtseying all round, and a
little more ease — especially as Mistress Penelope and
the other visitors felt that their curiosity must wait,
and took leave, to burst out in wonder and commiseration outside the front door.

The house was really Captain Aylmer's own, therefore his wife's; but his mother had always acted as
hostess and housekeeper, and thus the arrival and
bestowal of all this unexpected party of Caroline's
friends was rather a delicate matter. If it had been
only her cousin, it would have been easy to arrange;
but the sudden arrival of three professed nuns might
well be a difficulty between the two ladies, and it was
well that the elder had more hospitality and delicacy
than Caroline would have met with from her aunt.

The newcomers were disposed of in two adjoining
bedrooms, with Zélie waiting on them. Caroline
promised her cousin to come to them again, and was
running down to see after Denny, when she was

impeded on her way by screams from Eustace and
Nancy, who, awakened by the unwonted movements
in the house, had ventured out in their little night-
dresses and bare feet, pit-a-pat, pit-a-pat, looking like
little ghosts themselves, and catching a sight of the
black hoods thought all their worst terrors realised,
and vied with one another in shrieks.

Mother and grandmother met, and each caught up
one little mortal. "Oh! my dear darling boy, they
won't hurt, they are dear good ladies on a journey."

"Dear Nancy, hush; no, they shan't hurt her! Bad
people have driven them away. Oh, Carry! what
shall we do?"

"We must try to help them. Yes, yes, dear boy —
all right. Mamma loves them so much. Shouldn't
you like to see them and kiss them?"

"No — no — no — ugly — old — black ——"

"So you said about Zélie! You love her now.
That's my brave boy."

Which he was not, for he was infected by his
grandmother's consternation; but his mother was
determined to conquer the terrors, and the grandmother, though fearing that the boy would be frightened into convulsions, held her peace, while Caroline
carried him to the room — where Cécile and Félicité
were both divested of their head-gear — and as they
flew at him with "*Le petit ange!*" he understood the
smiles and tones, though not the words, and let himself be kissed.

"Yes! you are a brave sailor boy to take care of
them," said his mother. "Make your salute and tell
them so."

Félicité could interpret the lisped assurance, and
pretty gesture, and there was a fresh transport.

"Well, Caroline. I could not have done that!" said Mrs. Aylmer, when the children were safe in their cribs, patted off to sleep.

"The boy must learn to be brave."

"But tell me, tell me, Carry, what are we to do with these ladies? Will they stay long with us, and board with us, and do they always wear those dreadful hoods?"

"My dear madam, I cannot tell yet. I have not heard half their story, and I must go and see after that good man, their escort and mine, or Bond will arrest him for a deserter! If you would go — be so kind as to go — and forbid Bond."

"In my house! No, that would never be," exclaimed the old lady, fully sensible of all the claims of hospitality; and off she set to mitigate Bond's zeal for the British flag, by persuading him of the rights of their voluntary guest. He certainly would have found none of the women of the house on his side, for Caroline found the cook, who had braved him so unwillingly, and the housemaid, sitting by perfectly entranced by his manners, conversation, and the story of the rescue of the ladies. The housemaid begged to make up a bed for him. "She was sure he deserved everything they could do for the friend of the distressed," and the cook chimed in with an emphatic, "To hear him talk was as good as the players in the barn, and all true besides!"

Nevertheless, it was far safer for the chivalrous deserter to be out of reach, and so Caroline was obliged to tell him most unwillingly.

"The saints' blessing be on you, madam, but never take it to heart. Sure and it is nothing but the luck of an honest free-trader, and what I've had to do

night by night, over and over again. A hedge-side
or the lee of a hay-stack is as good as I'd look for on
land, nine nights out of the week; and now the holy
mothers is brought into port, I have the prayers of
them, blessings on them, and one of them, Mother St.
Hilary, she give me this medal, which has been blessed
by the Pope, and is not that enough to keep a man's
heart warm ? "

And more than content with that reward, the Irishman disappeared into the night; and Mrs. Aylmer did
not envy Bond, exposed to the tongues of the women,
though he heeded them little, "wrapped in his own
integrity," and thinking of his own two ladies as no
better than the rest. A ship was the only *she* among
them all that knew what discipline meant.

Repairing to her cousin's room. Caroline found that
Sœur Philomène had been called to join the two
elder nuns in their compline devotions, but Madame
de Henisson was still in the outer room, waiting for
her. Might she *veiller* with her ?

Caroline thought sleep would be better than watching for Cécile, but she longed to hear her adventures,
and took her to her room, where the children were by
this time fast asleep. There, installed in a low nursery chair, Cécile told of the alarm, and the flight, with
the disappearance of the Prioress, and of Sœur Françoise, then of the miseries of the journey, though
mitigated by the devotion of good Denny. "But oh,
my dear Caroline, such a frightful thing has happened.
We were joined by that Beaudésert ! "

" Beaudésert ! What, the lover ? I thought he
was in America."

" He came home on his affairs ! So he said, but I
believe myself he was drawn by the notion of danger

to the convents. However, to do him justice, he was
denounced and reduced to fly, when he joined us at
Rouen; and judge of my dismay when I recognised
him and thought of the scandal."

"Alas! there are few that care about the scandal
in these days! But Fé — Sœur Philomène, did she
know that he was there?"

"I am sorry to say I fear she did, though I kept
too good watch over them to allow them to speak to
one another."

"Poor things!" Caroline could not help exclaiming.

"Ah, you are a Protestant! and she had quite con-
quered all the past folly, and resigned herself to
her life, as if she had a vocation originally, so that
it is a thousand pities that all should be freshly
stirred."

"What has become of him? Is he here?"

"Here! My dear Caroline, could you suppose that
I should have allowed him to come here, though I
own that his whole conduct was irreproachable, and
the care he took of us all, the mothers and myself,
was perfect! I shall never forget it, but I could not
let him come on with us! Imagine the scandal and
impropriety!"

"Did the mothers know?"

"Only that I had met him in the world. I would
not let them know of the former relations between
the young people: it would have shocked them too
much. They were absolutely charmed with his attentions."

"And where is he?"

"What do I know? Gone to London, I believe, or
wherever he meant to look for miners," and Cécile

waved her hands to show that she had done with him.

" Poor fellow," sighed Caroline, "and now, Cécile, we must lie down and sleep."

"Ah! it is the first bed I have slept on for fifteen days."

CHAPTER XV

Come, pensive Nun, devout and pure,
Sober, steadfast, and demure.

MILTON.

CAROLINE AYLMER's first morning hours were spent in obtaining that Zélie should compound and carry to each of her guests a cup of coffee and a slice of bread, as much according to French taste as could be contrived, and therewith she used all her persuasions to keep them in bed; and as they had by no means recovered from the manifold distresses and sufferings of the voyage and journey, all obeyed her gladly except Félicité, who insisted on getting up and waiting on the rest.

Then came the breakfast with her mother-in-law, who was almost as much disturbed by this strange invasion as the visitors themselves could be, though she was thoroughly kind and hospitable, but "How did they come, and what was to be done with them?"

Caroline was now able to explain their history, which drew tears from the kind old lady. "Driven out with violence, and destitute, from the home of their life, and that after all had been sent away who had the semblance of a home within reach! Poor

things! Oh, they must stay for the present, till we
see what can be done. They shall have every kindness, I am sure they ought! But will they sit in the
parlour and be like company?"

"I do not think the nuns themselves would wish it,
grandmamma. They will be quite as happy as we
can make them if we give them up a couple of rooms
upstairs, where they can live as if they were in their
convent; Cécile, my cousin — Madame de Henisson —
may like to be with us. At any rate, I must make
her the offer."

"Oh yes, by all means. she is your cousin; but my
dear Caroline, do you think George, your husband,
will approve of our taking all this expense?"

"Oh, he will not grudge it! Besides Cécile will get
remittances from Guadaloupe, and all mine I am sure
will go to help. Zélie will wait on them. They shall
be no trouble to you."

"Well, my dear, I am sure that it is right to do
what we can for the poor ladies. They are quite welcome, but oh dear! I wish George was at home. I
wish they were not Catholics. And what will your
aunt say?"

"Oh, never mind my aunt. It was she who sent me
to them. so she has no right to object."

"Well, I wish they were not Catholics," repeated
Mrs. Aylmer.

To wish that nuns were not Roman Catholics was
beyond Caroline, so she could only answer that they
were very good women, and she could answer for it
that they would give no offence. She heartily re-
echoed the wish that her husband were at home, but
alas! there was no chance of that for at least three
years to come, and she could only thank her mother-

in-law for her kindness in the matter, to which Mrs. Aylmer responded that her heart bled for the poor ladies, and any one was welcome who was driven away by these dreadful French people.

Then came down the children, plainly forgetting the night's alarm, or else confounding it with evening recurring terrors. which, with the curious reticence of childhood, were never to be mentioned to grown-up ears. However, they retained for a long time a terror of the door where the "black hoods" lived, and for months were not quite convinced that plots for burning them, or blowing them up, might not be hatched behind it. In fact perhaps their nurse and the housemaid. by mysterious whisperings over their cribs, conduced to the impression.

Caroline looked in on her guests, and assured them of their welcome, then was a little mortified that all, except Cécile, seemed to take it as a matter of course, and to have no notion that an importation of four might be a serious thing in a quiet English household —and Cécile might have means. She wrote to the notary at Paris, though it was quite probable that means from thence might be obstructed (as in truth they were), since she was an emigrant, but there were hopes from her brother-in-law, from whom Caroline had actually received a small remittance direct from Ste. Marie Galante. The nuns were to be served upstairs, but Madame de Henisson undertook to get up and come down to the dinner which was to be at three o'clock.

Caroline had to go out, with a commission from the elder lady to do some marketing. " You know what sort of green stuff the ladies will like. They don't eat anything else, do they ? "

She took her basket on her arm, and went forth, but just beyond their fronting row of limes, cut in arches, she saw a figure unmistakably French in the general aspect, and still more so in the graceful bow with which his cocked hat was taken off and flourished to the ground as he spoke in foreign English, " Have I the honour of addressing Mistress Aylmer ? "

She curtseyed again, with an instant conviction, which was strengthened by his next words, " May I ask whether the ladies of Ste. Lucie have arrived safely under madame's roof ? "

" Yes — oh yes," she exclaimed, unconsciously speaking French, " they are safely here. You are Monsieur Beaudésert ? Then you have not met Denny ? "

" No, madame, that heart of gold went his own way. The lady would not hear of my escorting them, and in truth there was no room upon the diligence ; but I could not but make my way hither to know whether they had been safely received, and that your goodness had sheltered them."

" They are quite well, and safe, and I hope will soon be recovered," said Caroline, in some doubt how she ought to answer, or what was to come next ; but her heart was drawn towards the young man, with his attractive, clever, though not handsome face, his courteous French manner, and the eager gestures which he could hardly restrain.

" Madame knows me — my history," said he. " Ah ! I see she does ! She is my — our friend. May I ask if I could see Mademoiselle de Monfichet ? "

" Did she know that you accompanied her, monsieur ? " said Caroline, considering.

" One glance, like a beam from heaven, was granted

to me; but she held aloof from me, I know not whether she has forgotten me."

"That she has not," burst from the imprudent woman.

"Ah! madame has been the guardian angel of the situation. It is from her and her narration that my relations at Rouen knew that her vows were never really made. It was that which inspired new hope, or I would never have returned from America."

"I cannot tell how far she thinks them binding," returned Mrs. Aylmer. "Tell me, monsieur, what did you think of doing?"

"If I could win her consent, all would be clear. I would make her my wife and take her to Louisiana. where our own religion is practised, and yet no one would know that she had been a professed religious. Truly professed she is not."

"Not in heart. Scarcely by the lips, and under protest."

"Then, madame, you will grant me to speak with her! This is a land where there is true liberty. Remember I have travelled in company with her for eight days — never spoken to her — only once seen that face so beloved."

"You shall! you shall!" cried Caroline impulsively, bringing him back to the house, where she shut him into the dining parlour, and, without a thought of scruples or difficulties, ran up to the nuns' rooms, and called "Félicité — Sœur Philomène — come, I want you."

Félicité, without her veil, her dark short hair in waves all uncovered, was helping the sisters to dress; but she obeyed the summons without hesitation. except a "Mais — mais. madame," as her hostess held her by

the hand and took her down stairs. In another second,
Henri Beaudésert was before her, holding out both
hands, and advancing on her in ecstatic joy. She
retreated in alarm on Caroline, who would have left
them together, as naturally as if they had been English lovers; but Félicité in dismay and shame cried,
"Oh no! no! don't leave me," holding both hands
over her face, unveiled after the three years' habit.
Perhaps her first sense was of a treason in her friend.
She scarcely even saw, as Beaudésert threw himself
on his knees before her, and cried, "Oh lady, most beloved, grant me a sight of that face, you, whom I have
adored for years! You are free at last."

"Oh no, no. It is sacrilege! Go away. Oh! take
me away, madame."

She was close to the door, but Caroline set her
back against it to prevent an escape. "No. Félicité."
she said, "you ought to hear him. Remember what
he has risked for you. Remember all you have said
to me of your doubts if yours were a valid profession,
and your longings to escape."

This was said as much for his sake as for hers,
but she faintly said, "Ah! I had given all those profane desires up, sinner that I am. Awaken them not
again."

"Ah! you cannot, cannot deny that you felt them."

"It was a sin! I thought I had killed them."

"You had not. They were no sin, since in your
heart — nay, by lips and pen — you protested against
the cruel profession. You are *not* bound." She had
let him grasp her hand, and see her blushing face, and
he proceeded, "There is nothing — nothing to hinder
you from being made mine, and coming with me to
those new lands where there is liberty."

"No! no!" she cried in horror, withdrawing her hand. "Let me go, madame, I ought not to listen."

"Nay, listen once. There is a Catholic chapel at that old house half-way here. It was pointed out to me."

"I know it," said Caroline, "a French priest is there."

"He would wed us, in your own name, dear sweet lady mine. He need know nothing of the cruelly imposed title."

Félicité had rallied a little after the first shock. "No!" she said. "Hear me, monsieur. It is true that the semblance of a vow was forced from my weakness, and that my heart revolted against whatever was put into my lips. I was no willing handmaid of the Lord, who saw my heart. But I had tried to bend my will and do His service, as a reluctant slave might do, and I do not know what right I have to draw back now. Certainly, and you, an upright Englishwoman, madame, agree with me, it would be most unfair to ask a priest to give the nuptial benediction without knowing that I am a religious, outwardly at least professed."

"She is quite right," said Caroline. "It would be very wrong towards the priest."

"The ladies must forgive a *misérable* half-maddened," cried Beaudésert. "Alas! what is to be done! Must we remain thus torn apart for ever by cruel tyranny and religious scruples? Might not we be married by one of your Protestant clergy who would ask no questions?"

"That would not be the benediction of our only true Mother. We may not be traitors to her," said Félicité. "No, there are Catholic Bishops in this country, both

English and French. If monsieur could bring me the opinion of *one* that my vows, such as they were, are not binding, and that I can be absolved from them, then I shall not fear to transgress in——"
Her voice faded away, but in a transport, Beaudésert mastered her hand, kissed it, and declared, " Such assurance you shall have, if I go through fire and water for it!"

Félicité, frightened at a passion such as she had never witnessed before, loosed her hand with some vehemence and darted out of the room, nearly upsetting in her flight old Mrs. Aylmer, who was leisurely proceeding on her way, and stood amazed to see another French refugee, evidently in a state of much emotion, in conversation with her daughter-in-law.

"Monsieur Beaudésert, grandmamma," said Caroline. "He kindly looked in to assure himself that our guests are safe. I think I have told you of him."

Mrs. Aylmer made her best curtesy, but looked bewildered, dreading perhaps a fifth destitute claimant of hospitality.

Beaudésert perhaps guessed, for he said in his best English, "I go on to meet the coach of which I have been told. I go to London on affairs. I will do myself the honour to write to madame."

"Pray do so, and if there is occasion to write to you about — these ladies — where shall I direct?"

His answer was ready — to the care of an American banker in London; and then with much politeness, he bowed himself out.

"Well," said the mother-in-law, "I am thankful that he, at least, has a banker; not that I grudge anything to these poor destitute ladies! But what is this about that young nun? I met Félicité rushing to the

stairs like a mad thing, though she did stop and say
' *Pardon, madame.*' "

"Félicité! Oh, grandmamma, do you not recollect?
I told you about my seeing her professed, and how
she fainted and never quite spoke the vow."

"Poor girl! Yes I remember. And do you mean
that that was the young man she was in love with?
Dear me! But they can be married now."

"Dear grandmamma, I hope it may come about, but
there is a good deal to come first. You know she is
really reckoned as a professed nun."

"But they might turn Protestants, and a blessed
thing too."

"I don't think they would," said Caroline, almost
smiling, "they are a long way from thinking us right,
and you would be the last person to wish them to act
against their conscience."

"Why yes, certainly, but if we could convert them.
Perhaps the good doctor could."

Caroline, who had been obliged to know a good deal
more than her mother-in-law did of the gulf between
the tenets of the two Churches, could not entertain
any warm expectations of the kind, and was thankful
to recollect her marketing.

CHAPTER XVI

The Paip, that Pagan full o' pride,
Hath blinded us fu' long.
— *Ballad.*

THE two Mistresses Aylmer did not find their hospitality to the nuns of Ste. Lucie led much to their
ease and comfort, and the younger certainly had the
worst of it, for she had the misgivings of every one to
hear, as well as displeasure at times from the nuns
and Madame de Henisson.

They were far too well-bred ladies to utter a word
as to their accommodation, but they were dreadfully
distressed and angry when they discovered that Sœur
Philomène had been allowed to see a gentleman —
nay, one who had been her lover. Poor Cécile disclosed the fact unawares, and then found that it had
almost destroyed their confidence in Caroline. "But,
que voulez-vous? She is a heretic!"

"And no Catholic could be more good and kind to
us," said Mère de l'Annonciation.

"Though she might have known better than to
cause such a scandal!" added Mère St. Hilaire.

Accordingly they insisted on Félicité doing severe
penance by the repetition of Penitential Psalms upon
her knees. She submitted, for she knew that, as they

said, she could have refused all answer, and in many
moods the bounding hopes within her heart seemed
sinful and profane.   Nor would they let her speak to
Mrs. Aylmer, nor go into the garden, till Madame de
Henisson, alarmed by her looks, declared that they
were ruining her health, and that the crime would be
on their souls, for they were immuring her more than
ever had been done at Ste. Lucie.   Mrs. Aylmer undertook that the coast should be clear when the poor girl
was out of doors in the high-walled garden.

"Though," as Mr. Darpent said, laughing, "I am
much tempted to act Peeping Tom of Coventry!"

For the good ladies, unaware of the perplexities that
they were bringing on their generous hostess, had gone
to the utmost of their powers in making their abode
as like a convent as possible.

Their apartment consisted of two rooms and a pow-
dering closet; for Madame de Henisson had been placed
in a chamber of her own, in the secular side of the
house, where she lived, as she was quite willing to do,
as the guest of her cousin.

The windows of these rooms looked out on the
street, or rather on the tops of the lime-trees, and
therefore they were closed entirely, with the shutters
admitting only a little light at the top.   The dressing-
closet was towards the garden, but did not fare better,
for the sisters converted it into a temporary chapel.
They took the curtains down from their beds and
made hangings of them for the windows and the walls;
and they contrived a sort of temporary altar, over
which was arranged, on a raised cushion, a little brass
crucifix, which Mère de St. Hilaire had brought round
her neck, and at the sides a tiny reliquary, and likewise
a very small china image of the Blessed Virgin.   Each

of the three sisters and Cécile had had a sacred "object" committed to her charge, and these were now
put together on the little draped table, before which
it was the effort of the sisters to keep up continual
orisons for not only their exiled selves, but interces-
sions for that miserable country of theirs which
seemed for the time to be the sport of demons; also
for their own scattered sisters, for their chaplain, for
their families, and, above all, for their King, his wife,
and children.

But that poor little chapel was the cause of much
consternation. True, no servant but Zélie was ever
lawfully admitted there, but peeping could be accomplished, and reports spread all over the town that the
Papists were always worshipping their images there.

Even Mrs. Aylmer had her doubts whether it was
right to permit such doings under her son's roof, for
to her old-fashioned Calvinist training it seemed like
encouraging idol worship, and she consulted the rector
whether she ought to suffer it. Happily he was a man
with more instruction and some largeness of mind; and
though he could not make her understand the distinctions of worship, she accepted his dictum that it would
be cruel to interfere with the religious habits of her
unfortunate inmates, and that she might be satisfied
that they believed the same creed and worshipped
God like herself. But when she proposed to him to
try to convert them he only laughed, and told her
to let them alone. It was, he said, an excellent and
charitable deed to shelter such poor fugitives, and it
ought not to be spoilt by persecution.

He was thus satisfied, and Mrs. Aylmer had her
answer to those who blamed her and imagined by
force of scandal any amount of malpractices behind

those blinds.   Mrs. Darpent was most especially irate.
Gossip had swelled on tongue after tongue by the
time it came out to Walwyn, and the upshot of it was
that she sailed into her husband's study in wrath, and
insisted on his coming with her to put a stop to her
niece Aylmer's Popish practices.

" I hear that they have a whole nunnery in their
house, all in black hoods, and that old Sukey Shrimper,
up from the Creek, has orders to call every Friday ! "

" Good for Sukey," quietly observed Mr. Darpent.

" You are in one of your vexatious moods, Mr. Darpent.   I tell you that Rhoades, the butcher, does not
send in one pound of meat more than he did before
this lot came down on them.   It is high time some
one interfered.   In her husband's absence, too, letting
those Popish locusts sponge her out of house and
home."

" By your own account that is just what they are
not doing."

" Oh, depend upon it they knew what they are
about, when they came down all of a sudden, and
with a notorious smuggler — yes, and a smart young
gentleman, if you please, with them — and invaded
the house.   Poor old Mrs. Aylmer had no choice except to let them in, though the poor children are
frightened out of• their wits, and there they creep
about the house afraid of their lives for the black
hoods; while those nuns set up all their Popish practices, and they have got an altar and two or three
images set up as large as life, and there they are saying mass all day long.   What are you laughing at,
Mr. Darpent ? "

" At the nuns saying mass, my dear.   Don't you
know that only a priest can do that ? "

"Then you may depend upon it one of them is a priest in disguise, and it is your duty to look into it, Mr. Darpent, or some day Captain Aylmer may come over to find his wife and children turned into bloody-minded Papists. I tell you it is your bounden duty to go and see what your niece is doing, instead of sitting grinning there enough to make a cat sick."

"I grin, as you politely express it, to think who it was who induced me, nay, compelled me to place my niece under the charge of these same wicked nuns."

"There you go. I only said that her aunt ought to share the charge of the girl. I never told you to put her in a convent."

"Though you were aware that such was the usual style of education."

"Come, Mr. Darpent, you know I only said the girl was their niece as much as yours, and it was their duty to do something for her. The question is, are you coming over with me to see what is to be done to put a stop to these Popish ways? I have ordered the coach to be round at eleven o'clock, so you had better take off your dressing-gown and put on your wig."

Mr. Darpent as usual teased his wife, but meekly complied in the end, and besides he had a real curiosity to know the foundation of all these dreadful rumours. So, in due time, the family coach, to be more dignified and impressive, lumbered up to the door behind the lime-trees at Downford, and presently they were ushered into the parlour, where they found a bright-looking lady in mourning sitting at her embroidery-frame, and little Nancy standing by her holding a skein of rose-coloured silk, while her mother was apparently busied on more homely needlework.

Caroline's French breeding was equal to the occasion. She rose and greeted with curtsey and embrace her uncle and aunt, explaining with three words to Cécile who they were, and adding in English to them, " My cousin, the Countess of Henisson. I think you saw her as a little girl, Uncle Darpent, when you took me to France to the care of my aunt ? "

There was a little premeditation in this speech, for the sense of her obligations would tell upon her aunt's courtesy, and due genuflections were exchanged on either side, Madame de Henisson dexterously relieving Nancy's hands of the skein, and suggesting something about *belle révérence*, after which Caroline sent the child away to find her grandmother. Her boy, as she explained, being delicate, still took a mid-day sleep.

Mr. Darpent's French was not so far to seek but that he could make his civilities to the stranger lady, and understand her when he had drawn her into an account of the terrible alarm at Ste. Lucie, of the escape and the miserable journey, as well of her exceeding gratitude to her good cousin, and that dear " Mistriss Aylmer "—all given with gestures of hands and play of countenance that exasperated Mrs. Darpent, because she did not understand in the least. She might comprehend a single word or two, or a phrase here and there; but a rapid interchange of conversation was Greek to her, and the lively French action seemed to her mere coquetry meant to captivate her husband.

She could hardly command herself enough to be moderately civil to the elder Mrs. Aylmer, so anxious was she to catechise both mother and daughter-in-law, and happily her language was equally incomprehensible to Madame de Henisson; but the real delicacy

of Mrs. Aylmer would not discourse on a personal
matter in the presence of one of the subjects. She
invited the visitor to come upstairs and take off her
hat before the early dinner. This, of course, the good
lady had intended, as a huge bandbox in the hall,
containing her cap, could testify. Caroline rose to
conduct her, but grandmamma, kindly guessing what
was in store, signed to her to remain still.

"Well, ma'am," was the beginning, as soon as they
were outside the drawing-room door, "so Caroline has
been turning your house into a convent."

"It is my son's house."

"And I wonder what he will say to such doings
when he comes home."

"I think he will say that his wife was quite right
to give an asylum to the friends of her childhood."

Whereat Mrs. Darpent snorted, and was about to
turn to the door of the guest-chamber. "Not there,
if you please, ma'am. Come into my room."

"Oh-h! You are giving them up half the house.
Well if they leave you room for yourselves!"

"They have only the red and blue rooms, and the
closet."

"What, for ten nuns?"

"There are only three besides Madame de Henisson.
The rest stayed behind."

"I declare! Mistress Penelope Swan vowed there
were eight, and old Mistress Howland ten!"

"There are but three. We are very anxious about
the rest, who would not leave their convent."

"Quite enough of them. I shall see them at dinner,
I suppose?"

"I think not. They prefer to have their meals
alone, with Zélie to wait on them."

"Oh, the black woman! A use for her! But I shall see them, no doubt."

"They do not wish to admit strangers."

"Oh!" These exclamations were in an indescribable tone, varying between pique and surprise. "But at any rate I can see this chapel they have put up in this house, that I may — I mean Mr. Darpent may — understand what Popish things you have here."

"Indeed, ma'am, I do not see how you can. They have made a little oratory in the powdering-closet, and there is no way into it but through their rooms."

"You do not know it yourself, and you are satisfied!"

"I spoke to the rector, and he advised me not to interfere with them."

"Oh, good easy man! I pity the captain when he comes home and finds you all Papists. And pray who is bearing the expense of all this?"

"There is no great expense. The house is large enough. Zélie suffices for attendance, and as to food, it really grieves me to find how very little suffices them."

"Ah! fasting, no doubt, or some such Popish foolery."

"I believe they do fast for the sake of their poor country and their sisters, and above all, their poor king and queen."

"Highty-tighty, you are half-way to be a Catholic. What good do they expect to do their king and queen that way?"

Mrs. Aylmer thought it best not to answer, though she was actually so much of a true Catholic, that she bethought her of the many times in the Scripture that

fasting had given wings to prayer; and that every
native of unhappy France might well fast in humili-
ation, while the country seemed to be given up to
foes, the retaliation in bloodshed and anarchy for the
accumulated sins of generations past.

Poor woman, she had endured the worst of Mrs.
Darpent's very conscientious scolding, for Caroline
dexterously kept out of a *tête-à-tête*, and Mr. Darpent
was not only fascinated with Madame de Henisson's
pretty manners, but as he told his niece in private,
"Of course she could not have sent the poor things to
the workhouse, and if it were all right with her husband and his mother, of course all was well." Nay,
under all her grumblings his wife was of the same
mind, though she was greatly disappointed at not
being allowed a sight of the nuns, who were quite as
much a matter of curiosity to her as if they had been
in Exeter Change.

The old-fashioned respect for the presence of servants obviated family discussions at dinner-time, after
which she went out shopping and making calls; but
she contrived, when going up to put on her walking-
dress, to (willingly) forget her way and get a peep into
the red room, where she had one glimpse at the dreadful sight of a black hood and white scapular, and a
young dark-browed face under it, apparently mending
a tablecloth.

She mumbled "I beg pardon" and retreated, satisfied so far, but ashamed. Her husband had been satisfied about the notorious smuggler, as the brave man
who had aided the escape, and brought the ladies to
the door. And as Mrs. Darpent's silk shawl, and even
his own best brandy, came from unmentionable sources,
it was better to pry no farther. Moreover, he had an

interview with the rector, who knew that it was in consideration to raise a fund for the assistance of emigrants, partly private and partly from Government, and this intelligence did a good deal to pacify Mrs. Darpent, since it showed that Caroline was swimming with the stream.

Whether she would ask for a share in the subsidy or not was a different question. In the meantime Downford should have been grateful, for the nuns, though unseen, afforded admirable food for gossip; and such stories as could be picked up from the children or servants went the round of the card-tables, and enlivened the "dish of tea" in half the "genteel" abodes of the neighbourhood.

CHAPTER XVII

They love her best who to themselves are true,
And what they love to dream of dare to do.
                                        LOWELL.

TIME went on, and terrible reports came at intervals
of the doings in France. Monsieur Beaudésert wrote
from London that he was striving to find a French
bishop who might relieve Félicité from her scruples,
but he had not hitherto succeeded, and he had urgent
letters from America which compelled him to pursue
his arrangements for obtaining experienced miners.
Meanwhile he entreated Mademoiselle to believe that
his heart was still at her feet.

Caroline delivered the message, but Félicité only
smiled and shook her head. "He will never succeed,"
she said; "I had better resign myself."

It was soon after this that, on a warm August day.
Mr. and Mrs. Tresham were announced. They were
the Roman Catholic neighbours with whom both
Darpents and Aylmers were slightly acquainted, but
who generally held themselves aloof, partly from old
family habit, partly from actual poverty. They came
eagerly to call on Madame de Henisson, and after
greetings had been exchanged, the lady said, "I understand that you have had the honour of receiving some
fugitive Religious."

"Indeed we have, ma'am," said Caroline, "they are old friends who educated me."

"Ah! then you are of us."

"No, madame, but I was sent to Ste. Lucie for education. Madame de Henisson is my cousin, and brought the Religious here, knowing of the welcome."

"Indeed it is a good work, a blessed work. I am tempted to ask whether I may share it with you."

Knowing what the relief to her mother-in-law would be, Caroline could by no means refuse the proposal, and Madame de Henisson went upstairs to ask the ladies to see their English co-religionist. This they did gladly, and, moreover, it appeared that a priest was waiting in the carriage. He was presently taken upstairs. Mr. Tresham meanwhile sat and told the shocked and sympathetic ears of the two Mrs. Aylmers of the horrors of which the Abbé had brought the tidings. He had escaped, as it were, by the skin of his teeth, having been hidden in an old boat among the reeds of the little tributary of the Seine, and feeling immensely grateful to the wild duck's brood that swam about in front as if no human being lurked there. Thus he had escaped being either torn to pieces at once by the *sans-culottes*, or being committed to the Abbaye — the Carmelite Abbey — which had by this time become the shambles of his brethren.

He had thence made his way down to the river, and had fallen in with a good bargeman, Irish, who made it his business to assist the escape of the persecuted.

"Denny Molony!" cried Caroline; "the same who brought the nuns and Madame de Henisson."

"The same, madam. A man who merits immortal honours."

"Indeed he does. We all owe infinitely much to him. But did he tell the Abbé, your friend ——"

"The Abbé de Pont de Loire."

"Oh, I know him, I know him! He was chaplain at Ste. Lucie. How glad the ladies must be to see him!"

"Alas! though, he brings them sad news — more than sad, incredibly shocking," said Mr. Tresham.

"Did he tell you what became of those who were left behind, the dear Mother Prioress, Mère Dominique, and the young Sister?" cried Caroline.

"So far as I gathered the history, the elder nun had had another stroke, and was dying. They carried her down to the vaults below the chapel, where the Abbé gave her the last rites, while the cries of the raging mob sounded above, as her face was settling into perfect calm. The priest was the object of the search; the lives of the Sisters were not held to be in danger from the law (or what was called such), and the Prioress insisted that he should follow the lay-sister who could show him a secret passage from the vaults to the garden sheds and thence to the river.

"And did not they take it?" exclaimed Caroline.

"They remained doing the last offices to the poor body."

"And did he leave them? Oh!"

"Remember, he was in far more danger than they, and the Mother Prioress insisted."

"And then?"

"I believe the mob found them kneeling on each side of the corpse, and were overawed for the moment, leaving them there. And the next night, when all was quiet, but only the remnants lying sacked about them, he returned, and they committed the body to

the grave by the lights of the smouldering fires of their
furniture."

Tears might well come to Caroline's eyes as she
pictured to herself the cloister and buildings she knew
so well lighted up by the flaming remnants of the old
woodwork, the school lesson books, and furniture, and
the Prioress and Sœur Françoise with her heavenly
face kneeling in the midst of desolation. She only
asked, however, " And then ? "

" The Prioress decided on putting on a secular disguise which she had ready and endeavouring to make
her way to some relations in Anjou, taking with her
the young Sister. The Abbé parted with them on the
high-road, and, as you heard, lurked in cottages and
among the marshes till he could escape."

" Did he hear no more ? "

" He much fears that they were the two whom he
heard of as seized as intending to emigrate. In that
case they would be taken to Paris."

It sounded like a death-warrant, for the massacres
in the prisons, done under the cowardly terror of an
invasion by the emigrants, had been known by this
time in England.

" Ah ! " said Caroline, " dear Sœur Françoise. She
had the spirit of a martyr. I saw her face when she
made her profession, and it was that of one dead to
the world ! "

" Still," said Mrs. Aylmer the elder, " we may hope
for the best. They may have been saved from those
slaughterers, who, by all accounts, fell chiefly upon
the clergy and on gentlemen."

This was true, though it was not till long after that
the history of the slow "Passion" which the sweet
and gentle Sœur Françoise willingly, nay cheerfully,

was enduring at that very time in the prison of La Force, where no sufferings seemed to check her bright, kindly, and even playful spirit, since she endured all with joy as the footsteps of her Lord.

For the present, however, no more was known, and Caroline could only hear the same history in other words from the Abbé when he came down with Mrs. Tresham and Madame de Henisson from their visit to the recluses above.

It appeared that the Treshams were ready and eager to receive the two elder nuns; but as they already housed the Abbé de Pont de Loire and another priest, they really had no room, nor perhaps means, for also taking Sœur Philomène. Caroline was very glad it should be so. Grandmamma would be much relieved by the absence of the two old ladies, with their thoroughly monastic arrangements, and they would be infinitely happier in the Tresham surroundings; but it seemed to her well that Félicité should lead a freer life, and not be surrounded with all their conventual restrictions.

The Abbé must have been of somewhat the same opinion. He came over the next day to fetch the two nuns, and had a long interview with Sœur Philomène, for whom there had scarcely been time while the Treshams were calling. Meanwhile the mothers were pouring out their warm gratitude to their hostesses, whose goodness seemed to them beyond all price, and only to be rewarded by prayers that they might be brought to the Holy Mother Church into which Caroline had been baptized.

"Tell them," said Mrs. Aylmer, "that you were indeed baptized into the true Church, which is above all these divisions. You can put it clearly enough."

Caroline tried, but doubted whether she had done so, for Mère de St. Hilaire only shook her head, and said that her dear pupil was " *Catholique malgré elle*," and they-parted with tears and embraces such as had been cut short at the real break-up.

The Abbé was a good man, but not a rigid, nor perhaps a courageous, one; and he had known, better than any one perhaps, all the anguish of mind, the doubts and sense of expediency, as well as of deference to Episcopal authority which had been undergone by Félicité and by the Prioress before her profession had been made.

Such considerations might have been with him when he took upon himself to relax the Benedictine rule, and permit the girl to live as a guest with the family, only observing certain times of devotion in the oratory, going out in the town, and wearing an ordinary dress, as well as returning to her own name. She would come with Madame de Henisson to attend Mass at Court Tresham on days of greater solemnity, but it was too far off to do so every Sunday.

Of Félicité's own family he knew nothing, and it remained absolutely uncertain whether they remained in their château, had escaped over the border into Switzerland, or had been arrested. The Bishop of Charmilly had probably been among the slaughtered priests at La Force, but there was no knowing. And the doubt did not seem to burden Félicité's mind. Liberty was a strange new boon to her, such as she had not enjoyed since those happy days when she had been under the English governess at home.

"I like you without the great black hood," said little Eustace, coming up to her for a kiss.

He could not say " Félicité," and his mother told

him to call his new friend Joy. "I hope it is a good
omen for this and further joy," she said.

She had dressed Félicité as well as she could from
her own wardrobe, and neither Mrs. Aylmer nor
Cécile at the first moment knew the slim young lady,
with dark hair uncovered except by a little round
lace cap, who shyly descended the stairs. The brows
were very black, the face more resolute than beautiful;
but when the children came and caressed her, showing
the wooden doll and the spotted horse, there came a
charming bright responding smile, such as Caroline
had never beheld before in all their eighteenth months'
acquaintance.

Madame de Henisson had been reviving ever since
she had been at Downford. She had thought it a
duty of good manners to conform to the habits of
her cousin's household; and when no longer under
the shadow of the convent and the first associations
of her widowhood, she had begun to brighten, and all
her French vivacity, so long dimmed, asserted itself,
when with Caroline, the playfellow of her girlhood.
She picked up enough of English, too, to understand
and make herself understood, and it was no wonder
that the rector and the doctor, the pupil and the son,
as well as others, also held Mrs. Aylmer's to be the
pleasantest card-parties in the town; while several
elders and half of the young people sided with Mistress Penelope Swan, and declared that poor old Mrs.
Aylmer's evenings were quite spoilt. "It was intolerable to see that Frenchwoman's airs, making fools
of all the men! Teaching them *trictrac*—a Jacobin
French game! What would they bring in next?
And as to the young one. They say she is a nun,
and she sits up vastly demure, but depend on it she

Q

is up to some mischief. I saw her making eyes at young Chalfont."

What was chiefly concerning the two ladies for the present was their entire dependence on their hostesses. Madame de Henisson had hopes from her sister, but Félicité was absolutely destitute. They were not much disturbed as to food, but when Félicité had to be fitted out entirely, and winter was coming on, anxiety began. Both, as well as Caroline herself, and all the pupils of Ste. Lucie, were excellent needle-women and fair house-keepers and cooks, and to the arts there taught many of the delicacies of Mrs. Aylmer's suppers were owing; but Félicité could not feel that there was any equivalent for the hospitality she enjoyed purely out of compassion.

They made and trimmed all the hats and caps, and embroidered whatever dresses they could lay hands on, besides dressing a doll for Nancy most elaborately, the very pockets beautifully stitched; and they also contrived to offer, through the servants, to work for the mercer's shop in the little town; but ladies did so much plain work and embroidery at home that there was not much opening, and at last the doctor's wife, edified by hearing Nancy air her scraps of French, made the proposal that Mademoiselle de Monfichet should teach her little girls French history and music.

Cécile was shocked. "Really, my cousin," she said, "you should know better than to convey such a request from the wife of a mere doctor to a demoiselle of quality."

"The demoiselle is happy to do something for her own expenses," said Félicité, smiling, "and as to the doctor ——"

There she broke off short, blushing and ashamed to

show how much her thoughts were roaming to the son
of a doctor of medicine. She accepted the proposal,
and ere long had made the two children very fond of
her, and chatter French to the general admiration of all
who did not think mischief must come of all the for-
eigners. Zélie attended Mademoiselle to the door, and
fetched her back, otherwise Madame Henisson would
not have been pacified; the town laughed at the governess escorted by the negress, but Félicité was evidently happy, quite a different creature from the
broken-hearted girl whom Caroline had first known;
and when she talked of "Monsieur le docteur," it was
plain that she liked him the better for his profession,
great, rough, plain-spoken country doctor as he was.
Yet Gallic temperament and power to enjoy the present were needed to keep up the spirits of the two
guests as winter brought on the terrible year 1793,
and with it the execution of the King, the captivity
of his family, and the daily murder of all that was
noblest in France; while the nation seemed as it were
drunken with blood, and the long course of ancestral
crimes were being visited on many an innocent head,
and many a frivolous character was redeemed and rose
into nobility through that terrible ordeal of suffering
which made the scourge into a palm of martyrdom.

To Caroline's surprise, her French friends did not
seem to feel it as deeply as did her uncle, easy-going
country squire as he had always seemed. They wept,
sometimes even sat up at night to weep and pray when
any fresh appalling news arrived, but then they put it
from them and were as lively as usual; but he — when
he came to Downford — used to come and sit with his
niece and Mrs. Aylmer and talk over the horrors that
he had heard. Traditions of the Huguenot persecu-

tions had descended in the family, and he had learnt the history of those later endeavours in the days of the Fronde, which had sent his great-grandfather, as an exiled man, to find a new home in England.

"Every striving after truth, every attempt at justice and mercy has been stifled," he said. "And here is the consequence! God forgive us if we are tempted to run in the same course!"

CHAPTER XVIII

FOR CONSCIENCE' SAKE

Our life is turned
Out of her course, wherever man is made
An offering or a sacrifice.

WORDSWORTH.

In the spring Caroline received a long letter from
Monsieur Beaudésert. He had heard tidings, he said,
which he could not bear to communicate to Mademoiselle de Monfichet; and he therefore begged his
good friend to let her hear them, and have time to recover from the blow before he attempted to see her,
as he hoped to do before taking out his miners to
America in the course of the next month.

He had met in London a gentleman who had formed
part of the army of emigrants in the Low Countries,
which had been defeated at Valmy. From him he had
learnt that the Duke of Drelincourt, Mademoiselle's
brother-in-law, had been killed in that battle, while his
young wife and her little girl were in Germany. The
Marquis de Monfichet and his wife had been taken in
their château, carried to Paris, and their names had
been found in the lists of the *ci-devant* nobility sent to
the guillotine. One of the persons whom Beaudésert's
friend had seen in the Low Countries knew the fact

229

with absolute certainty; so that no loophole for hope remained.

He added that it was no fit time to mention his hopes to Mademoiselle de Monfichet, and, in fact, he had nothing certain to lay before her; but he could not help telling Mrs. Aylmer, who had been so good a friend to them both, that he had taken advice, and obtained an assurance that his hopes might be legally and validly accomplished, though on the side of the Church, the bishop whom he had seen declared that the lady could not be absolved from her vows without reference to the Pope. He expected to have the honour of coming down in the course of the next fortnight to explain the matter, and he could not help entertaining hopes of overcoming her scruples.

The terrible intelligence had to be carried to Félicité. She saw in a moment that there was some such communication to be made to her, and her first question was, "Who is it? Is it all of them?"

Then on the answer came the wholesome showers of tears, more violent perhaps than an Englishwoman's would have been, but evidently a safe outlet. When Caroline ventured to leave her, Mrs. Aylmer was the first to propose that she should go to pour out her sorrows to her friends the nuns and priest at Court Tresham. Caroline might take her thither in a chaise, and, if she were asked, leave her there for a few days.

Accordingly this was done. The poor child accepted the proposal with all the gratitude her choking sobs allowed her to show, and they set out on their melancholy drive; when, after the first mile, she revived enough to talk of her mother's tenderness and her father's petting affection before those unhappy proposals of the Duke of Drelincourt had made everything into bitterness.

She told of them brightly, then relapsed into tears, and when they arrived at the old house with its octagon side, turrets in red brick, and its iguana-like crest of tiles, she fell into a fresh agony of weeping at the thought of what she had to tell the sisters.

Mrs. Tresham was out, but Caroline went upstairs and told the nuns her grievous news, before fetching in Félicité, and their sympathy was vehement—indeed, Sœur de l'Annonciation fainted away on hearing the tidings, but her faintings were not infrequent; and Caroline had not been able to help agreeing with her mother-in-law that they were due, partly to constant fasting and partly to her thinking a swoon the proper tribute to bad news—for she revived in a very short time, and both nuns vied with each other in leading Félicité into the room and weeping over her.

Though the lady of the house was out they made no difficulty about keeping Sœur Philomène, especially as they were sure to *veiller* all night. And so the orphaned girl was left, waiting to see the Abbé and to participate in the masses and prayers that he would offer in the chapel. He was out at this time, having obtained a few pupils in the neighbourhood for French and Latin; but the sisters promised his ardent sympathy, and indeed Mère de St. Hilaire showed herself so much disposed to keep the latest sister for ever that Caroline almost doubted whether she should see her young friend again, and wondered how she should meet Monsieur Beaudésert in that case.

However, at a fortnight's end, the Abbé and Mrs. Tresham brought her back in deep mourning, looking very white and thin, but as cheerful as before. She

was soon on the floor, acting mouse to Eustace's cat,
and her laugh quite scandalised old Mrs. Aylmer, who
truly supposed that it was French to recover the surface spirits so easily. Such a blow, as she truly said,
would have crushed her to the earth for a much longer
time, if not for ever; yet Madame de Henisson did not
seem surprised at the girl's brightness, and readiness
to go out as usual to her pupils. Father and mother
both executed. uncle murdered, brother-in-law killed,
how could she ever be happy again ?

"You should recollect, grandmamma, that they persecuted her dreadfully before she went into the convent, and after that she hardly ever saw them."

"Ah, well! to have painful remembrances would
make it all the worse to me."

"That I think they do, or have done, but it seems to
me that the first days which we did not watch were
spent in grief more violent and more strained than we
should have thought right or becoming fit resignation;
and now the sorrow has in a manner exhausted itself,
and she can look to the present and the future."

"Ah, well! to be sure if that poor unfortunate lover
comes again, there will be no question of duty to parents to stand in the way."

"I doubt whether that has occurred to her," said
Caroline. "She was supposed to die to them as to the
world when she was laid down within that pall."

"Ah. poor thing! I don't understand it, but I suppose you do! At any rate I hope she will see her way
to making the poor man happy."

Caroline wished it most heartily, and in a few days
more Beaudésert arrived by the coach, looking well
and prosperous, though saddened by the news of the
death of the Queen, which had just taken place. He

was not naturally on her side, having heard many of
the over-true tales of her frivolity, and the calumnies
on her character which were afloat not only among
the populace, but among the more disaffected of the
nobility. Moreover, he had learnt that his relations,
Monsieur and Madame Normand, were in prison, in
danger, if not actually denounced by the monster that
had begun to prey upon its own children. But all the
justice and pity of his nature had been roused by the
barbarous history of Marie Antoinette's imprisonment
and trial, though as yet the full atrocities were little
known in England. Madame de Henisson was so
overwhelmed with the tidings that she retired to her
room to weep there, and evidently expected Félicité,
who was gone to give a lesson, to join her in her
seclusion.

But when Félicité came in and found the visitor in
the parlour, though the colour flushed into her cheeks,
so as to give her the one beauty that she lacked, under
her black hat, she did not turn and flee as Caroline
had feared that she would.

She let M. Beaudésert approach, bend low over her
hand and kiss it. He knew English manners too well
to make his greeting either more distantly courteous or
more ecstatic before the eyes of the other ladies, but
his countenance expressed all that he durst not utter.

The first words were, however, on the fatal tidings.
"Ah, yes! I saw it posted up at the bookseller's shop!"
she said. "It is too — too terrible!" and she clasped
her hands as she had done on the news of her own
bereavement. "Ah, there are so many to grieve for,
one knows not how to mourn for any!"

"Truly that is the feeling of all my compatriots
whom I have seen," said Beaudésert.

" Horror upon horror seem to deaden one's mind and feeling," said Caroline.

" Does Madame de Henisson know ? " asked Félicité.

" Yes, she knows all. She has gone to her room," said Caroline.

Félicité moved a step as if she thought she ought to follow, but lingered as Beaudésert began to tell more particulars. It was a gruesome form of approach of love, but yet hearts beat high even while cheeks paled, and tongues spoke of misery and horror; acquaintance and friends were inquired for, and the best answer was uncertainty. The young man's voice of grief and sympathy was drawing them all the closer. Mrs. Aylmer sat and listened, and lifted up her hands in dismay and pity as her daughter-in-law interpreted each frightful piece of intelligence of what may well be called the Reign of Terror. then at the height. Mrs. Aylmer begged M. Beaudésert to remain to dinner, and Félicité went to summon Madame de Henisson, who would not come, having shed too many tears, and given way to too many outbursts to appear. She expected Félicité to remain with her, but the young lady decided that she could not do so out of *bienséance* towards Madame Aylmer, and Cécile admitted the plea, even though she suspected that there were other considerations.

Yet the dinner was, as far as the two guests were concerned, an empty ceremony. Each knew what was coming, and neither could eat, though Beaudésert made not unsuccessful efforts at conversation on matters indifferent. Afterwards, the grandmother escaped to amuse the children, and their mother would have done the same, but that Félicité caught her by the gown and entreated her not to go away, or she must follow; and Caroline was recalled to her French conscience enough to perceive that propriety demanded her presence.

She retired as far as possible into the window-seat, trying to work diligently and to efface herself, but it was not possible not to listen most anxiously, and to be aware that she was witnessing a scene of passionate love such as she had never seen approached, except when her husband had taken her to Drury Lane to see Mrs. Siddons. Theirs had been a quiet, undemonstrative courtship. George Aylmer had come for her as for a property that belonged to him, and she had nestled into his love and tenderness as that which had been lacking to her ever since she lost her father. Her uncle and aunt had been glad enough to give her to him, and nothing could have been more tranquil; though, however, their affection for one another was ardent and constant. Here, however, she saw first Beaudésert eagerly expounding the situation to his lady-love, who sat upright in her chair, her brows contracted over her dark deep eyes, her hand pressed over her lips as if to prevent them from involuntary betrayal, listening to all that he had been able to learn in London, among lawyers of either nation and priests of his own.

Lawyers, English and French alike, had assured him that there was no danger of the legality of their union being disputed, certainly not even in France if there were ever to be a restoration of the old régime. So many clerical personages had married, that there would certainly be no examination into previous vows. What should hinder her being united to him the very next day, and sailing with him in the ship where he had taken his passage, having sent on the miners with their foreman to Charleston in an American ship. He tried to seize her hand to put his ring on her finger, but she held it back. "No, no," she said, "not yet. You have told me what the world says; what does the Church say?"

Priests and bishops alike allowed that there had been very hard treatment, and that the Bishop of Charmilly had no right to stifle the young lady's objections, and to insist that she had a vocation. On that they were agreed, and one of them said that, considering the manner of her compulsory vows, he should not object to marry her, and she might do penance afterwards and get absolved.

"Do penance — what for?" asked Félicité.

"Ah! what know I? For anything the priests choose to lay on a scrupulous conscience."

"What do they lay?"

He talked on, with vehement gesture, of what the priests had no right to say — of enforced half-uttered vows being mockery, and much more; but at last he was brought to tell that all the clergy whom he had been able to consult in London, except that one liberal-minded one, half a Protestant, half an Encyclopedist, had agreed in saying that the tyranny which had compelled the faltering, barely pronounced vows, had been most improper, and contrary to all the safeguards provided by the Order and the Church; but that even thus extracted, as the maiden had accepted herself as bound, and lived the life of a novice first and then of a professed sister, she could not give it up without being solemnly absolved from her pledges as the Bride of Christ, and this — by the constitution of the Order — could only be done by the direct or delegated authority of the Pope. Most reluctantly was this drawn from Beaudésert, and therewith he launched into every imaginable persuasion. The vow was no vow in the sight of Heaven, extracted as it was by absolute compulsion; nay, it had never been uttered at all; she had appealed against it from the first; it was absolutely null and invalid. Why should she drive him to distraction by clinging to it? — him who had loved her fervently from the first. Still she shook her head; she could hardly speak, but she still declared, "Not without absolution."

Then he talked of the new country, where no one would know of her profession, no one would blame her even if they did.

" I should blame myself."

Then he talked wildly of the desperation to which she was driving him. To be rid of the priests and their scruples he would turn heretic or Voltairian, he would plunge into all excesses in his despair, and it would be her doing. His blood would be on her head. Would she not save him? He actually threw himself on the floor, beat his forehead and clutched his hair, so that Caroline looked about to see that there was nothing that he could do himself a mischief with near at hand. Félicité meanwhile shed floods of tears, and murmured, "No, no," and "Je vous prie," at intervals; but finally she seemed to brace herself, drew her dark eyebrows together, made her voice clearer, and said, "To transgress a law of God through the Church cannot bring a blessing. To break a promise to my Lord and Christ, even though forced from me, must be a crime. It would so remain on my conscience."

He broke in, was it not a greater crime to drive him to despair and murder his soul. He swore that ——

She interrupted now. "Silence, sir! To cross one's sense of conscience to save another must be fatal to both. It is a delusion. Listen to me. You *will not act* madly and desperately. You will remain the man whom I learnt to love and esteem. You will go out and do the appointed work that you have undertaken. I will meantime do all that is possible to obtain my release from our holy father the Pope. There is hope now. There is no one to intercept my letters, and if I do not obtain an answer, I will go to Rome as a pilgrim, and throw myself at the feet of the Pope, who, I think, will hear me. Will this content you?"

There was more approach to raving, but the force which Félicité put upon herself evidently constrained her lover, and he ceased to threaten her with his own desperation, only pleading the misery and uncertainty he should suffer after his long years of patience; but he finally accepted her promise, and himself gave his pledge that he would do nothing to render himself unworthy of the favour that she was to obtain, and to which she looked forward with a certain confidence. They even exchanged pledges at last. She did not refuse to wear the gold ring he had brought, in hopes of a closer bond, and she gave him the little pearl cross from her rosary, and made him promise to look at it daily, and remember that she was striving for him.

They parted at last. Félicité fell back in a dead faint, and was very ill for several days, the strength of her resistance telling on her. And Caroline had to defend her, for Mrs. Aylmer thought her scruple all superstition, and very cruel to the poor young man; and there were others who said that it was really shameful to refuse these means of relieving Mrs.

Aylmer of the expense of her maintenance. " Beggars should not be choosers," openly quoted Mrs. Darpent. Indeed Félicité had felt the sting of this herself, for she implored Mrs. Aylmer and Mrs. Tresham to assist her in getting a situation as resident governess or French teacher in a school. But there were far fewer openings for governesses in those days, and French teachers were a drug in the market, and nothing was heard of except the few daily lessons that she gave in the town ; and as her two friends would accept nothing for her board, she saved almost all these scanty gains for her journey to Rome.

There was really no one who did not think her mistaken, except, of course, her friends at Court Tresham, and even they thought the scruples might have given way under such circumstances. The rector came and talked it over with the elder Mrs. Aylmer, and cited the example of Luther, a much more effective one in those days than in the present; but, as Mrs. Aylmer said, Luther and Catharine acted according to their conscience, whether right or wrong, and Mademoiselle de Monfichet was withheld by her conscience, perhaps foolishly, and with a burthen on it wrongly imposed, but anyway to her own great detriment, both of worldly prosperity and of the yearning, loving heart.

" And," said the good old lady, " I cannot help recollecting, ' Whatever is not of faith is sin.' "

" You are right, madam," said the clergyman. " We may be sorry for her, but we must respect her."

And the Abbé at Court Tresham assisted her in writing her appeal to His Holiness, and promised that means should be found for forwarding it, though in the state of the Continent, he could not give her many hopes of its finding its way either quickly or securely.

CHAPTER XIX

What'er my desire is, in thine may be seen,
I am King of this household, and thou art the Queen.
                                    LONGFELLOW.

NEWS, even to those who kept their eyes on the
Gazette, was slow of travelling, and it was with as
much amazement as joy that a letter was received one
morning at Downford, absolutely dated from H. M. S.
Oudenarde, Plymouth harbour. Short and sweet it
was, bearing the tidings that the *Oudenarde* had been
sent from Bombay to carry home the ex-governor.
Captain Aylmer hoped that his wife, and, if possible,
his mother and children, would come down and see
him at once, for he understood that he was likely
to be sent out again immediately to join the fleet in
the Mediterranean, which was endeavouring to assist
the loyalists at Lyons. He was to hoist his flag in the
Leopard, a splendid new ship, as soon as the *Oudenarde*
was paid off. It was time, for she had had a touch
with a hurricane, besides a sharp affair with a French
brig. To describe the gladness and thankfulness of
mother and wife would be impossible; but poor old
Mrs. Aylmer was in the midst of an attack of rheuma-
tism, and both children had whooping-cough, so there
was nothing for it but for Caroline to go alone, laden

with kisses for papa, and the handkerchiefs that Nancy had been hemming for him for the last six months. She travelled by post-chaise to meet the Exeter coach, and in due time, after many a hill had been climbed, many a valley splashed through, the coach drew up at the hotel; and at the same moment one blue-and-gold uniform, one cocked hat, flashed before her eyes, the coach-door was thrown open, and those blue arms were clasping her and lifting her out.

"Oh, George, George!"

"Well, Carry, my love! What, all alone?"

"Grandmamma grieved so! She is rheumatic, and the poor dear children have whooping-cough."

"Never mind. I've got you all the sooner. You're enough for any man! Come on; gig is off the jetty. Better luck than I looked for when I came ashore, though I ran up to meet the coach for the chance. Davis, bring her box down," to the sailor, who touched his hat. "So, old lady, you look — look as pretty a darling as ever you were."

"And oh, George! how brown you are, and how thin!"

"Is that the best word you have for me, madam? Knocking about in the Hooghly is not the way to mend one's complexion."

"But are you well?"

"Well, to be sure! You'll see how we punish the English bread and butter and the fresh beef. And how is my mother? I must run up and see her if only for a day. And the little ones? The boy out of petticoats?"

"Oh yes, and as proud as Punch; says he is Joy's beau. Joy is what they call Félicité de Monfichet. You had my letters about the poor ladies?"

R

"Aye, aye! Quite right to take them in out of the way of those devils let loose!"

By this time they were nearly at the jetty, struggling through the crowd of sailors, fishwomen, bumboat women, and the like, till they came in sight of the trim boat keeping a little off the jetty. Up it came with measured plash of oars. "Oh, that's music!" cried Caroline, and she recognised the boy midshipman she had parted with as the grown man with blue stubbly chin. But a greater surprise awaited her. When they had reached the *Oudenarde*, and she had sprung up the companion ladder with the dexterous hand and foot of one at home in such places, the first person she beheld among the circle of officers drawn up to greet her was no other than Henri Beaudésert himself.

She could hardly listen to the hearty welcomes of the lieutenants and midshipmen, for her astonishment and eagerness to know how he came there.

"I owe my deliverance and life to Monsieur le Capitaine," he answered, bowing low.

"I told you we had a brush with a couple of French brigs off Brest," explained Captain Aylmer. "There she lies — as pretty a brisk little craft as ever I set eyes on, and we found this poor fellow lying in the hold in irons."

"Expecting the guillotine," said Beaudésert; "unless the rogues lost patience, and hung me beforehand to the yardarm. My life, my liberty — everything I owe to Monsieur votre Mari, madame, as I owe all my hopes to you."

"Ah! I found out that you were old acquaintances," said the captain, "though there was no time to prepare this lady for the meeting."

"As joyful as it was astonishing!" said the ever
polite Beaudésert. "May I be permitted to inquire
for all the dear friends at Downford?"

Caroline hastened to reply that she had left all in
good health. She waited for a quieter, less public
moment to give the account of the illness that her
firmness had cost Félicité, and of her actual letter to
the Pope.

All, and a great deal more, had to be explained to
her husband, while they were arranging her accommodation in his cabin. He quite agreed to its having
been perfectly right to receive the poor exiled nuns,
and laughed over the old sailor butler's notions of
duty and discipline to the generous French-Irish
smuggler. As to Félicité de Monfichet, he whistled
a little, and then said, "Pity she could not see her
way to marry the poor young fellow out of hand and
have done with it; but as those Romans call the old
Pope the captain of the ship, and she has sworn to
the articles, she is a good girl to stand by them, and
you were quite right to help her — like your father's
own child. We will do what we can for them in
their fix."

It was not till supper-time that Caroline heard the
story. Beaudésert was the captain's guest, and messed
with him, and the two lieutenants were likewise invited in honour of Mrs. Aylmer's arrival. She was
a great favourite on board, being far too good and
experienced a sailor to give trouble, and the sight
of a lady, after all their months and years at sea, was
no small enjoyment. The governor, whom they had
taken home, was gone off, posting to London, and
there was more ease and space in his absence; so as
they sat round the table, enjoying an English goose,

Devonshire apples, and Devonshire cream, the tale was told how Beaudésert had embarked in an American ship for Charleston, and had made a good voyage for nearly a week, when the *Miriam* was overtaken and boarded by a French brig. The Americans had not attempted resistance, being in alliance with the French, but as there was war with England they had to submit to examination to find whether there were British on board. The crew tried to shelter their passenger by mispronouncing his name, and explaining where he had shipped, and what was his business; but he was claimed as an emigrant and deserter, hauled away, put into irons, and thrown into that noisome den, the hold, where, day after day, the ruffianly crew came to insult him as a bad citizen, an enemy to liberty, only worthy of the guillotine, which was waiting for him as soon as he arrived at Brest. So horrible was the place, so infested by rats, so wretched and scanty the provisions and water, that he almost expected to escape a public death, and wondered how soon his friends would cease to look for news of him and mourn him as dead.

Then came the yells announcing a hostile ship, and the welcome thunder of guns. If a ball actually crashed through the ship's side, and ended his misery, it would have been welcome; but there were other hopes which began to grow upon him, as the cries sounded like consternation amid the shrieks of agony.

As Captain Aylmer and his lieutenant related the history, the *Oudenarde* had been attacked by a flotilla of three brigs, which had ventured to measure themselves with a British frigate. The fight had been sharp, but without loss, and two men still lay wounded. One of the enemy had been blown up, a second crowded

on all sail and escaped, the third had been disabled
and boarded, and the sounds of the trampling, shouts,
falls, and shots penetrated to the dark hole where the
captive lay. Hours passed, or it might have so seemed
to him, during which he heard a gurgling, and began
to feel that the bilge water in the hold was deepening,
while the cries and commands above made it seem as
though the vessel were to be left to founder. He
gave a few shouts of entreaty, then tried to resign
himself to die, truly like a rat, he thought, as the
creatures scuttled over him. A tread came near;
there was a shout demanding if any one was there.
On his response, there was a hasty struggle to get the
way open, and stiff, chilled, loaded with irons, barely
able to help himself, he was dragged out by an English sailor, thrown rather than helped into a boat, and
up the side of the *Oudenarde*, where such of his countrymen as had not been sent below received him with
yells of execration as a deserter, an emigrant.

That was testimony enough to cause his fetters to
be instantaneously struck off by the smith, while a
glass of grog was administered by another hand; and
thus enabled to stand and speak, he made himself
known to the captain, and explained his circumstances, how he had been seized in an American vessel,
after having long been working in the United States.
He also stated that Mistress Aylmer had been a friend
to whom he should be for ever grateful.

Letters were so slow of exchange with India that
Captain Aylmer was no farther on in his wife's history
than the arrival of the nuns. Her letters, telling of
Félicité's affairs and Beaudésert's importunity, were
probably somewhere on the Coromandel Coast looking
for the *Oudenarde*, and the captain was too busy to

understand the nature of M. Beaudésert's obligations, only that there was some extra claim of friendship. Indeed, the liberated prisoner was so ill from the sufferings he had endured in that horrible den that he had only come from his berth the morning before the arrival at Plymouth, and as he sat at the table he looked ten years older than when Caroline had parted with him at Downford — thin, worn, and haggard, coughing painfully, and the marks of the irons on his wrists.

He was glad to retire early; and the lieutenant left the captain and his wife to consultation. What was to be done with him? It was now late in October, and very few vessels plied between the United States and England in the winter, nor indeed did poor Beaudésert seem to be in a state of health for the discomforts of an autumn voyage in a chance merchant ship, nor for beginning his mining work, which in point of fact would have to wait to commence in earnest till the spring.

"In fact," said Captain Aylmer, who had taken a fancy to him, and wanted to understand his plans of electric conductors, "the wisest way would be for him to take a trip in the *Leopard*. Will you have him for a guest, Carry, and add to the favours of madame?"

For the idea had been already started, but scarcely examined, that Caroline should accompany her husband as far as Gibraltar. Wives were not at that time absolutely prohibited articles on board, especially for short voyages. It was intended that the *Leopard* with other ships should reinforce Lord Hood's fleet, then endeavouring to succour the loyalists of Toulon; but Captain Aylmer meant to drop his wife at Gi-

braltar, and let her establish herself there while he
was cruising in the Mediterranean. She had been
enchanted at the proposal, without quite promising to
remain contentedly at Gibraltar if he was to go into
action; but at any rate it was better than being in
England, and now she wanted to take her children.
"I was away from them a whole year, and only think
of their growing up without knowing either of us —
poor little dears! And it would be so good for them
after the whooping-cough!"

"Ah, poor things! Poor mother! Sailors' wives
have sometimes to choose between husband and children! What do you say, Carry?"

"I want my husband, and my children want me!
Ah, and I want them too! Can't I have both?"

"Well, we must see what space we find on board
the *Leopard*, and what my mother says, — yes, and
what the officers may think of a nursery on board."

"Oh, they always like children. Besides it is only
for a fortnight."

The *Leopard* came round from Portsmouth, and
proved to be a splendid ship, with plenty of accommodation. As soon, however, as the crew were paid off,
and a few of them had declared their willingness to
sail again with their captain — but he went previously
to London to report himself to the Admiralty — Caroline was dropped on the way at Exeter to cross to
Downford, and make her arrangements; and Beaudésert remained at Plymouth with the ship's surgeon to
recruit.

Old Mrs. Aylmer was very averse to her going with
her husband, and still more to her taking the children,
representing that Nancy was too old to be made the
pet of a ship's company, and to have her education

standing still; and reminding Caroline of certain episodes which had given her more trouble than the young lady herself.

But Eustace — he had pined for his mother before, he looked as if he would pine again, he was a delicate child, and the cough hung about him; and Caroline was sure that the southern climate would be good for him. When his father came home for three days, all that he could allow himself, he soon decided that it would be best to take the boy to be heartened up, and to be Caroline's comfort if she were left in solitude at Gibraltar; but to leave the little girl to cheer her grandmother, and "sew her sampler."

He was devotedly attached to his Caroline, and had loved her from what she sometimes called her " reefer times "; but somehow he did not want to see them repeated in his daughter, and Mrs. Darpent gave him her approval, only wishing he would keep her niece at home. " She was too fond of gadding about in foreign parts."

Caroline was considering whether to take Zélie, or leave her to attend on Madame de Henisson, and take the whole charge of the little boy, when Félicité came to her room with the entreaty, " Oh, madame, I entreat you, let me go with you as *bonne* to the dear little Eustace."

" You, Félicité ? "

" Yes, dear madame, I entreat you.   He will want a *bonne*, and I would dress him and teach him, and watch over him when you are occupied.   Think; I have been looking at the map, and there is only a stretch of sea between Gibraltar and Rome.   It would be so far on my way.   Oh, I entreat you! — you who have always been my best friend, the only person who gave me hope."

To which Caroline could only answer, "We must see what the captain says."

The captain whistled, then said, "That young mamselle, is it? Poor Beaudésert's love, eh? Well, I'm not the man to hinder the course of true love, only she must not hinder him from putting his conductors, or what you may call them, in order, in case we should fall in with a gale of wind and thunder. Don't let 'em be philandering together."

"Never fear, she is much too correct a person. Besides, she has undertaken to look after Eustace."

"You imagine she will," said the captain, smiling.

"Of course I do. She is determined enough, as I have often seen. Besides, he has me. Zélie is really too old, and a young nursemaid —— "

Captain Aylmer held up his hands and laughed at the notion of a young nurse. So Félicité was accepted; though, as her friends observed, the way to Rome was not exactly clear from French ships or Algerian pirates.

And the captain, after a few days at Downford, went on to Plymouth, to be followed by Caroline and little Eustace with Félicité so soon as he was ready to sail, in fact as soon as he had done his press-gang work. This was by no means entirely the cruel kidnapping of peaceable fishermen, or even landsmen, of which we are told, but a kind of hide-and-seek with veteran sailors who fully meant to ship again, but were bent on their frolic to their utmost, and made it a matter of honour to give the officers as much trouble as possible. It was a brutal captain, or one hard pressed for men, who would not listen to the plea of being unfairly captured; and George Aylmer was liked enough to make up his crew without much difficulty. Thus by the first week in November he was able to summon his wife, child, and "*bonne*" to join him, as well as Beaudésert, who had written to Georgia to explain that he hoped to come out in the spring, when the working of the mines would begin. Meantime he supplied the masts of the *Leopard* with lightning conductors, such as anticipated the apparatus with which the navy is at present supplied.

CHAPTER XX

But I heard on the gale a sound of wail,
And tears came to my eye.

UHLAND.

BEAUDÉSERT's conductor had a trial sooner than was expected, for a terrible storm overtook the *Leopard* when she was scarcely beyond the Channel. Of course no one could tell where lightning would have 'fallen, but it was all in a blue glare round the ship; and the boatswain and his fellows, who had been most averse to "that there Frenchy's conundrums," and had almost thought them a device for betraying them to the enemy, were fain to confess that they had seen the lightning run down the line into the sea, and the mast remained unshattered. The captain declared that he believed it owing to his guest that he was not putting into Falmouth for repairs, instead of beating round Cape Finisterre a good deal closer than he wished.

Caroline saw little of him just then. She was too practised a seafarer not to know that the best thing she could do was to keep out of the way, and ask no questions; and though thunder and waves roared fiercely round her, and she was dashed about the cabin in a furious manner whenever she endeavoured to change her position, she still consoled her frightened

251

boy and the still more frightened Félicité by declaring that if there were pressing danger her husband would come or send. Poor Félicité had been miserably ill ever since they had passed the Sound, and was prepared to think that a reluctant, half-emancipated nun was a kind of Jonah, who might sink the ship by her guilt; and Caroline had fairly to laugh at the morbid fancy, and call on her to join in prayer.

A midshipman was sent down at last to tell the ladies that the danger from the storm was over, and that very little damage had been done, but the captain could not come, as they had been driven over near to the rocks of Brittany, and all his seamanship would be needful to prevent being wrecked, or driven into the jaws of the French. The lad told Mrs. Aylmer so in an important whisper, and it made her shudder with the thought of the fight, possibly unequal, and the peril to the two fellow-travellers.

However, the gale did not cease with the tempest, and the same wind that blew them towards Brest hindered French ships from coming out; while it kept poor Félicité a wretched captive to her berth, all over bruises. Eustace, in his mother's arms, had fared better, and was fast asleep when his father came down with news that the worst was over, and though the sea was rough the wind had veered round, and they were scudding merrily before the breeze, and he should be glad if they were past the mouth of the Loire before daylight, as no one could tell what vessels might be lying off Nantes, and they were too near to the coast. When the tide turned, the current of the Loire would not help them, so he was crowding on all sail.

Daylight had come; and Caroline ventured on deck,

carrying her weary, sleepy little boy for a breath of fresh air. His father came to meet her, and took the child in his arms, while he said, "Very good, Carry, you have learnt to be a sailor's wife."

"It was very dreadful, but I had to be comforting poor Félicité, and could not think about myself," said Caroline, as she leant against the bulwark.

"And this young reefer, too," said the captain. "What do you think of the white horses, sir?"

"I don't see their faces, papa," said the boy. "I wish they wouldn't jump up and down so, and shake the ship."

"They must, my man, till we get beyond the Bay of Biscay, oh! So much the better, or we should have you flattening that little nose against the bars of a French prison."

"Is that France, or is it a fog-bank?" asked Carry, as the sun rose in his glory above a grey outline.

"France it is, bad luck to it, and I'd fain give it a wider berth." Then followed some shouted orders, and "Aye, aye, sir!" and the like, and a cry from the masthead, "Boat astern!"

Eyes and glasses were directed in the direction, where a speck was seen tossing on the waves, apparently carried helplessly outwards between the ebbing tide and the current of the river.

"From a wreck!" said some.

"Shall we lower a boat?" said the first lieutenant.

The chances were for a moment debated. The ship must lie to, to enable the boat to examine the forsaken fragment and then overtake the ship again; and to tarry so near off the French coast involved peril.

"And all for the sake of a brutal murderer of a Frenchy," as the sailors murmured.

But Captain Aylmer would not hear. He had confidence in his *Leopard* and her crew, and he remembered that the good Samaritan had tarried within reach of the robbers; so the boat was sent off under the command of the second lieutenant, and anxious were the eyes that watched it, while the motion of the ship made Eustace complain that she jumped more than ever, and his father had to carry him up and down. Rising on the crests of the billows, then disappearing, the boat made its way, evenly in the midst of the swell, and by and by the glasses disclosed that the rescue party had reached the broken shattered remnant, reduced almost to a spar, and that a figure was being, with great difficulty, lifted from it, and lay prone at the bottom of the boat. Then rowing swiftly, the return was made — Beaudésert, who had come on deck on the report of what was passing, forgetting all his *"mal de mer"* in the intense interest of watching the arrival.

"He's alive, sir," shouted the lieutenant; "unless he died after we picked him up," he added anxiously, for the figure, that of an elderly man, with ragged grey hair, and a still more ragged black dress, was quite helpless, and the face deadly white, the eyes closed, when hoisted up and laid on the deck. The surgeon called for spirits, Caroline chafed the hands, Beaudésert raised the head. "Here are signs of the tonsure," he said; "it is a priest."

The spirits were put between the pale lips, it was swallowed in part, and the first murmur was — "*De profundis clamavi.*"

"Ah!" said Beaudésert, "you need not fear that he is a Jacobin. He is nearer being a martyr."

The poor priest, under the tender hands of the lady

and Beaudésert, and the somewhat ruder ministrations
of the surgeon, a rough-and-ready fellow, presently
murmured again, "*In manûs tuas*," but after another
interval opened his eyes, and looking round in utter
confusion, said, "It is not paradise!"

"No, not yet, *mon père*," returned Beaudésert. "It
is an English ship, where you are safe."

"Ah, it is a miracle — praise and thanks!"

They carried him to a berth, and changed his
clothes, giving him food as he could bear it, and re-
fraining from questions till he had slept.

It was not till the next morning, when the sea had
subsided, and the *Leopard* had recovered the ordinary
bearings, that Beaudésert came into the state-cabin,
where breakfast was laid, and to the inquiries for his
patient, replied, "He will be here in a few moments.
He is the Abbé Casaforte, originally from Antibes,
but on a mission to Nantes, where he has undergone
even more horrible cruelty than I had heard of yet at
the hands of my miserable countrymen. He is delivered by a true miracle. Shall I present him to you,
madame?"

"Is he enough recovered?"

"He wishes to come. I have dressed him as best I
might, but he is very weak, and much exhausted. I
have not heard all his story, but there must have been
frightful atrocities at Nantes. He had broken sleep
at first, muttering fragments of the prayers for the
dying, and names of others."

There was a knock at the door, and with the word
"*benedicite*" there came forward an elderly man, pale,
haggard, and wasted, his limbs trembling, and his white
hair trimmed (after Beaudésert's best abilities) into the
clerical tonsure, his dress an adaptation of Beaudésert's.

All rose in reverence to misfortune, and Félicité threw herself on her knees to crave his blessing, and long, worn, bony fingers were held over her head. "Thanks to God, I am among the faithful! Ah, sir! ah, madame! how shall I express my gratitude?"

"Let that pass," said the captain. "Make him sit down, Carry; tell him he is the best prize I could have taken in these waters, and it is we that are thankful."

The two ladies, with ready tender words, persuaded him to sit in the easiest chair, and drink a cup of coffee before he attempted to say more than something about a true miracle. Beaudésert, who knew a little more, then said, "Monsieur l'Abbé tells us of the utter overthrow of the loyalists in La Vendée."

"I feared they would never stand against regular troops," returned the captain.

"No, truly; save for their noble devotion we should call it madness," said Beaudésert.

"The madness of saints," said the priest, understanding his words in part. "Ah, you should have seen them and watched them, Lescure, La Rochejacquelein, Bonchamp, Cathelineau — true martyrs."

"You were among them, Father?" ventured Félicité.

"I was sent on a message of encouragement from the Holy Father to the resolute clergy," replied the Abbé. "I have the honour to be secretary to Monsignore della Crusca, and as French is native to me, I was selected, and thus witnessed heroic courage and piety worthy of the first ages of the Church."

"And you were taken, monsieur?" asked Mrs. Aylmer.

"Yes, madame, the Blues surrounded the village where we had taken refuge, and we surrendered in hopes of obtaining mercy for the women and children. Alas, no! We could hardly give them absolution before they were mowed down by the muskets, the little innocents in their mothers' arms! Ah, they are with the Babe of Bethlehem! We were marched with hands tied together to Nantes, and there thrown into a loathsome vault beneath a church, where hundreds of us pined in misery till there came down from Paris an executioner rather than a commissioner — one Carrier. He devised a readier way than even the guillotine of ridding the prisons of their population. There was no tribunal. We were simply taken out in boats upon the Loire, tied together, a plank was removed, a door opened, and there we were! I was one of a troop of ninety-four thus disposed of!"

"The fiend!" cried Captain Aylmer, as he understood.

"The monster!" exclaimed Caroline.

"Ah! rather say the miserable given up to demons," said the victim.

"But how did you escape, Father?" asked Félicité.

"At Antibes the boys are well-nigh amphibious. I am the son of a trader between that port and Genoa, and I had not forgotten my old powers of diving and swimming. We were taken out at night, as many as the boat was able to hold, whispering absolution to one another, while our guards blasphemed. God forgive them; they knew not what they said. A dear brother was with me; we exchanged a kiss; we were the last in our boat. No doubt the ropes were used up; ours was rotten, and broke even as we fell. The water restored my old instincts. I let myself sink, and swam on as far as I could under water, then floated so as to be undistinguishable from the bodies

s

that, alas! likewise floated. It was night, and by the
time my strength was exhausted I was beyond the
environs of Nantes. I landed on the other bank, and
by and by Heaven guided me to the hovel of a good
Bretonne woman, who gave me food and sheltered me;
but the Blues were apt to search her house. She
could not keep me, but she showed me where lay the
broken remains of a boat, which, by the help of a
couple of old oars, might carry me down the river —
perhaps to a fisher's boat, perhaps to the dwellings of
merciful folk. I drifted on, but no sooner had I
reached the sea than the tempest came on. My oars,
already frail, were broken and swept from me. I was
tossed hither and thither, and gave myself up for lost;
yet by divine mercy the boat did not fill, and kept
afloat till the weather calmed, but I was past knowing
when or how. M. le Capitaine's goodness and courage completed the miracle of my safety. Oh, for
what can God reserve me among so many?"

It was known later that among the thousands, literally thousands, who perished in the *noyades* of Carrier
at Nantes, men, women, and children alike, only one
was known to have escaped or half escaped, a priest
named Brianceau, who swam out like Casaforte,
reached land, but was given up by the wretched peasants to the murderers, who threw him in again with
his hands cut off, to prevent his being able to swim.

CHAPTER XXI

Ever as Earth's wild war-cries heighten,
The Cross upon the brow will brighten.

KEBLE.

CASAFORTE'S history was listened to with tears of burning indignation and sympathy, such as could only find utterance in such words as Milton's —

Avenge, O Lord, thy slaughtered saints, whose bones
Lie scattered on the Alpine mountains cold.

Caroline and Félicité longed to get farther out on the Atlantic, always imagining that dead corpses might be washed up against the ship; and the Abbé spent all his time in prayer for his brethren who might still be perishing at the ferocious hands of the boatmen and the cruel behest of Carrier.

All his own books and clothes had been taken from him, and he was glad to borrow Félicité's breviary. He also asked, with some apologies, if madame had not an English Bible. He could read very little English himself, though it appeared that he had been at one time in the establishment of Cardinal de York, or as he said with a smile, Henry IX. of England, though the good old gentleman never allowed himself to be called by that title.

What the priest wanted was to have the terrible tenth chapter of Ezekiel found for him, and where

the angel with the inkhorn marks those who are not
delivered to those with the slaughter weapon. He
could not read the English, but Caroline translated it
to him. He clasped his hands and said, " Ah, verily,
it is as though the angels with the weapons of death
had been let loose in our miserable country; and who
am I, and for what am I reserved by God, that I
should be saved alive out of so many ? I know not
that I have grieved at popular sins more than they."

The fact seemed especially to overcome him; he
could not believe himself anything like so good a
man as some of the victims, and then he thought himself unworthy to be a martyr like them, and hoped
that he should do some future work, if he did not win
a crown like theirs.

He spent all the time he could in prayer, and
Félicité often joined in his devotions, and Beaudésert
likewise once a day. When he joined the company
in the state-cabin he showed himself a thoroughly
agreeable man of the world, full of conversation, and
trying to keep from recalling too many melancholy
recollections of the noble loyalists of La Vendée and
their fate.

Ere long he knew the whole past history of Beaudésert and Félicité, backed by the captain's declara-
tion that he believed the safety of his ship to be owing
to the former, for had not the boatswain, the chief
grumbler against "that there Frenchy with his devil-
ments," sworn that he had seen the blue-forked flame
light a-top of the flagstaff, and instead of shattering
the mast, run down bodily into the sea ? "As to the
Mounseer having whistled up the storm, don't talk to
me!" Thus the captain was anxious to do anything
for Beaudésert, and the Abbé Casaforte was equally

ready to do anything for the captain. In fact he took such interest in the story, and showed so much sympathy, that Caroline could not help guessing that disappointment in some such love-story might have had its part in making a priest of the amphibious son of the skipper of Antibes.

On arriving at the Lion Rock of Gibraltar the first news that the *Leopard* met was disappointing. New vigour and strategy had been developed by the Jacobin besiegers of loyal Toulon, under the guidance, in fact, of that rising young captain of artillery, Napoleon Bonaparte. Point Grasse had been seized, and the fire thence so directed that the allied fleets — English, Spanish, and Neapolitan — had been obliged to retreat, after blowing up as much as possible of the fortifications, and trying to destroy the French fleet.

Every one in the English service was absolutely convinced that it was all the fault of the chicken-hearted Spaniards. Perhaps they were not far wrong; but plentiful abuse was showered on the allies in the little house on the slope of the hill where Caroline Aylmer had taken her boy and Félicité, while the *Leopard* was refitting after the storm, which had tried her severely, and waiting for further orders from Admiral Lord Hood.

Naval and military society gathered there, much to her enjoyment, and every day vessels were coming in with reports of the siege, and with freights of fugitives from Toulon, where 15,000 persons, who could reasonably believe themselves to be obnoxious to the Committee of Public Safety (*i.e.* of public desolation), had been embarked on board the allied fleets. The victors, however, were not to be balked of slaughter, and killed promiscuously on their bursting into the city, beginning with two or three hundred Jacobins, who had come out in procession to receive them.

It was very difficult to dispose of such numbers of fugitives. Savoy was far from safe, and the most part were landed in Spain or Naples, for Genoa and Tuscany were divided between mortal fear and sympathy with the Revolution; and wherever the poor creatures went, it was destitution to once prosperous families.

One day Captain Aylmer brought up with him a friend, saying that he had a request to make. "I understand," said the sailor, "that you speak French as easily as English."

"Certainly, I was educated in a French convent."

"Then you would be able to speak to my poor passengers. I brought away three of them at the last — born ladies by the cut of their jib — just in time, for their house had a mine under it; but I cannot for the life of me understand what they want. One points to England on the map, and another to Rome, and that's the utmost I can make out!"

Caroline gladly undertook to solve the good commander's perplexity, and presently was enjoying the motion she professed to like above all, the measured beat of the sailors' oars, wafting her over the smooth waves of the harbour, while she listened to the ever-repeated tale of the inefficiency of the Spaniards.

"Well done, madam. Plain to see you are a sailor's daughter," laughed the commander, as she sprang up the side of the *Woodcock* without assistance, followed by her husband and himself. In another minute he had introduced her into what was properly his own cabin, now given up to the three ladies who rose politely at her entrance. Behold, in one of them she

saw the Prioress of Ste. Lucie! There was a cry of
delight on both sides, and they flew into each other's
arms, both sobbing for joy and grief together.

"Old friends, it seems," observed the two captains,
hastily retreating.

"*O ma mère, ma bonne mère reverende!*" cried Caroline. "How little I ever thought to see you again!
Is Sœur Françoise here?"

"Alas! no; she is with the saints, *la bien heureuse.*
These are my cousins at Toulon, Madame de Jolimont,
Mademoiselle de Frémont. Let me present Mistress
Aylmer." They curtseyed, as in convent days, and the
Prioress eagerly asked for the other sisters.

"All well: the two mothers are with Catholic friends
in England; Félicité is here at Gibraltar with me."

"The good God be praised who has left us a remnant; and our good father, the Abbé, did he escape?"

Caroline told of his arrival at Downford, but then
asked eagerly how the Prioress had come to this place
of safety. She looked sadly aged and worn, and wore
no remnant of a monastic habit; though her dress,
very shabby and stained like that of her friends', was
the costume of a lady.

She told what was known already, of the death of
Mère de St. Dominique, and then of her own attempt
with Sœur Françoise to reach Anjou. "There is no
telling how brave and good she was. She looked rav-
ishing in her peasant's dress, her little short curls
peeping out under her white cap, and her figure like
that of one of the shepherdesses of Watteau, only that
her face was more and more like that of a saint; and
she was always cheerful and joyous, treating all our
little adventures as matters of mirth, and keeping up
my courage with her unfailing hope. Ah! it was not

hope of anything here below that inspired her; yet how merry she was when that old peasant offered us a ride in his rough country cart. While I could only think how my poor bones were shaken, so that my teeth might almost fall out, there was she making friends with him and learning the names of all his grandchildren! That night we slept in his cottage, and were treated with distinguished care by his daughter-in-law; but on the next night we were less happy. I fear our disguise was too easily penetrated, for as we sat outside a little country cabaret, eating our bread and drinking wine under the vine, two fellows in red caps came out and denounced us as *ci-devants* attempting to emigrate. We had no passports to show, and a *gen d'armes* was called, who took us in a cart rougher still to Chartres, and there accused us; and we were sent back to Paris, and thrown into the Luxembourg—Françoise all the time, as bright as could be, almost disarming our guards by her good-humoured submission. '*Comment ?*' said one. 'Other women weep and lament, and give as much trouble as possible, but you, *citoyenne* (he tutoyed her, the wretch), have taken it all in good part.'

"'And why not?' she asked; 'you do not want to hurt us, monsieur; you are too good; you are only obeying orders, and doing your duty.'

"The poor man muttered his doubts whether it were his duty, and consoled himself and us by declaring that our detention could only last a short time, till the Convention were convinced that we were harmless.

"So, indeed, we believed at the time, little imagining that the monsters who had tasted blood were about to revel in it. He became very friendly to us; and Sœur Françoise, finding that he had a bad hurt on

one arm from a bite of the horse, which was getting
much inflamed and very sore, undertook to bathe and
dress it, with some help and direction from me, made
a poultice for it at night, and gave him infinite relief,
so that he declared that '*la petite*,' as he always called
her, ought to have been a poor man's wife or a sister
of charity. When he gave us up to the authorities,
such as they are, at Paris, he told us to reckon on him
if he could do anything for us.

"We found ourselves in the old palace of the
Luxembourg, converted into a prison, and full of the
most noble — the Duchess de Tarente, Monsieur and
Mademoiselle de Cazotte, with many ladies and priests;
and we were not ill-treated, and were glad to be with
friends. We were too much crowded, five or even
ten ladies in one room, and the air in these summer
months was most oppressive and very foul, so that
there was much illness. Sœur Françoise attended
those who were sick most tenderly, and filled them
with her own resignation and even gladness. She
loved to tell them of St. Perpetua and other blessed
saints, in whose steps she said it was granted to us
to tread. For rumours reached us of the arrival of
the Marseillais tigers, and there were whispers that
something dreadful was intended. The jailer, who
had been good to us, removed his wife and children
from the prison. We all prepared for death before
the priests. Dinner was served to us earlier than
usual. You may imagine what appetite we had for
it; and when we had done, all the knives and forks
were taken away. Then began sounds of the tocsin,
and horrid shouts and howls in the streets. The turn-
keys said that the people were trying to force the
gates; but it was three hours before they succeeded.

A good priest collected some of us round him, and
chanted the Miserere and other psalms as for the
dying. How sweetly Françoise's voice sounded in
the responses! As evening fell all the women were
separated from the men, and shut into one large room ;
but through the windows we heard savage roars and
howls, mixed with cries and groans. The jailer told
us that he had been obliged to abandon some of the
priests to the fury of the Marseillais in order to slake
their thirst.

" ' Our holy fathers ! ' we cried.

" ' Let us sing of their triumph ! ' exclaimed Françoise, and she began to sing —

> Cælestis O Jerusalem,
> Mansura semper civitas,
> O ter beati quæ tuis
> Cives reconditi mœnibus.

" You know how she loved those hymns in the
breviary, and the sweet young voice went on, verse
after verse, through all the terrible sounds, and the
shrieks and sobs of the women within. She only
paused to go and try to soothe a poor lady whose
brother had been called out to the slaughterers, and
as she looked up and declared that she knew the
angels were flocking to bear away the happy spirits,
her face was as the face of one of them. At first
we thought the women safe, and that it was only the
priests and gentlemen who were dying on the plea of
conspiring with the emigrant army. Alas ! by and by
names of ladies were called, and mine came at last,
my own original name, which I hardly recognised,
Françoise de St. Luc. My dear daughter clung to
me, whether mistaking really or wilfully I cannot

tell. I bade her go back into the hall, but she said,
' No, no — with you, with you, mother'; and linked
her arm in mine as we were hurried along between
men armed with sabres and pikes, along a dark entry
to the turnkey's chamber, where behind a table sat a
man stained with blood, ferocious-looking beyond description, who demanded our names and occupations.
As we answered, he howled at us, ' Maintainers of
unnatural superstition! About to join the enemy,
traitors to liberty and their country!' Something
we said in answer of having refused to leave the
country because we were attending a dying sister;
but he shouted us down, and cried, ' Go, go back!
Push them out.'

" But another voice, close to my ear, said, ' No, no.
That is destruction! I will get you through. Come,
petite.' Then I knew it was the friendly *gen d'armes*.
I clung to him and shut my eyes to avoid the horrible
visages, and the weapons streaming with blood. We
struggled through, I know not how, only that I hung
upon his arm, and heard him answer one after another
who pushed against us, till, after a final crush, we were
in the open street, and then — O heavens! — I was alone
with him. I cried out, ' My child, my daughter!' I
heard him say ' *Hein!* it is not *la petite*.' I believe I
fainted. I think he carried me into a back street, for
when I came to myself an old woman was bending over
me, sprinkling me with water. It was a cellar, scarcely
lighted, for the shutters were shut to keep out the terrible sounds. She told me that Jean was gone back to
endeavour to save the other, but — oh, it was too late!
Sick with horror I lay on the floor till the good man
returned, and striking his forehead cried, ' Too late!
too late! Alas, the angel!' Then when he could

speak, he told how, in the thickest of the crush in the passage, near the fatal door, he heard a voice say, 'It cannot be both. Take her. I follow.' He thought it was I who spoke, as indeed it should have been. I blame myself for ever, but I was hardly conscious. She had turned aside, she let herself be dragged into that dreadful court. There the angels were waiting for her, there she fell beneath those pikes." The Prioress sobbed so much that she could not speak, and Caroline wept with her over the sweet life so heroically closed in the true spirit of martyrdom. How little had they thought when they heard her vows that they would be so fulfilled.

When the Prioress was able to finish her history, she said that after the massacres of September there was a comparative pause, and the old woman, the mother of the *gen d'armes,* had been able to conduct her in tolerable security to a house where her daughter and her husband were left as concierges. They sheltered her for a few days, and as she had decided on going to Toulon, where she had relations, they helped her to the dress of a *bourgeoise,* and obtained a pass for her in that character, sending her off by diligence. She had never been stripped of the means that she had secured in the break-up of the convent, and these were honest people, shocked at the atrocities around them. Her friends at Toulon made her welcome, and she had lived with them and shared in the reaction of the south against the cruelties of the north. Then had come the savage vindictive ire of the Parisians, when Couthon wreaked his ruthless fury upon Lyons, and Toulon trembled at the frightful reports, and the decree that all who resisted the republic must perish. The help of the allied fleets was accepted, but had not

proved as effectual as was hoped; and when the be-
sieging army of "patriots" was directed by what
proved to be a master hand, hope failed, and there
was nothing to be done but to embark all those who
were in any special danger in the allied fleets, hoping
that the rest might be spared. The Prioress and her
two cousins, having no man to protect them, had
nearly been crowded out of the boats taking out the
fugitives, and had only at the last moment been
brought on board the *Woodcock*.

CHAPTER XXII

Yet nothing stern was she in cell,
And the nuns loved their Abbess well.

SCOTT.

IT was necessary to dispose of the three ladies on shore, and as there was a Spanish nunnery not far from the lines, it was decided that they should seek shelter there. Caroline much wished to keep the Prioress, but she felt sure that as she belonged to the same order of sisters, her presence would be needful as an introduction. Caroline promised to bring Sœur Philomène, as the mother still called Félicité, to see her the next day; and Beaudésert, who had picked up a little Spanish in the course of his wanderings, went beside the little mule carriage in which they travelled, to speak for them. Beaudésert returned in time, somewhat angered, for it had not been a ready welcome that the poor exiles had met with. The Spanish nuns seemed to have a general idea that all the French were rebels, murderers, regicides, if not "Luteranos"; and though the Prioress, Madame de Ste. Lucie as he called her, had convinced the portress, and afterwards the Superior by the passwords of the Order that she belonged to them, they were horribly disgusted by her secular apparel, and could not understand that it had been necessary even in Toulon, which in fact had been more like the Girondin republicans than actually loyal.

They had taken all the three in for a few days at the utmost, on Beaudésert's assurance that means for disposing of them elsewhere should be found as soon as possible. He had found out on the way that one lady wanted to join her son and daughter-in-law, whom she believed to be in London, and that another had relations at Madrid, while Madame de Ste. Lucie wished to go to Rome to present herself to the head of the Order, and give such account as she could of her "daughter in religion." "Indeed," said M. Beaudésert, "I am glad of it, for if she will give a candid account of the coercion used with Mademoiselle de Monfichet, nothing would tell so much in our favour."

"Ah!" exclaimed Caroline, "I verily believe that Providence has brought us all together for the purpose."

"And the generous goodness of the best of friends," returned Beaudésert, with deep sincerity if with much gallantry of manner. All the next morning was spent by him and Captain Aylmer in looking for a vessel to transport Madame de Jolimont to England; and at length they found one of the swift "orange vessels," which made their voyage too quickly to be caught by Moorish pirates or French privateers. The poor thing would be very uncomfortable, but it would not last long, and it could not be helped. The other lady was despatched with a sort of caravan of muleteers to Seville, where she would find a coach to take her to her friends, to whom she had written, and who per-

haps would meet her there. The Prioress would be
the Aylmers' guest.

"Poor woman, let her come," said the captain, "we
shall not be the worse for it. She was your school-
mistress, Carry, and I would give a good deal more
than an old lady's board to get your pretty little
Félicité out of this tangle they have made for themselves, though I can't for the life of me see why the
poor things should not get Casaforte to marry them
out of hand and make the old Pope give leave when
it was done."

"As if you would serve Lord Hood in that way,"
exclaimed Caroline, with a little playful slap.

But the captain, when on shore, was the most courteous and hospitable of hosts, and the Mother Prioress,
though she knew not a word of his language, could
not help contrasting his gentle, respectful tone with
that of the Spanish nuns, from whom she was glad to
escape; for they were nearly ready to make her do
penance for being willing to consort with "Luteranos";
and really she thought that save for the neighbourhood of the English, she might have had to give an
account of her faith to an official of the Inquisition.
She suspected, too, that they were poor, for though
there were splendid jewels and plate in the chapel,
and the meals were served on silver, there had appeared no food but beans dressed with oil and garlic.
The convent of Ste. Lucie had kept the rule; but with
the daintiness of French cookery and after all the
mother's terrible experiences, the bill of fare of Santa
Eulalia could not but be remembered with disgust,
coming as it did, when she needed refreshment after
the disorders of the voyage. But she was a good
woman, and this time of chastening had caused her to

leave behind her much of the worldliness of Madame
de Ste. Lucie, bred up to keep terms with the nobility
and higher clergy, and to manage her estates and their
tenants. She shared the same room with Félicité, and
Caroline suspected that they wept together all night.
Little Eustace, who had believed grown-up people
never cried, had his opinions on that head a good deal
modified; for the two ex-nuns could hardly speak of
their sisters without tears. The Prioress knew the
fate of some who had joined their own families, but
of others she was uncertain; and it was a great consolation to see one of her daughters and to know that
two more were in such good quarters.

But the real comfort was with the Abbé Casaforte.
Both he and the Prioress met as those delivered won-
drously from the very jaws of death, where so many
had perished; and the lady with the additional sense
that her life had been, all unwittingly to herself, pur-
chased by the self-sacrifice of her companion, whom
plainly the *gen d'armes* thought he was saving.

Of their fellows they could only think in the words
of the Book of Wisdom, "In the sight of the unwise
they seemed to die, and their departure was taken for
misery, and their going from us to be utter destruction, but they are in peace."

The Prioress told Caroline that there was nothing
for which she so thanked Heaven as that Félicité de
Monfichet was not sharing her perils, and that the sin
which had pressed most severely on her conscience
had been her connivance at the compulsion which
had brought about the young girl's reluctant profession. Everything had pressed her. She was a relation of the Monfichet family herself, quite near enough
to feel a personal interest in their affairs, and to be

T

willing to do anything to avert the disgrace of the *mésalliance*, and to save a large proportion of the daughter's *dot* for the son and heir. On the other hand the convent was poor enough to make the portion a matter of importance, and the Bishop of Charmilly impressed on her that it was a duty to overcome the sinful scruples of the recreant maiden. So with severity, that she then thought her duty, but by and by beheld as mere worldliness, she had silenced entreaties and representations from the girl, she had suppressed appeals, and answered for the vocation that was utterly wanting, all as she thought piously for the good of the child and of the Church.

Such fallacies had fallen away from her as she crouched in a corner of the Luxembourg in momentary expectation of the pike. It was brought home to her the more what *was* a true vocation, as the devoted virgin, as she watched Sœur Françoise. Through all they had undergone together, the whole impression left on her mind was of the maiden's perfect happiness and unfailing joy, even to that last smile of encouragement with which she went to her death.

And now it was with extreme joy that she learnt that such expiation might be open to her as the power of pleading for the release of Félicité from her vows, and of giving her own testimony to their imperfect utterance.

"Truly," she said to Mrs. Aylmer, "it would seem as if my life had been given to me in the stead of that sweet martyr that I might be able to plead for the undoing of the wrong to those poor lovers, and thus atone in part for my share in the sin."

As the Prioress meant to go to Rome, where were

the headquarters of her Order, Captain Aylmer saw no necessity for his wife's accompanying Félicité, and was better pleased that she should be out of reach of any seductions, or indeed claims, of the Roman Church, since there was no denying that she had been baptized by a West Indian priest. The Inquisition still existed, and no one could guess where its powers might extend. Caroline was disappointed, laughed, and said there was not much fear with H. M. fleet no farther off than Cività-Vecchia, but he used his authority, and she had to submit and see her friends sail away in a Spanish ship, guarded from Moorish pirates by the English fleet. How they wept, and declared that their lives, and more than their lives were owing to their brave English friends can well be imagined. It was a final parting with the Abbé and with the Mother Prioress, who meant to remain at Rome, but Beaudésert declared that he should return to America by way of England, and, as he trusted, bring his wife with him.

"Ah!" said Félicité, as she gave her last embrace to Caroline, "I shall never forget what you said to me about prayer when I was in my deepest trouble."

CHAPTER XXIII

'Tis well! from this day forward we shall know
That in ourselves our safety must be sought,
That by our own right hands it must be wrought.
                                        WORDSWORTH.

NOTHING had been heard from the lovers when the
Leopard was ordered home to join Lord Howe's Channel Fleet, and Caroline, with her little boy, was welcomed by her mother-in-law and daughter, now grown
out of her baby charms into the lank, growing girl to
whom "multiplication was a vexation," and nouns and
verbs were the trying business of life, or rather trying
interruptions in the affairs of life, the doll's domestic
economy, and whoop hide in the garden. Eustace had
grown old enough to despise the doll, and insist on
naval battles in the pond, with the fleet constructed
for him by the crew of the *Leopard*. "Mamma" was
by far his best antagonist, far above the little boys,
his neighbour's small boys being far inferior to her,
not only in knowledge of the subject, but in spirit
and enterprise; but their mothers and aunts were
greatly scandalised at seeing Mrs. George Aylmer
sailing toy boats, among a flock of little boys.

The fleet was in the Channel, so communication
was easy, and mother and wife were so far happy,
though they suffered from every storm that blew in

the knowledge that the *Leopard* was exposed to it.
They did not know, when off Cape Finisterre, the
English fleet, on the 1st of June, was winning a brilliant victory over the French. The first tidings that
actually reached them was in a note to Caroline sent
from Plymouth.

"All well. Thank God. *Leopard* a good deal
knocked about, and her captain too. Contusion in
left side, broken arm, ten men killed, twenty and
lieutenant wounded. Thanks from Lord Howe. You
will not be contented without coming to see me and to
share the honours, so I shall expect you.   G. A.

"Love to mother and children. No cause for
anxiety."

Caroline found her husband on a couch in his cabin,
in a good deal of pain at times, but in high spirits,
and only regretting that the victory had not been
more complete, owing to the mistakes of some of the
captains, of whom, however, he had not been one, but
the *Leopard* had done her part in breaking the French
line. Battered and bruised she looked, though her
masts and cordage had been repaired, and Mrs. Aylmer
was able to make prize of a French cannon-ball, which
was brought to her in triumph by a little midshipman.
Both the *Leopard* and her captain were, however, so
dilapidated that they were to be paid off for the present, and there was to be an interval for recovery at
home.

"How are all your old French ladies?" asked the
captain.

"Very well; your mother has grown very fond of
Cécile de Henisson, and would miss her very much if
she went out to Guadaloupe; and as for the two
mothers, they wept rivers of tears over the history of

the Prioress, but they are fully occupied and fairly cheerful."

"If I am sent out to the West Indies, I may get some news of your cousins there; what's their name?"

"Nidemerle. On Ste. Marie Galante."

"Old Jervis will have a hand upon the islands by this time. Never fear, we shall not touch civilians. They will be better off than under your French devils."

"I wonder if I could write to Mélanie?"

"Of course. Give your letter to the first captain commissioned to the station, and he will get it to them."

"Shall we ever hear again of Félicité? I should dearly love to know whether she was successful at Rome."

"Or clapped into the Inquisition. No, no, that is not likely in these days, even in the very den of Giant Pope. But I cannot say I ever expect to hear of her or Beaudésert again."

"Oh, George! what do you think can have happened to them? Not the Inquisition?"

"Hardly, though, by the bye, Spanish or Italian sailors would be apt to think his dealings with lightning had a spice of the black art. But suppose they succeeded, letters are not easy of conveyance; and if they were, a crew sailing before a fair wind is apt to forget who helped them through the shoals."

"I don't believe it of Félicité."

The words had hardly passed Caroline's lips, when there were sounds to be heard, and the captain's servant came to the door, saying, "If you please, sir, there's a boat alongside with the French lady and gentleman who went out to Gibraltar with us. They want to see you and madam."

"There!" in triumph cried Caroline, "you are equal to seeing them?"

"Of course I am. Bring them down at once."

Caroline hastened on deck, where she found the second lieutenant superintending the drawing up in a chair of a lady, looking so bright and happy that she was hardly to be recognised, till, unheeding all the crew, she threw herself into her friend's arms, scarcely able to utter a greeting for joy and emotion, while Beaudésert, climbing up more freely after her, seized Mrs. Aylmer's hand, and kissed it, exclaiming, "Our benefactress." Then ensued an eager inquiry for "monsieur le capitaine" and his wound, on which Caroline led the way to the cabin, where her husband rose with outstretched hand, and there was a whirl of congratulation and inquiry, before the newcomers sat down to be served with wine and cake, and to tell their adventures.

Landing at Cività-Vecchia, after a very comfortless voyage in a Spanish ship, far from clean, the Abbé Casaforte had first escorted the Prioress and Félicité to the Abbey of Santa Lucia, where they were welcomed, and he most especially, as if they had come back from the den of lions. There he left them, and Félicité became Sœur Philomène again, resumed her veil and the monastic customs, though this was an easy-going convent, far more so than the French one, where the influence of Port Royal had been felt.

Beaudésert meantime had been, through all his anxiety, infinitely struck with Rome, chiefly, perhaps, on the classic side. If they had but known it, this was the very last view of mediæval Rome. Already when he was speaking the French were at the door, and soon the Pope would be a fugitive, and Napoleon's tyranny, that tyranny which would bring about universal innovation, was about to begin.

But when Beaudésert was there the majestic relics of the great days of the empire, and of *Senatus Populusque Romanus*, still were in strange contrast or else adaptation with the mediæval splendours. St. Peter's reigned supreme; the Vatican, adorned in the Renaissance perfection of art, was still the centre of a magnificent ecclesiastical court of prince cardinals and bishops, and the tall castellated palaces of the old historic nobility frowned along the streets, with Italian verdure showing over their walls and in the loggias.

Beaudésert was in a world of enchantment as he was carried along to be presented to Cardinal de York, at the beautiful villa at Frascati, laid out in terraces shaded with vines, ornamented with trees, and with exquisite flowers in borders.

The descendant of kings, a mild-faced, stout, indolent, elderly man dressed in purple, and with touches of scarlet enough to show his ecclesiastical rank, moreover with the blue ribbon of the Garter round his neck, was sitting at his ease under a bower, with a priest reading his breviary to him while he nodded through it. But on the announcement of the Abbé Casaforte, he rose with outstretched arms, and with the exclamation in Italian, "My son, my dear son, miracles do not cease." embraced him heartily.

Beaudésert was presented, and His Eminence desired to hear the story of the rescue, which had been told by letter; but to Beaudésert's acute eyes and ears it did not appear to have been entirely taken in, and even during the narration it might be doubtful whether the old man were thoroughly awake; but there was no question of his gladness to welcome his secretary.

Supper was served in great state, and in most dainty fashion, but it was long and tedious, and cards and coffee seemed the only subsequent resource. Beaudésert owned that he could not help recollecting what the Pope was alleged to have said, after an interview with the last of the Stewarts, that he did not wonder that the English had expelled them.

Still, when not taken unawares and half asleep, Cardinal Henry of York was a stately, noble-looking prince, and a very kindly man.

"It seemed to me," said Beaudésert, "that he took refuge in apathy from dwelling on the misfortunes of his race. To me he was very kind, all the more that I do not think he ever quite understood that I was not English, and could not lay claim to the honour of saving the Abbé."

"It made him all the more friendly to our suit," said Félicité.

"I believe it did, though I was always trying to undeceive him, and did not always know when I was addressed as Signor Capitano Inglese; nor why he was so much pleased to see me kneeling in his chapel *come buon Catolico!* However, he was very good and kindly to us, greatly owing to good Casaforte's mediation. On the next day we set forth in his carriage, with the purple liveries, four horses, and all the ornaments of state, that he might see the Prioress and mademoiselle. It was like being in a dream to see all the splendour and grandeur renewed that I remember in former times at Paris, and the convent in like manner, a great castellated building, while the streets were thronged with priests, monks, and friars, black, white, and grey. The adulation with which he was received at the convent was a perfect revival of what might have been seen in Paris. The nuns were ready to prostrate themselves in delight at the honour of a visit from a Cardinal of royal birth. Our friend, the Mother of Ste. Lucie, came forward as he was admitted within the *grille*, and was about to prostrate herself, but he raised her, and told her he regarded her as a martyr. We waited without — his chief chaplain, Casaforte, and I — while he had private interviews with our Prioress and with Félicité. I do not think he was insensible to Félicité's *beaux yeux*, for he ended by letting her kiss his hand, and promising to make the case known to His Holiness. We meantime were entertained by the Prioress of the convent, and though her French was imperfect and my Italian still more so, I could perceive what a graceful, courteous woman of the world she was, and how delighted to do honour to the two confessors."

"They could not make enough of us," said Félicité. "Our Mother was quite distressed at the luxuries they insisted on giving her. She told me that she should resist, or else seek another sisterhood, and withhold her name and history, so as to be permitted to mourn all her life for what she now calls her worldly rule."

"And the Cardinal?" asked Caroline.

"He was very good and gracious, only he laughed a little as he heard of my resistance, and winked with his eyes, in a way too like some of the pictures that your uncle has. But he promised to represent our case, and to present us to His Holiness."

"And he did?"

"Oh yes. We waited long and long, and we were told that there were whisperers representing that Monsieur de Beaudésert's inventions were inspired by demons," said Félicité.

"Yes, it is true," interposed her husband; "but happily there were others more enlightened, and the Cardinal himself enjoyed my experiments, though I cannot say he seemed to understand them. At last, however, came intelligence that His Holiness wished to see the Abbé Casaforte, as a confessor who had actually suffered and been resuscitated. I believe the Abbé pleaded our cause effectually, and answered for my orthodoxy, for by and by the Prioress and Félicité were summoned to the Vatican."

"Did you go as a nun?" asked Caroline.

"Yes," said she; "I had resumed my habit in the convent. The good Cardinal called for us in his carriage, and took us to the palace, where we went up marble stairs on stairs, through galleries lined with gorgeous Swiss guards, swarming with clergy, a coming and going enough to make one dizzy, till we reached a small inner room, where sat His Holiness all in white, with a sweet and loving face. We knelt to kiss his foot, but he raised the Mother at once, and said he could not receive such homage from one who had suffered martyrdom. He asked her a few questions — in French — about the dispersion of her nuns and her own adventures, and then he turned to me. I should say that I had drawn up a statement which had been translated both into Latin and Italian by Monsieur there, and the Abbé Casaforte."

"'Is this true, my daughter?' he said, as I knelt before him.

"'Ah! your Holiness, every word is from my heart.'

"'You were coerced and compelled and never uttered the vows.'

"Then, after a word or two more, he laid his hand

on me, and gave me his blessing, delegating his authority to the head of our Order to absolve me from my
vows! I kissed his hand, he blessed us both, and I
recollected happily to ask his blessing for three
crosses for Mères St. Hilaire and de l'Annonciation,
and their kind hostess. That was all, I think; the
Cardinal took us away. The absolution followed in
the Church of our Order."

"And the next day it was Casaforte who united us,
and the Cardinal who gave us his nuptial blessing,"
added Beaudésert.

They had afterwards made their way to England
by a devious course, through Switzerland and Hol-
land, and arriving in London had secured a passage
in an American ship which was about to sail from
Plymouth, trusting to the security from French vessels likely to prevail after Lord Howe's victory.

"And Félicité is prepared to live the rough life of
an American engineer's wife after all the luxuries to
which she was brought up as *fille de qualité*," said
Beaudésert, looking at her tenderly.

"Ah! what joy the life will be!" she said, "now
at last my name becomes appropriate!"

"Nay, it is I who can say 'my Felicity,'" returned
her husband.

So Monsieur and Madame Beaudésert took their
leave for the present, still in all the joys of their
honeymoon, though the period had well-nigh departed.
When they were gone Captain Aylmer held up his
hands saying, "That is well. They have gone through
a good deal before getting into harbour, but it is hard
to see how the blessing of an old Italian sets them at
their ease."

"Ah, George, you never grew up to think he stood
in the place of the Head of the Church."

"No! thank God, I never did. I look higher. I trust you do, Carry, for all your bringing up."

"Indeed I hope I do. But remember what your mother says: 'Whatever is not of faith is sin'; and Félicité has held to her conscience."

"Yes. Obeyed her orders, and no doubt she was right, and he is an honest fellow, and the cleverest I ever came across yet, except perhaps little Horatio Nelson in his own line. I hope it will go as well with them both as they deserve."

And as far as could be gathered from their letters, so it did in their new home, where Beaudésert became a prosperous director of the mines, and Félicité presided over a château as like that of Monfichet as the climate would permit, with a chapel served by a fugitive French priest, and whither French-speaking workmen and peasants gathered from the New Orleans neighbourhood.

They soon knew that Félicité's release was one of the last authoritative acts performed by poor Pius VI. ere he was driven from Rome by fears of the French aggressors, who seemed to have been sent to chastise all Europe, after the awful devastation of their own country. The last of the Stewarts, Cardinal Henry of York, shared in this suffering, having contributed all his property and jewels to assist in raising the sum imposed on the Pope by Buonaparte, and afterwards, on the second French invasion of Italy, being stripped of all his property, so that he would have been reduced to absolute want save for a pension granted him by George III.

The Abbé Casaforte was reported to have been last seen tending the wounded at the battle of Marengo, and was thought to have died by a stray shot. He had lived a most ascetic life, entirely among the many sufferers of the time, as though convinced that his rescue from the *noyade* had been for the sake of letting him show his repentance for his former diplomatic courtly life.

The Nidemerles returned to their former home with diminished fortunes, and Madame de Henisson joined them, but Captain Aylmer — or rather Admiral Aylmer, for such he became after the battle of the Nile — declared that he would never let his Caroline again risk herself among her French kindred; and when the Peace of Amiens was suddenly violated, she knew he was right.

THE END

www.ingramcontent.com/pod-product-compliance
Lightning Source LLC
Chambersburg PA
CBHW020851020726
47497CB00005B/1361